THE TWO OF US AGAINST THE FAMILY

There we were, just me and Sofia, right? Over at the house there were fifteen to twenty guys, maybe more by now, who had guns and no hesitation about using them. The good news was that they didn't want to kill me because once I was dead, the five million bucks was out the window. But the bad news was that they could sure take it out of my hide while getting me to sign over that five million, and once I did, bye-bye Benny.

"Sofia," I said into the darkness, "can you lead us back to the house?"

"Now?" she asked.

"Now," I told her. "In the dark."

She moved off and I followed closely behind her. I didn't feel scared at all, maybe because my Irish and Jewish blood had finally fused into the right combination. Or maybe it was because I really did have a plan. . . .

DIRTY MONEY

"Benny is a likable hero, wise and often funny, and Bass knows how to trigger the reader's emotions. It will be fun to watch the series grow."
—*Chicago Tribune*

⊘ SIGNET   (0451)

DEADLY DEALINGS

☐ **THE MOVING FINGER by Milton Bass.** Half-Jewish, half-Irish, Benny
Freedman is not Everyman's image of a cop: A poetry-reading martial-
arts disciple with a great appreciation for beautiful language and
beautiful women. Now he's got to crack a case involving a murdered
used-car mogul with a missing finger, a gorgeous widow, and a religious
cult that worships money and makes a sacrament of slaughter....
                                                      (141105—$3.50)

☐ **DIRTY MONEY by Milton Bass.** Benny Freedman liked having six millin
bucks in the bank. But now he was caught between the Mafia, who
claimed it was theirs and wanted to write out their claim in his blood,
and an overheated lady of the family who wanted to use him to make
her sexual fantasies come true.... Now with six million dollars worth of
tsouris, Benny's life wasn't worth two cents....   (144805—$3.50)

☐ **SWITCH by William Bayer.** Someone had decapitated the two women and
switched their heads. It was a grisly work of art, a crime as perfect as it
was pointless. And it was Detective Frank Janek's job to get inside the
mind of the lethal genius who committed it ... to become as cold, as
creative, as insanely brilliant as his killer prey....   (143337—$3.95)

☐ **WHEN THE BOUGH BREAKS by Johathan Kellerman.** Obsessed with a
case that endangers both his career and his life, child psychologist Alex
Delaware must plumb the depths of a seven-year-old girl's mind to find
the secret that will shatter a grisly web of evil that stretches from the
barrio of L.A. to an elite island community ... coming closer and closer
to a forty-year-old secret that makes even murder look clean....
                                                      (142497—$3.95)

Prices slightly higher in Canada

Buy them at your local bookstore or use this convenient coupon for ordering.

NEW AMERICAN LIBRARY.
P.O. Box 999, Bergenfield, New Jersey 07621

Please send me the books I have checked above. I am enclosing $_____
(please add $1.00 to this order to cover postage and handling). Send check
or money order—no cash or C.O.D.'s. Prices and numbers are subject to change
without notice.

Name_____

Address_____

City_____State_____Zip Code_____

Allow 4-6 weeks for delivery.
This offer is subject to withdrawal without notice.

DIRTY MONEY

Milton Bass

A SIGNET BOOK

NEW AMERICAN LIBRARY

PUBLISHER'S NOTE

This novel is a work of fiction. Names, characters, places, and incidents either are the product of the author's imagination or are used
fictitiously, and any resemblance to actual persons, living or dead,
events, or locales is entirely coincidental.

SIGNET TRADEMARK REG. U.S. PAT. OFF. AND FOREIGN COUNTRIES
REGISTERED TRADEMARK—MARCA REGISTRADA
HECHO EN CHICAGO, U.S.A.

SIGNET, SIGNET CLASSIC, MENTOR, ONYX, PLUME, MERIDIAN AND
NAL BOOKS are published by New American Library,
1633 Broadway, New York, New York 10019

First Printing, September, 1986

1 2 3 4 5 6 7 8 9

PRINTED IN THE UNITED STATES OF AMERICA

For Elaine and Jimmy

and

Stell and Alan

*friends who have lovingly paid attention
to my words for a long, long time*

*D*ead!
     She had not placed undue emphasis on the word, and her voice had been low-pitched and pleasant, as was correct for all good receptionists, but it gonged in my head loud enough to make me look wildly around the entire lobby to check the reaction of all the others who were present.

They were going through their normal business, standing patiently and impatiently in the teller lines, or conferring with other employees at the desks placed strategically on the marble floor. A bank is a mausoleum for money, and only the death of money, either through financial crisis or robbery, ever creates a stir within its polished walls and columns. The news that a man was dead, a man I had met only once, briefly, had nothing to do with the lives of these good citizens of Upsala, New York.

"Is there anyone else who can help you?" she asked.

"Heart attack?"

"I beg your pardon."

"Mr. Wenker. Arnold Wenker. Did he die from a heart attack?"

"No, sir. He was in an automobile accident."

She was beginning to look at me peculiarly, tilting her head as she gazed up, her eyes sweeping the lobby to see where the security guard was positioned. She was young, maybe twenty-two, and attractive, but she had also been well-trained, and her antennae were starting to wiggle in the breeze.

"I would like to see whoever has taken over his

accounts," I said, trying to retreat into the aura of regular customer.

"That would be Mr. Woodbridge," she said, smiling now that the situation had normalized. "Follow me, please."

She threaded us across the lobby, her pert ass my beacon to an office set against the back wall, where a young man in what had to be a brand-new dark gray flannel suit sat behind an oiled walnut desk while perusing, his brow furrowed, a black-paneled loose-leaf notebook. Although he had to know we were there, he did not look up as the young lady stood in the doorway, me close behind her behind.

"Mr. Woodbridge," she said quietly. He took a few seconds before he lifted his eyes in our direction. This young man had obviously thought out the attitude he was to assume for what had to have been an unexpected promotion, since Wenker couldn't have been much past his middle thirties, and I might have thought it funny if the accident hadn't so disrupted my personal situation. I was there to get information, not give it, and Wenker was to have been the Rosetta Stone.

His arched eyebrows indicated both acknowledgment and questioning of our presence. I hadn't been particularly taken with Wenker the one time I met him, and his successor gave indications of being an asshole. It could be that the Bay City Bank and I had little more in common than my trust account.

"This gentleman would like to see you," she said, gave me a small smile, and removed herself neatly from our presence.

The young man continued looking rather than talking, so I walked uninvited into the office, sat down on the chair that was placed on the opposite side of the desk, and looked at him, prepared to stick it out on that front if it took all summer. It turned out he wasn't that good at it, and he finally said, "Yes?"

"I was looking for Arnold Wenker," I told him, "but the young lady informed me that he had died in an

automobile accident and that you were handling his
accounts."

"You have a trust account here?"

"Yes."

"Your name?"

"Freedman."

One time in a restaurant, my wife and I were following the waiter to our table when a man jumped up to
block our path, and he had the same look on his face
that appeared on Woodbridge. I had immediately swung
behind the man, encircled him with my arms, and
whacked him in the solar plexus with the Heimlich
maneuver. Out had popped a piece of half-chewed meat
from his windpipe or esophagus or wherever it had
been stuck, and the management had bought me a free
drink and the guy had picked up our dinner check,
which included a fairly expensive bottle of mediocre
wine, plus other strangers had patted my shoulder
throughout the evening as they passed by our table.

"How did you know what his problem was?" my wife
had asked.

"He had that look," was all I could come up with.

Woodbridge had the same look and I wondered for a
moment if he had been sucking on a hard candy or
something, but came to the conclusion that it wasn't
quite the same thing and because of his snotty attitude,
I wasn't going to save his life anyway.

"Benjamin Freedman?" he finally managed.

I nodded. I could also be chary of words when the
situation demanded.

He stood up from his chair and came around the desk
to shake my hand, which he pumped enthusiastically.

"I am delighted to meet you, Mr. Freedman," he
said. "I have already familiarized myself with your account and have several suggestions to make that I think
you will find most constructive. When did you get in
from California, and what is the purpose of your visit?"

I couldn't resist. It was a small thing to do, perhaps
nasty, but I was disturbed that my one known link,

Wenker, was dead and that I now had to deal with this pompous ass, who, I was sure, was going to be sticky about what I wanted to know. So I laid it on him.

"I'm thinking of moving my account," I said.

His ashen face and the weak-kneed shift of his body gave me more than the satisfaction I had anticipated. Here this wimp had just taken over another guy's job and he was about to lose a six-million-dollar portfolio that had to be a major asset of his department in a bank this size. What was he going to tell the boss? I decided at that moment that it would be a waste of time to dance around with this schlemiel, and the best thing would be to go right to the top. As he opened his mouth, uncertain of what to say, I beat him to the punch.

"I'd like to speak to the president of the bank," I told him.

"But, Mr. Freedman," he said, "Sergeant Freedman, if there is anything that I can . . ."

"No," I said, "I'd rather not discuss it on your level. I want to speak to the head honcho."

"I'm sure Mr. Sinclair would be delighted to discuss whatever problems you think there might be," he said, "but if you could give me an idea first, we can probably work them out here and now."

"Is he available?" I asked sternly.

"I'm sure, I'm sure," he answered, scurrying back around the desk and punching four numbers into his phone base.

"Ah, Sally," he cooed, "I have in my office Mr. Benjamin Freedman, who wishes to consult with Mr. Sinclair as soon as possible."

His voice changed at her answer.

"Sally," he grated, "this is very important. I want you to ring in there and tell him who is here and what he wants. Now! No, I'll hold."

He smiled over at me, or at least what he thought was a smile. Strain had changed it into what I would describe as a grimace. The game was beginning to lose its fun, and I decided I would have made a lousy slave owner.

"Thank you, Sally," he said. "We will be right up."

Sinclair turned out to be a big man somewhere in his mid-fifties, his face ruddy from golf and tennis in the summer and either skiing or racket tennis, or maybe both, in the winter. He was handsome almost to the point of prettiness, and there was just the hint of a paunch to indicate that business lunches and dinners were beginning to make their permanent impression. He was the kind of WASP who could get to be president of a bank without having a brain in his head.

He was smart enough to detect almost instantly that I desired a private conversation, and once the introductions were out of the way, he eased Woodbridge from the office with a quiet "Thank you, Marvin."

"Well, Sergeant," he said, once I had refused the offer of a cigar and we had settled into our chairs, "you have been much in the news of late. How does it feel to be a national hero?"

I allowed a modest little deprecating smile to trickle across my face.

"I was just doing my job," I said. Duke Wayne always got to drawl that line to a female, so he could say "ma'am" at the end of the sentence, and I had come damn close.

"Quite a job," said Sinclair. "Solving a murder, holding off a bunch of fanatic loonies, and saving the lives of all those other police officers. Quite a job, I'd say. Your face was on television for a whole week. For a man who insisted that this bank keep his affairs secret, you sure didn't cooperate much on your end."

He smiled softly and I decided he didn't get to be the head of this bank because of his good looks.

"Somebody didn't keep the secret somewhere," I said, and tossed on his desk the letter I had received the day before on the Coast. It had been typed in capital letters, and there were only two sentences: "YOU

HAVE FIVE MILLION DOLLARS THAT BELONG TO US. WE
WILL BE IN TOUCH."

He studied the sheet carefully, even bringing it up
close to look for a watermark. Bankers and detectives.

"You have no idea who sent this?" he asked.

"None."

"One of your California friends playing a joke perhaps?"

"I have no friends."

He looked up quickly to see if there was a smile on
my face, and seeing none, resumed his study of the two
sentences.

"There are only four people besides yourself who
know about the trust fund your wife left you," he said,
"and one of them is dead. Although I cannot vouch for
it, I am sure that neither Arnold nor Marvin nor our
lawyer in California, Mr. Hamilton, told anybody, and I
certainly haven't. It is doubtful that anyone connected
with us sent this because we know that there is six
million in the fund rather than five. I will double-check
with Marvin, but as you know, Arnold died in a tragic
accident just a week ago and he is beyond our reach."

"Tell me about it," I said.

"What?"

"The accident. Tell me about the car accident."

Sinclair didn't smile but there was almost a touch of
amusement in his voice.

"If you're asking as a sergeant of homicide," he said,
"it was a one-car accident on a foggy night where Arnold went off the road on a bad curve with a soft
shoulder and hit a huge oak tree. He was probably
knocked unconscious and the gas tank exploded. They
were unable to determine whether he was killed by the
crash or the fire."

"Because the body was burned so badly?"

"Right. But the police said there were no suspicious
circumstances."

"Everything was all right here at the bank? Everything was all right at home?"

"The audit checked out to the penny. And Arnold

and Ann and their two children were a model family. He was a friend of mine as well as an officer of this bank, and I would have known if the slightest thing had been out of kilter."

"Where did my wife's money come from?"

"I don't know."

"Come on, Mr. Sinclair. Wenker said that according to the conditions of the trust, he was not allowed to tell me where the six million dollars came from. And you're telling me the same thing."

"I'll be frank with you," he said. "Wenker obviously wasn't exactly frank with you. It wasn't that he wasn't allowed to tell you where the money came from, which, by the way, was originally five million dollars. The other million came from the investments we made."

He paused to give me time to digest the fact that this bank knew how to handle trust accounts, just in case I had come to bitch about something along that order.

"The trust was set up for her by a Swiss bank, which didn't tell us where the money came from, and, frankly, we didn't push it. Because we are so close to the Canadian border, we do a lot of international business, some of which in the past, to be honest with you, has been a trifle shadowy. Any bank that wanted to spread its wings a little had to play that game. But since the Bank of Boston stuck its assets up its ass with the billion in footsies it played with the Swiss and the seven million it exchanged with the Mafia bunch, we've been toeing the line to the millimeter. There were times in the past, and as I said, we weren't alone in this, where we blinked at certain things, didn't fill out certain papers, ignored federal regulations, didn't go by the book. We didn't do anything basically dishonest, mind you, but we could be made to look bad if somebody hauled us up before an investigating committee. I'm laying it on the line to you even though"—he smiled—"you're a policeman, because I want to keep your account with us, and I want you to know that we are an honest bank as well as one that will go out of its way to please its clients."

"Did you know my wife?"

"We met her once, just before she moved from New York to the West Coast. After that we just talked with her on the phone. She seemed like a lovely person as well as a most attractive one. I was sorry to hear of her tragic illness and death."

"She had told me she was living in New York before she came to the Coast," I said. "Do you have any kind of an address listed?"

Sinclair stood up and pulled a key from his right pocket, which he used to unlock his middle desk drawer, from which he lifted a ring of keys. He walked over to a side cabinet in the wall, which he unlocked with two separate keys, and withdrew one of the black-jacketed folders from the top shelf of the case. He opened the folder on his desk and turned two pages.

"She never gave us a New York address," he said. "The only address she ever listed with us was Wackowick Heights, New Jersey. W-a-c-k-o-w-i-c-k. The Swiss bank instructed us to call her at a New York City telephone number, and that's where we reached her at the time. But before she moved to California, the only address she gave us was 1934 View Drive, Wackowick Heights, New Jersey."

"The envelope I received was postmarked New Jersey," I told him.

"Ah," he said, "that might be what you would call a clue, but we never contacted anybody at the New Jersey address. There was no need to. It could be that the people who set up the trust live there, but I don't really know. And after she married you, she drew up the will that mentioned only you and nobody else."

"What you're telling me then is that out of the blue a Swiss bank contacted you and said they were transferring to your bank a five-million-dollar trust fund for a young lady who lived in New York City at such and such a telephone number? What the hell happened when you contacted her? Was she surprised? Did she know anything about it?"

"Arnold handled the contact, but I asked him those same questions. He said she obviously knew about the fund that had been set up for her, but she just as obviously had no idea that this bank was the one that had been designated to handle the trusteeship. I don't know if the Swiss bank had already contacted her, or whether it had been done by the person or persons who set up the trust fund, but it all worked according to plan, and there have been no hitches since then. Nor should there be any hitches in the future. Marvin Woodbridge is an excellent trust officer with an excellent track record, but if for any reason you are uncomfortable dealing with him, you can work directly with me. I'll be happy to go over the whole portfolio with you right now or at any other time that is convenient. Perhaps we can have lunch or dinner, or both, and discuss it then?"

"What is the name of the Swiss bank that set up the trust fund?"

The pause was very slight.

"I can't tell you that."

"Can't or won't?"

"Won't."

"Suppose I were to say that if you don't give me the name, I'm moving the whole damn thing out of here?"

"Then I would have to tell you, much as I would regret it, to move the whole damn thing out of here."

I smiled and stood up.

"Well, I'm telling you to keep the whole damn thing in here. I like your style, Mr. Sinclair."

"Don," he said.

"What?"

"I know we've just met, but I'd like you to call me Don."

"And I'm Benny. And if you don't mind, I'd rather deal directly with you than with anybody else. I'd also like a checking account with something around two hundred thousand dollars in it, and I'd like a couple of thousand in cash. And do you think it would be possible for me to visit Mrs. Wenker? I want to pay my respects."

He looked at me quizzically for a moment. Brains. The guy had gotten where he'd gone by brains.

"I'll arrange about the money and I'll give Ann a call," he said.

"Is there a car-rental agency close by?" I asked. "And which hotel do you recommend?"

"You can use one of the bank's cars while you're in town," he said, "and we'll book you a room in the Sheraton. What about dinner?"

"There are some things I have to do," I told him, "and I'd like to get settled in. Maybe tomorrow."

"Whatever is convenient," he said. "Why don't you sit and have a cup of coffee while I see to your money and arrangements."

As I sat there sipping from the real china cup, I thought about a line from a Mel Brooks movie:

"It's good to be a king," he kept saying, leering directly out from the screen.

There weren't any mirrors on the walls in that office, and it was just as well that I couldn't see the look on my face. I might not have liked it.

2

The car the venerable security guard led me to was an Oldsmobile Toronado with power windows and seat, leather that smelled like a club that limited its membership to the chosen few, and a stereo system that could pull in Bangkok on a clear day. I had the feeling that Sinclair was going to be using some annoyed vice-president's car for the duration of my visit. The guard stowed my soft suitcase in the rear seat and gave me directions to the street where Ann Wenker lived.

I knew better than to try to classify the price of the houses by San Diego standards, but figured they were somewhere in the neighborhood of $150,000 in Upsala. Nice. Clean. Well-maintained.

There was a medium-size Ford station wagon in the blacktop driveway of the address I had been given, and I took a chance and parked right behind it. If it belonged to a visitor, I might have to move, but if it was the family carryall, I had saved myself steps from the street. "Live for the moment" is my motto.

The woman who came to the door was dressed in a pale purple dress of some kind of fluffy material rather than widow's weeds, but I figured from the circles under her eyes that this was Ann Wenker.

"Mrs. Wenker," I said, "I am Benjamin Freedman."

"I know," she said, and I could tell from the way she pronounced it that she knew everything, that her husband had kept no secrets from her, including ones that had to do with bank business.

She started to lead me into the living room but

stopped still after two steps and turned quickly to face
me. She was almost my height and I was forced to lean
over backward to avoid an awkward embrace. As it was,
I had to put both my arms up to her elbows to maintain
equilibrium.

"Have you had lunch?" she asked.

It was peculiar to be standing this close to her, but
any move would have made it even worse.

"No."

"I was just about to sit down to a sandwich and a cup
of tea," she said, moving around me and heading back to
the hallway. "Come join me."

The kitchen counter was loaded with cakes of various
types, each one covered with wax paper or plexifilm.
There was also a stack of empty casserole dishes and
five boxes of candy and nine fruit baskets, some still
unwrapped. The Wenkers obviously had not lacked for
friendly neighbors and neighborly friends.

On the kitchen table was a tuna-fish sandwich on
whole-wheat bread and a steaming mug of tea. She
pointed at them with her hand and I nodded. As she
busied herself duplicating the lunch, I realized I was
hungry. The steward on the jet I had chartered had
offered me some crackers and cheese, but I had been
too preoccupied to eat them. For what the jet had cost,
they should have shampooed my hair with caviar, but it
was a small matter to a man who at that moment had
two thousand dollars scattered among his pants pockets,
and a checkbook with assets of two hundred thousand dollars in his jacket pocket. But I was still me and the thought
of plain old tuna fish with mayo was enough to start a
hunger rumble in my stomach.

Once we sat down, she didn't waste any time in
establishing a polite relationship before plunging into
personal matters.

"Your wife died of cancer," she stated.

I had just taken a big bite of sandwich and used the
time to chew my way to a reply. It turned out to be a
simple nod.

"I have been thinking about you since Don called this morning," she said, "thinking about the difference between you and me. Arnold said you had been married not quite a year and that your wife was sick for most of that year. We were married for almost fifteen years and except for the two boys having strep throats and assorted bruises and the family having bouts of flu, we enjoyed a good life, a damn good life. I suppose I should be grateful for what we did have, especially in comparison to you. But I'm not; I wanted more, much more. I'm thirty-seven years old and in good health and my parents are both alive and in good health, and I could tell by the way that everybody looked at me this past week that they expect I'll remarry sometime in the future. And you know what, the thought went through my mind every time an eligible man came to pay his respects this week. What do you say to that?"

"Can I have your sandwich?" I asked her.

Her jaw dropped open as she gazed at me. Tears had started running down her cheeks from the dark pools of her eyes after she had started her speech, and her face glistened in the afternoon light.

"I am still hungry," I said, pointing to my empty plate, "and you obviously are not. But my main reason for asking is that I wanted to shut you up for a minute. My wife died slow and your husband died fast. She and I had the opportunity to discuss our time together and you didn't even have one split second. You feel cheated. Maybe you even think you envy me. It's something you couldn't tell your family or friends this week because you've been too busy being brave and setting an example for your boys and being a good banker's wife. So when this stranger comes along who is not really a stranger because your husband told you all he knew about him and his wife and his six million bucks, you thought at first that here was someone who could share your grief, but then you decided that I had a better deal in the way my wife died. Well, it wasn't a better deal. I watched her turn into a living skeleton and after we had gone over the few good months we had together three or four times, we ran out of words. Which is better, Mrs. Wenker, going fast or slow? I tell you, neither. They both stink."

She exchanged her full plate for my empty one, wiped her cheeks with a tissue from the box on the table, took a sip of her tea, and smiled at me. It was a real smile, undoubtedly her first one in a week.

"Why did you come here?" she asked. "Why did you want to see me?"

I took a bite of her sandwich and chewed a bit. Maybe I should always carry a tuna-fish sandwich on my person. Then, whenever I wasn't quite sure of my ground, such as being on the witness stand in a murder trial with a smart defense lawyer going after me or when the captain asked me how I could be such a dumb son of a bitch, I would just haul out the sandwich and munch away until I came up with some satisfactory answer.

"First of all," I said, "I'm sorry about your husband. I just met him that once for a few minutes, but you obviously had a good marriage and I wish you could have gone hand in hand right into very old age. But essentially I'm here for my own purposes. I'll be frank with you because I am sure your husband made a big deal about the confidentiality of bank business, and you will respect that. Someone told somebody about the trust fund my wife left me, and I received an anonymous letter informing me that the money belongs to them and they want it. My deduction was that your husband had to be the source. But when I got here to ask him about it, he was gone. Automobile accident. Body burned so badly that cause of death could not be determined. I'm a policeman, a homicide cop. I'm not satisfied with the circumstances and I want to know more. I know how horrible it is for you to even think about it, but you may know something that can help me. It won't do you any good, it won't change any of your circumstances, but it could help me. It could lead you into areas that you don't want to visit now or ever. If all you're willing to go for are two tuna-fish sandwiches and a cup of tea, I'll understand and thank you for your hospitality and leave. But if you're willing to let me ask you some questions about the past couple of weeks, it might help me tremendously."

She sipped from the mug of tea, using it the way I had utilized the tuna-fish sandwiches.

"Are you saying that there might be more to my husband's death than a car accident? That it might not have been an accident?"

I nodded.

"But why? To what purpose? What would anyone gain from killing my husband? What kind of people could they be?"

"I don't know," I told her. "I don't even know if they exist. But my wife left me a trust fund of six million dollars, and all we know is that it was set up by a Swiss bank. The antiseptic Swiss have become banking middlemen for some of the slimiest people in the world, ranging from the heads of nations to the Mafia. I have come to the conclusion that my wife's money was dirty money, that it was taken unknowingly from people who had no idea they were giving it up. Now they want it back. Somehow, maybe through contacts in Switzerland, they learned that it had ended up at the Bay City Bank. And somehow or other, they could have put the squeeze on your husband to find out what had become of it. Sinclair said both the car and the body were burned"—her hand went up to her mouth—"beyond the point where the police around here could learn anything of the circumstances."

"They said they found glass from a broken fifth of whiskey in the front-seat area," she said, "and the two policemen who told me about it gave each other a look when they said it. He drank, sometimes more than he should have at parties, but he never carried a fifth of whiskey around with him in the car. I would have known."

"It's an old trick," I told her.

"What?"

"You see it on television all the time. The bad guys pour whiskey around the victim and then . . ."

Jesus, I thought to myself. Maybe I'm not just rambling. Maybe. Maybe.

"Did anything occur in the week before he died?" I asked, getting a little excited, telling myself to slow down, not to spook the witness. "Anything that was out of the ordinary? Did a stranger come to visit him? Did he get any weird phone calls?"

She started to shake her head, then pulled herself up short.

"One night," she said, "one night we were watching television in the den and the phone rang and we let it ring a few times because it's almost always some fourteen-year-old girl calling Jeff, but finally Arnold picked it up and said hello and the strangest expression came over his face. He listened for a few moments and then he said, 'Look, I told you no at ten thousand and at twenty-five thousand and I'm telling you no at fifty thousand. It would be the same at fifty million. Don't call me again.' 'What was that all about?' I asked him, and he shook his head and didn't answer me. 'Who was that?' I asked him. 'Insurance,' he said. 'There's this pest who's trying to sell me some insurance.' It still didn't sound right to me, but we were watching Bill Cosby and I let it go. I almost asked him about it again when we were getting into bed that night because it hadn't sounded right and we had all that bank insurance to begin with, but I was tired from playing tennis and I let it go. I let it go."

I pulled the little set of index cards out of my shirt pocket and jotted down what she had told me. I always did that when I had a gut feeling that what had been told me might come in useful someday, but I also wanted to give her time to rework it in her mind for a minute. There was no change in her face and I could tell that was the end of the story.

"Did he ever get another call? Was there anything else that happened?"

She took another minute, then shook her head.

"No, nothing. No more calls, no incidents. When you think about it, when you go over it in your mind, our life was pretty standard and if something else out of the ordinary had happened, I would have noticed, I would have remembered."

"You didn't remember that phone call."

"Yes, I did. It popped right out when you asked me to think of anything different. That was different. That was the only thing that was different."

"Mrs. Wenker," I said, standing up, "I'm going to be staying overnight at the Sheraton before I move on. If you think of anything tonight, anything at all, would you please give me a call? If I don't hear from you, I'll call you in the morning before I leave. Thank you for the sandwiches and the tea."

She escorted me to the door and I turned back toward her as I stepped out on the porchway.

"Thank you again," I said. "And I'm sorry if the events in my life have caused you tragedy in yours."

That shocked her. Her eyes narrowed and for a moment I thought she might raise her hand and strike me. I wouldn't have made a move to stop her. But all she did was close the door firmly without saying a word. I really was sorry if her husband was dead because of my six million dollars, but I also wanted her to think deep that night on anything else that might have happened that would throw some light on the case. Because I was a cop and to my mind this had turned into a case. And if you're a cop on a case, quite often you have to act like a shit.

3

*W*hen I returned the car keys to Sinclair, he handed me in return a bank charge card.

"This is good for up to fifteen thousand dollars," he said, "and we'll handle the bookkeeping."

"If I stayed around her much longer," I told him, "I'd forget how to salivate."

He smiled briefly. Spit jokes were obviously not among his favorites.

"Ann called me last night," he said, "and I went over to see her. She was upset by some of the things you discussed with her. I'm upset by some of the implications you seemed to have made. I know homicide is your business, but to say that Arnold was murdered by somebody who wanted to find out about you and the trust fund seems irresponsible. The police were satisfied that it was an accident."

"What about the broken whiskey bottle?"

"I didn't know about that until Ann mentioned it. Arnold was at a Chamber of Commerce banquet in south county that night. Someone could have given him a bottle. It happens to us all the time in the banking business. We get presents from people who want something or who think we have done them a favor. A man sent me a dozen prime steaks just yesterday because he secured a loan that was given solely because of the merits of his application and security. He was insecure enough about it, however, so that he felt I had done him a favor. If I sent the steaks back, it would destroy or at least put a dent in our relationship. It could also be that my rationalization has to do with the fact that they are damn fine steaks. There were probably a dozen men at that banquet who had the same kind of relationship with Arnold. Any one of them could have presented him with a bottle of whiskey for any number of reasons."

"Mrs. Wenker seemed to feel that the cops thought her husband was drunk when he hit that tree. I stopped by the station and the sergeant on duty was good enough to show me the accident report. There was no indication of high speed, no brake marks on the road. True, it was foggy, but that car just ran into that tree. And then the car exploded and burned like an oil tank. Wenker might have been drunk, might have been nipping at a bottle while driving home. But nobody seems to have asked anybody at the banquet how many he popped and nobody has been asked if they gave him a bottle."

"Because there was no reason to," said Sinclair. "Until you came to town, the thought of anything but an uncomplicated car accident never crossed anybody's mind. I can understand your being upset by the letter you received, but there could be a very simple, very innocent explanation that has nothing to do with Arnold Wenker or the way he died."

"Have you considered asking that Swiss bank for a possible explanation?"

"We don't ever ask them for explanations of the business they send us. That's why they keep sending us business."

"But suppose there is illegal business going on? If you were suddenly investigated, is that what you would tell the examiners?"

"We have nothing to hide at the Bay City Bank. Our transactions are conducted according to banking rules, both national and international. But in addition to rules there are also customs, as I'm sure there must be in your profession, and we abide by those just as strictly."

"I take it you won't be devastated when I depart from Upsala," I told him.

He smiled. "Here's your hat, what's your hurry?" he said.

"What's the best way of getting to New York?" I asked him.

"We took the liberty of booking you on the noon commuter flight," he said, "and this is an AAA map of New Jersey with a circle drawn around Wackowick Heights."

"You ever run for president of these United States," I told him, "you can be sure of my vote."

"Just ordinary Bay Bank service," he said.

"Somebody picked up my tab at the hotel," I commented.

"Don't try paying for your New York ticket either," he said. "I would have driven you to the airport myself, but I have a meeting I can't get out of. Consequently, you will once again have the pleasure of spending a few minutes with Marvin."

"I want to thank you for your hospitality and information as far as it went," I told him. "I'm sorry I upset Mrs. Wenker but I'll go even further if necessary in order to get to the bottom of this."

"I would be interested in knowing what you do find out," said Sinclair. "At least I think I would be. Despite what I said about business and customs, I don't want this bank cooperating with crooks. Especially if a policeman knows about it. Don't do anything that will get you back in the headlines."

"I've had enough of that," I told him. "In two weeks I have to be back on the job and then I'll fade into the woodwork where I belong."

The commuter plane was one of those eleven-seater, twin-engine turbo-props that bounce around in a light breeze. What we encountered was a gale which the plane couldn't rise above, and I spent all my time trying to keep my stomach in the assigned seat rather than planning on what I was going to do about Wackowick Heights, New Jersey.

I asked the taxi man to take me to a good hotel and

ended up at Loews Summit because the driver said a lot of air crews stayed there. If I'd sought a good place to eat, I probably would have dined where all the cabbies rendezvoused. Pilots, of planes or taxis, tend to stick together socially as well as professionally.

When I spread the New Jersey map out on the hotel bed, I discovered that there was no Wackowick Heights printed on it. Rather, somebody had written the name on an area near West Orange. It had to be one of those suburbs that are part of a township without any official designation except to the people who live there. Or maybe just a development named by the builder for some individual or event in his personal life. I have this friend in Canada who bought a place called Piper Hill and for years she romanticized about some Scotsman who had immigrated there and played his pipes in sentimental memories of the auld country. Then a neighbor told her that the people she had bought the place from had a yappy dog named Piper, and when he died, they buried him up there on the hill. The name of this place probably came from some wacko who had his wick snuffed in New Jersey.

I rented a Cadillac convertible the next morning and crossed the river. It was amazing how quickly I was adapting to my new economic status. But also, people would tend to be less suspicious of a guy cruising around in a Caddy convertible. At least that's what I told myself.

The gas pumper in West Orange knew exactly how to get to Wackowick Heights, and it turned out to be a hilly suburb that had nothing but huge estates, all with high brick walls and locked gates, behind which there were curving driveways and acres of mowed lawn. Some had gatehouses, but none of the main houses was visible through the wrought-iron bars. These places had to be owned by people whose Great Danes wouldn't even piss on the tires of a Cadillac.

A couple of the places had names the equivalent of Piper Hill embossed on brick columns beside the gate and a few had numbers on the mailboxes, but I couldn't find 1934 View Drive anywhere.

So at three P.M. I drove back to West Orange and had a cheeseburger, a large fries, and a diet cola at a fast-food joint where I was the only Caddy in the parking lot. I needed that to build up my ego again after the experience of Wackowick Heights. If I told the people there I was worth six million dollars, it would probably bring on a yawning fit. That is, if there really were people in Wackowick Heights. I hadn't spotted one human being, and the whole place could have been a movie set of false fronts.

As I chewed my way through the indigestible, I pondered my next action. I could go to city hall and try to find the records for 1934 View Drive in Wackowick Heights. That would tell me who owned the place but nothing more. Or I could go to the West Orange police department and seek help from the brotherhood. One reason I had joined the cops was that it made me a citizen of one of the ruling nations of the world. The lawyers called each other brother in court, but it was a Cain-and-Abel relationship; doctors, despite all their piousness about ethics and their ranting about the high cost of malpractice insurance, never squealed on another doctor when he fucked up, but they also didn't go out of their way to help each other up the ladder of life.

Cops were different. They weren't better people than lawyers or doctors. In fact, too many of them were worse scum than the criminals they were supposedly policing. But when the chips were down, when the nightstick was beating on the sidewalk or the radio informed the official channel that officers were in trouble, the response was automatic. They came through. They stuck together. And that was a big reason why a nice half-Jewish boy like me became and enjoyed being a policemen. I knew that even the biggest half-anti-Semite of any police force in the world would come to my aid and succor under any and all circumstances with no questions asked. And if I had questions, such as in

West Orange, New Jersey, I had a place to go ask them.

I told the sergeant on duty at the desk that I would like to speak to a homicide detective, and when he asked me why, I showed him my identification. He made a brief call and then directed me up the stairs and to the left and to a door that had "Lt. Cibelli" marked on it.

Cibelli turned out to be one of those swarthy human tanks who probably had just made the height requirement but who could also walk through a door without opening it. He shook hands and stared at me for a long moment.

"It is you, isn't it?" he said finally.

"What?"

"You're *the* Freedman, the cop who was kidnapped by that nutty church group and then blew the shit out of them."

"It was the Navy napalmed the canyon," I said. "I just kept my ass covered."

"Bullshit," he exhaled. "I watched the TV and I read the stories and I read between the lines. You did one hell of a job. What can I do for you? I don't recall anything coming in about a West Coast case. But then again, I'm lucky if they remember to give me a paycheck around here."

"It's not a case," I told him, wondering how much to actually tell him. "It's a personal matter."

"Sit down, sit down," he said, "make yourself comfortable. Jesus Christ, Benny Freedman."

The way he said it, you couldn't really tell which one was the deity. I thought of what I had gone through with the Church of the Holy Avenger in the canyon fortress they had established to withstand the nuclear holocaust when it came, and what I would have given at the time to have never had to go through it. But now that I had survived in one piece, I kind of liked the rewards in the respect and even adulation I was receiving as a result of it. You can't make an omelet without breaking eggs, my mother used to say at least once a day. And she didn't even know about the cholesterol that was involved.

"It all has to do with my late wife," I told him. "She came from this area and she left me a bit of money. Now some relatives have put in a claim against her estate. I've heard from their lawyer, but I don't know anything about them. So I'm trying to dig up some background. All I know is that at one time before she came to San Diego where I met her she lived at 1934 View Drive in Wackowick Heights."

His eyes bugged out. It was like looking at a giant bullfrog, and I held my breath for a moment as I wondered if they would stop or would keep getting bigger and bigger until they burst like balloons.

"Your wife was a Marchese?" he asked, wonderment in his voice.

"No, her maiden name was Slater. Catherine Slater."

"Slater," he mused to himself. "Slater. Slater."

He stood up and went to a metal filing cabinet behind him and pulled out a drawer. He riffled his fingers over the tops of the folders, and then dragged out one that was so bulky he could barely hold it in his two hands. He cursed as it almost got away but then plunked it down successfully on the desk, where papers spilled out from all three open sides of the folder. He pawed through and pulled out two typewritten pages that were stapled together. His finger ran down the list on the first page unsuccessfully, and he flipped over to the second page, where his finger continued its exploration.

"Slater, Slater," he was mumbling. "Ah! Slotnick. Hermie Slotnick. Was your wife's name Slotnick?" he asked, his eyes moving up to stare into mine.

"No. It was just plain Slater."

"There ain't no Slater on the list," he said. "The closest is Hermie Slotnick. Sometimes the Yids—Jewish people—shorten or change their names. But it doesn't say anything here about his having a family anyway. The list ain't up-to-date; it's probably three years since anybody looked in it. There was a time when we even staked out the place, but they're penny-ante now and we don't have the manpower. They've got about nine hundred acres there, and if you fired off a cannon in the middle, nobody else would hear it. Christ, they got lakes and brooks and a swamp that looks like alligators live there. Once we got a court order and went out there with backhoes and all kinds of crap because the feds said some bodies had been buried there, but we didn't find nothing. Hell, you could bury Ethiopia there without anybody finding any bones. I'm sure there are bodies out there and it was used for a dumping ground, and that's how Marchese got his little slice of the action. I've always had the feeling that the big families subsidize him the way Saudi Arabia takes care of the little Arab countries that only have sand instead of oil."

"Who was this Hermie Slotnick?" I asked.

He shook his head as if trying to shake the cobwebs out.

"I'm not sure I remember him," he said. "He could of been one of the soldiers or a gofer or had something to do with one of the shylock operations. It's been maybe five years since I was out there. It's a half-ass bunch. They call Marchese"—he pronounced it the Italian way, Mar-*kay*-zay, with the accent on the second syllable—" 'the Don,' but that's only his own palookas do that. In the old days, when they used to call him to go to one of the big meets in upstate New York, he had to wait outside in the main room of the restaurant while the real business was done in the private dining room upstairs. It was his first wife's father was the real big shot. Marchese married into the power, and when she died, she left the property to him in her will. So he's still got some guys living in the big house and the little bungalows scattered all over the place, but they're all getting on in years. The big money ain't there no more so they don't have no fresh young punks joining up with them. I heard the Don married some young chick a couple of years ago, but I ain't never seen her. Christ, he's got to be seventy, seventy-five years old."

"What about this Hermie Slotnick?" I prodded again. "Do you know if he had a daughter who would have been somewhere around thirty years old?"

"I can't help you there," he said. "I think I remember Slotnick and at the same time I can't remember him. He could have had a wife, a daughter, I just don't know. And there's nobody else on the force who can help you either. The chief and Captain Forester were the only other ones who ever had anything to do with Marchese, and they wouldn't know as much as I do. You think maybe your wife changed her name when she went west? She died pretty young, huh?"

"Yeah," I told him. "Cancer."

"Too bad," he said. "I haven't smoked in four years now."

"I guess I'll hang around town for a few days," I said, standing up. "What would you recommend for a motel?"

"There's a good one right past where I live," he said, "which will make it easier for you."

I squinched my eyebrows and looked at him.

"You're coming to my house for supper," he said, "and then you won't have to go far to go to bed. You like pasta?"

"I like pasta," I told him, "almost as much as I like matzoh-ball soup."

He laughed but at the same time I could see that he was noting down not to let any more "Yids" slip out. I wonder what would have gone through his mind if he'd known that the other half of my genes was Irish.

4

Texans tell about the visiting Englishman who was given his first taste of four-alarm chili and went crazy for it, shoveling down huge amounts as he babbled on about how it compared to the hottest of Indian curries. When he finally sat back and reported that he couldn't down one more bite, his hosts insisted that he must eat a quart of vanilla ice-cream.

"No dessert," he protested, "I am literally chock full."

They told him that it was absolutely necessary; it went with the territory. So spoon by spoon he ate the vanilla ice cream and then toddled off to bed.

In the middle of the night, they heard moans coming from his room. They knocked, but when no one answered, they entered and found their way to the guest bathroom. There, sitting on the throne, was the Englishman, his brick-red face raised in anguish toward the ceiling, his mouth imploring over and over, "Come on, ice cream!"

I have a weakness for hot and spicy things—chili that makes the little sweat beads pop out on your forehead, Polish horseradish, Chinese food in the style of Szechuan or Hunan, tandoori chicken. But there was nothing, nothing, nothing that compared to Mrs. Aldo Cibelli's homemade hot sausage.

To be truthful, as she kept confessing to me during the long and delicious meal, it wasn't her sausage. It was made by her husband's father, Anthony Cibelli, and to her taste it was a trifle too hot, but Aldo and the children liked it, and the old man brought a batch once a month, and God help you if the previous month's

supply wasn't gone when he went to place the new
links in the usual spot in the freezer.

I ate three of them. With the pasta. After the minestrone and before the chicken and the braccioli. The
salad cooled the mouth a little, as did the rough red
wine, and for dessert there were powdered fried dough
and thick slices of navel orange that had been dripped
with olive oil and sprinkled with rough-ground black
pepper. Then came the espresso that had as much
coffee grounds as liquid.

And while we were sitting in the living room with the
twenty-five-inch color TV blaring away, Cibelli plied
me with grappa and questions about what it had been
like when I was kidnapped by the church group. I
didn't leave there till nearly midnight, and I wish I had
left my stomach with them because I couldn't handle it
all alone in that motel room.

I spent half the night tossing on the bed and the rest
of the time sitting on the john in hopes that the cool
parts of the dinner would pass through at some time. I
had once been accused by a former girlfriend of being
anally oriented, and if she had been present in that
motel room, I would have apologized to her. At that
moment in time it was both the sun and the moon. But
then again, the shape I was in would have caused me to
apologize to anybody.

The diarrhea finally hit at 7:07 A.M. according to the
digital clock that was chained to the motel bedtable,
but I was unable to exactly note the subsequent attacks.
At 8:15 I falsely concluded that there could be no more,
that all that might be left were the villi, those fine hairs
in the small intestine that I learned about in ninth-
grade science. I couldn't remember exactly what they
were, but I did remember they were important in
digestion. I figured I might be dying because my whole
digestive system seemed to be passing in front of me.

I tried to brush my teeth but couldn't, and finally
gave it up and packed my stuff into the suitcase. My
usual solution to both physical and mental problems

was to do push-ups, hundreds of them at times, but I
could barely lift my arms, let alone push with them. My
plan . . . I sat down on the bed and tried to figure out if
I had a plan. My plan was to go out to the estate by
means of the directions Cibelli had carefully written out
for me the night before, ask the people there if they
knew anything about the former "Catherine Slater,"
and then go back to New York for the night and wait to
see if my stomach had returned with me and then return
home to the Coast. In ten days the mayor of our city
was going to present me with a medal and if I had
figured it right, announce my promotion to lieutenant.
I never should have started out on this cockamamie
chase in the first place. It was just that my wife had
been dead only a couple of months, I had gone through
hell when the crazy born-agains had kidnapped me
during a tough murder investigation, and then I had
cooped myself up in my apartment alone for almost five
weeks while I tried to catch both my breath and my
bearings. Those church people had so scared me that I
wasn't sure about my manhood, my guts, and the question was still open for debate. My taking off on this
wild-goose chase had come about strictly from frustration. I had needed to purge myself. Well, the Cibellis
had finally taken care of that for me. My asshole had
spoken; it was time my head took over.

The morning was cool but I drove with all the windows down, and by the time I got to the estate shown
on Cibelli's hand-drawn map, I just felt lousy, which
was maybe a thousand times better than I had been
feeling. The Marchese place was on one of the side
roads I had not taken the day before, all alone on a long
stretch of two-lane blacktop. "This was the road not
taken, Robert," I said aloud to the trees as I struggled
to open the heavy door of the Caddy and pull myself
out into the fresh air.

The gate was as fancy as any of the others I had seen
in the area, but when I got out of the car, I saw that
instead of stretches of mowed lawn and elaborate plant-

ings beside the long, curving driveway, there was rough underbrush and weeds and stunted trees. Either I had read the map wrong and was looking at an abandoned estate or the Marchese group did not care that much about keeping up with the Throckmortons.

There was a doorbell set into the left stone column and I pushed it. There was no way to tell if it was live or hooked up to anything, but I was in no physical condition to do more than push a button. To me, right then, the gate and the seven-foot wall, topped with iron spikes and embedded upright shards of colored glass, were insurmountable.

It could have been five minutes later, more or less, that I heard a vehicle coming down the blacktop driveway, and it turned out to be a jeep driven by a burly fellow who could have been Aldo Cibelli's second cousin. When he crawled out, I saw that he was wearing one of those rainbow-colored sport shirts outside his pants, which is as good a way to cover a handgun stuck in your waistband as punks have been able to devise over the ages. Cops in hot climates do the same thing. Where the weather is cool, you can wear either a shoulder or hip holster under your jacket. One time, when they sent me back among the churchers during the standoff, they hid a palm gun in my asshole, but it's not regular procedure. Out of habit, I had taken my Police Special along with me when I had chartered the jet to come east, but it was still in the suitcase. I thought about it being there for a fleeting moment as the guy came toward the gate, but shrugged away any reasons for going back to the car and sneaking it out. Nausea is never an inducement to decisive action.

The gorilla stared at me for a minute and I stared back, my head floating a little and my mouth tasting like the sewer line behind Cibelli's house.

"Yeah?" the guy finally said. He hadn't bothered to shave that morning, and I was quite sure he hadn't washed, and I would have bet that his breath matched mine.

"I'm looking for Mr. Slotnick," I said. "Herman Slotnick."

"Hermie don't live here no more."

"Then I would like to talk to Mr. Marchese." I had forgotten to ask what Marchese's first name was.

"About what?"

"It's personal."

"You a cop?"

"Yes, I am. But this is a personal matter."

"Does he know you?"

"I don't think so."

"You from West Orange?"

"No, I'm from California."

"What do you want to see him about?"

I had a vision of this going on forever, like that gateman scene in *Macbeth* that's supposed to be so hilarious, or one of those jokes about getting into hell or heaven, and the devil or St. Peter asks you all those questions until it ends up with an unfunny punch line, almost always racist. I put my hand against the stone column because I felt I might fall down. Then I reached in my pocket and pulled out my wallet. His eyes had followed me down and his hand had moved close to the middle of his sport shirt. I extracted one of my official police cards giving name, rank, department, and phone number and handed it through the bars. He took it and glanced at it in a way that made me wonder whether or not he could read.

"Please give that to Mr. Marchese and tell him I would like to see him on a matter of personal business," I said.

He pondered the problem. His inclination was to tell me to fuck off, but there always was the possibility that the Don might want to see me as much as I wanted to see him, and then there could be hell to pay. It was not this guy's business to make policy decisions. His usefulness was a matter of abject obedience and physical power. I breathed carefully and deep into my lungs while I wondered about Mrs. Cibelli's thawing proce-

dures. It was possible that it wasn't the hot that was
bothering me, but that Anthony Cibelli's sausage should
be fed to every Mexican tourist who visited our country.

The guy got back in his jeep and after much clashing
of gears turned around and headed back up the driveway. He was obviously not the gang's wheel man, and
would drive the getaway car only in a Woody Allen
movie. I returned to the Cadillac, opened the door on
the passenger side, and sat down sideways in the seat
so that I could rest my feet on the ground while contin-
uing to breathe the outside air.

I might have dozed because I didn't hear the return
of the jeep until it was right at the gate. He must have
been going too fast because even though he jammed on
the brakes, the vehicle slid into the right stone post and
broke off the left headlight. I apologized to Woody
Allen; this guy was strictly Three Stooges.

He had a duenna with him this time, a lady whose
age was indeterminate. She could have been anywhere
from twenty-two to thirty-five, but her face was so plain
and so creased with unhappy lines that she had to be
younger than she appeared at first glance to be.

Her voice was lovely, low and soft and inviting. It
made me want to rest my head between her capacious
bosoms and have her talk nice to me until my tummy
felt better.

"Hello," she said as she approached the gate. "I'm
Sofia Marchese and I understand you want to speak to
my father."

I looked at the door of the Caddy and decided it
wasn't worth the effort to close. Later. I'd close it later.
It was enough of an ordeal just to walk to the gate.
Shigella. That was the stuff that was worse than salmo-
nella. I'd been trying to find the word in the back of my
mind all the time I was waiting. Shigella could kill you.

"My name is . . ." I began to say until I noticed she
was holding my card.

"Freedman," she finished for me. "Benjamin Freedman. And you are here looking for Hermie Slotnick."

"Well," I told her, "he's not my real objective. I was hoping he might be a lead to somebody else I am really looking for."

"Hermie's dead," she said. "He died in New York just a few weeks ago. He fell off the roof of a building."

Befuddled as I was, the significance of what she said did not escape me. The classic cop phrase "fell or was pushed" went through my mind immediately. In my town, we had maybe forty people *fall* off buildings in the course of a year. The male fatalities were usually mob-related. They held them over the edge of the roof by their ankles until they spilled their guts on what somebody wanted to know, and then they dropped them. Or they beat them to pulp first for one reason or another and then they dropped them to cover up the bruises. Or pimps did it to hookers who had held out on them or maybe just looked cross-eyed at the wrong time. Husbands did it to wives, usually for suspected or actual cheating. Kids did it to other kids while horsing around. And sometimes people jumped for their own particular reasons. Maybe one person a year actually fell off a roof or a balcony or out a window. You give any cop in the world one of those psychological word tests, and one hundred out of a hundred will answer "pushed" when you say "fell."

"I am actually looking for someone who might have known a girl named Catherine Slater who reportedly lived at this address at one time," I said, and watched the woman's hand go up to her mouth, clenching into a fist that she grasped between her teeth. This was some kind of an answer to my question.

The hand came out of the mouth, but it took her another few moments to get the words going. She had to swallow a couple of times first, think about whatever instructions she had been given where she had come from, and decide on what she could tell me. Somebody, maybe her father, had sent her down for a reason. It was just that she hadn't been briefed on my particular question.

"Hermie had a daughter," she said, "and her name was Catherine. Catherine Slotnick."

"Did she look anything like this?" I asked, once more pulling out my wallet and flipping the credit-card section until I came to the piece of plastic holding Cathy's picture.

Her hand went back up to her mouth, the teeth biting into the first knuckle.

"That's Catherine," she said. "She's changed her hair, and her eyes look sad, but that's Catherine."

I turned the wallet around and looked at it closely. The picture had been taken the week before she told me about the cancer. The eyes were different. I'd looked at that picture I don't know how many times, and I'd never before noticed how the eyes had changed from the first time I had looked into them. I felt the nausea come up in my throat again, and I could hear my teeth grinding against each other. Fucking cancer. Fucking, fucking cancer.

"Is she here?" the woman asked.

"What?"

"Catherine. Is she here? In West Orange? They wouldn't . . . I didn't go to Hermie's funeral. Nobody went from here. So I haven't seen Catherine since she left. Is she here?"

"She's dead."

I'm sure the hand went back up to the mouth, but I didn't see it that time around. I stumbled around to the other side of the Caddy and tried to throw up, but all I could manage was long strands of mucus. I thought of the routine that Bill Cosby does about going to the dentist and how people roared with laughter when they watched him do it. Christ, I could be a headliner in Vegas with my routine. Only instead of killing the crowd, I was the one who was dying.

The sound of metal groaning and then shrieking in protest at being dragged over something against its will brought me back around the car again, still slightly bent over but with my lips wiped dry by my handkerchief.

The jeep driver had activated some machinery that was supposed to open the gate automatically, but the gate must have warped over the years and he had to pull and tug to get the bottom over the rough spots in the blacktop.

The woman walked out to me, her eyes red and tears streaming down her cheeks.

"How did Catherine die?" she asked.

"Cancer," I told her. I was in control now, able to say it.

"And you were a friend?" she asked.

"Husband."

"She married a policeman?" she asked, and I couldn't tell if it was plain disbelief or perhaps sheer horror.

"This policeman. She was married to this policeman."

She straightened up, all dignity, not bothering to wipe the tears from her cheeks. The word "policeman" had obviously reminded her of something, maybe whose daughter she was.

"My father will see you and talk to you," she said. "I will ride with you in your car, and we will follow Angelo."

Angelo. The angel. And there are people who think that Italians don't have a sense of humor.

5

We did not exchange one word all the way up that driveway, which was exactly 3.2 miles long, according to the flight-deck instrument of the Caddy, which was situated in the area that used to be called a dashboard. It was like driving a pinball machine. It had taken me from the rental agency in Manhattan way past the George Washington Bridge to figure out all the digital gadgets that flashed colorfully in front of the wheel. Well, almost all. Like in that old toilet joke, there was one button I was afraid to experiment with for fear I would suddenly have something stuck up my kazoo. And I was in no shape for that.

Sick as I felt, I was still nervous about where I was and who I was going to meet, so I clocked the distance up the driveway and looked for landmarks. There wasn't much to see except for the underbrush. There was one small house that looked lived in mainly because there was a bicycle leaning against the porch, but the clapboards needed a coat of paint and there were no curtains in the windows.

Miss Marchese was silent for her own reasons, and sat there in the leather bucket seat with her legs pressed together and her hands tightly clasped. The guy in the jeep in front of us would drive slowly and then speed up and wobble from side to side on the road. It was necessary to keep half an eye on him so that I didn't run up his tailpipe.

Suddenly we broke out into a clearing and there was the house, a huge three-story gray fieldstone building that had turrets at each end. It looked like the kind of place the movie stars built in Hollywood in the 1920's, copied after somebody's idea of a palazzo. "How many rooms you got there?" I blurted out, surprised at what I was seeing.

"Twenty-six," she said. "There were a lot more people living here when my grandfather built it. They say it is like one he admired in Sicily when he was a boy."

The jeep had stopped at the entrance to the curved driveway that led to the front door of the house, and Sofia indicated with her arm that I was to go around it and drive up to the entranceway. As we reached there, the door of the house opened and a little old man in a white cafeteria-restaurant jacket shuffled down the stairs and opened the door of the car on the girl's side.

I got out on my own and stretched, which was a mistake because it made the blood rush to my head or something, and once more I felt dizzy. I wondered if I should excuse myself, drive back to West Orange, book myself into the motel again, and stay in bed until this thing went away. Or a hospital. Maybe I should see a doctor and get some blood tests or stool tests or whatever they did to check for poisoning. If I lived through what was wrong with me, it was going to be yogurt and a bland diet from then on. And I was definitely going to report one Anthony Cibelli to the federal Food and Drug Administration as a public menace. Jesus, I felt bad.

"Thank you, Tomaselli," said the girl to the little guy, who had to be somewhere in his eighties with one of those wizened little almost-black faces that look like an African Pygmy tribe has put it through one of their shrinking pots. He was watching me out of his beady little eyes, and I wondered if he had a gun hidden under his white jacket, which was really more grimy gray than white.

"Come inside," said the girl, and started up the stone stairs to the door that looked like it had been purloined

from a cathedral somewhere. The jeep driver was standing back at the entrance to the driveway with his eyes
focused on me, as were those of Tomaselli. I followed
the girl's thick legs up the stairs and into the house.

There was no doubt that everything inside was the
original furniture, and that nobody dusted much. The
floors were marble with worn scatter rugs all over the
place, enough to make it possible to step from rug to
rug without once hitting bare stone. Some of the rugs
were huge and some were small, and there was no
rhyme or reason to how they were laid out.

The furniture was all heavy pieces, gigantic side-
boards of walnut and chairs and couches with that stiff
brocaded material that looks itchy. The colors of most
of them had faded into indistinguishable browns and
reds, and the lighting was furnished by lamps that had
shades with fringes all around the edges. The first big
room we went into had a glittering chandelier on its
high ceiling, and the next big room had a mural painted
on the ceiling, one with angels and cherubs and clouds,
mostly in light blues and pinks.

The sun was shining outside but you could barely
distinguish the light through the windows in the dark
interior. Surprisingly, the whole effect was soothing,
and it calmed my stomach down a bit. You felt safe
behind those thick walls and in the dim interior, as if
the outside world couldn't get at you.

The woman finally stopped at the entrance to another
large room and waited for me to catch up. I looked past
her back, and there seated behind a desk the size of a
pool table at the other end was an elderly gentleman
with one of those bushy mustaches. He was wearing a
white linen jacket, a white shirt, and a white tie, and
there was a small resemblance to that actor who does a
routine in which he's supposed to be Mark Twain. Hal
somebody.

The desk was covered with papers, and the old man
was scribbling away on one of the sheets with a gold
ball-point pen.

"Papa," called the girl from where we were standing. She had emphasized both P's in "Papa," giving it a European pronunciation. It would have brought my head up with a jerk, but the old guy seemed not to hear it.

"Papa," she repeated, maybe a trifle louder, and the pen stopped its movement, and he slowly looked up to where we were across the room from him.

A smile came over his face, which I realized was damned distinguished-looking, as the full glow of the smile bathed his daughter and turned her face a little pink.

"Sofia," he said, "come in, come in. And bring your friend."

Jesus. It was as if I was courting this lady and I was there to ask for her hand in marriage. Friendly but formal. Or was it formal but friendly? One thing was for sure. This kind of greeting had nothing to do with my being a sergeant of homicide come to call for some information. According to Cibelli, the Don was nothing compared to his late father-in-law, but just a simple hello from him had impressed the hell out of me.

I followed her across the room until we reached the desk where I moved up to stand beside her.

"Forgive me for not rising," he said directly to me, "but I am an old man whose body is disintegrating."

"Papa," said the daughter, "your gout is acting up a little. There is nothing really wrong with you."

"Hah!" said the old man gently. "Heart, blood pressure, arthritis, glaucoma, shingles. A little gout, eh? I am dying and my family treats me like I have a hangnail."

She started to protest again, but he held up his hand and it cut her off like one of those comedians doing the applause routine. I wondered if all this guy had to do was raise a little finger and somebody died. What the hell did I know about the Mafia except what I read in the papers and saw on television? We had it in our own

city, but no one had ever gone beyond individual in-
dictments for drug-peddling or loan-sharking or prostitution or stuff like that. The feds were probably working
on the big picture of the families and high-level meet-
ings and all that crap, but we were lucky if the feds
gave us the time of day, let alone a rundown on how
the Mafia might be operating in our area. If the Don
really was a member of the Mafia, he was the first one I
had ever come up close to.

"Papa," the girl started again, and when he looked to
see that she was not going into his health situation, he
let her talk this time. She was holding my card in her
hand again.

"Mr. Freedman," she said, "Sergeant Freedman, is
married . . . was married to Catherine. To Hermie's
daughter."

The bushy salt-and-pepper eyebrows arched at that
information, whether in surprise or pleasure I couldn't
tell.

"Ah, Catherine," he said, "the pretty Catherine. How
is she?"

"She's dead, Papa," said Sofia. "The sergeant says
she is dead."

"Catherine?" said the Don. "But she's only . . . what?
. . . she's only a year older than you."

"Cancer," I informed him.

"Ah. My doctor tells me there is a suspicious spot on
the last set of X rays they took of me. I must have
further tests soon."

I didn't know how to answer that one so I just kept
quiet. I had the feeling that you could mention any
disease and this guy would top you by a virus, a blood
clot, or a CAT scan. And at the same time I wouldn't
have bet on the winner if I had to arm-wrestle him
three out of five.

"I had to come east on business," I said, "and on
impulse decided to look up Cathy's old haunts. This
was the address I had."

"Where have you come from?" asked the old man. "Where has Catherine been living these years?"

"California. We live in San Diego."

"She and her father lived here for many years," he said, "much of it right in this house. Catherine and Sofia were close, like sisters. It stayed the same even when they moved into their own house, didn't it?"

"I can't believe she's dead," Sofia blurted, tears popping out of her eyes and small sobs shaking her. "First Hermie and now Catherine. God has closed his eyes to us."

"There, there," soothed her father, "it's not for us to question. He'll be taking me before long."

"Oh, Papa," the girl wailed, rocking her body back and forth. Jesus, this guy was good. Dressed up in his Sydney Greenstreet whites, all he needed was Peter Lorre whining somewhere in the background. One thing about television was that it kept you up-to-date on all the old movies and all the classic acting techniques. I hoped I would get to see him doing a routine on the guy who drove the jeep.

"I have to be getting back to West Orange," I said.

"But you just arrived here," said the Don. "You must stay to lunch. We must talk. We want to know about Catherine. Since you are Catherine's husband, you are now part of our family. You must stay."

"Well, to tell you the truth," I said, "I'm not feeling very well. I ate some hot sausage at Lieutenant Cibelli's last night, and it didn't seem to agree with me."

I had been watching closely, and the name Cibelli caused a flicker in the old man's eyes. I was feeling very insecure inside this stone fort, which probably had several jeep drivers wearing sport shirts close by, and the way my stomach and head were feeling, I couldn't handle the pressure.

"You do look a little pale," said the Don, "but we'll fix you right up for that."

He pushed back his chair, stood, and went over to a sideboard on the left wall, which had dozens of bottles of liquor on top of it. He selected one, poured a healthy dollop of the dark liquid into a fluted wineglass, and brought it over to me.

"Drink this," he commanded, "and you'll soon feel better. My mother made us drink a glass of this every week, and we could digest nails."

The way I was feeling, Socrates could have handed me a small wooden bowl with liquid in it and I would have slurped it down. So I took the glass and in one swallow drained it. When the aftertaste hit, the shock was so great that I was paralyzed. If someone had given me the choice of a Cibelli sausage or another glass of this stuff, I would have had to think about it carefully. The lady or the tiger? It was the foulest, bitterest, most awful stuff that had ever passed my lips going down. Going up, of course, was another story.

I sputtered around the area for a few moments, unable to stay in one spot and so weak on my legs that I was afraid of falling. When I was able to clear enough tears from my eyes to see, there was the Don smiling benignly at me.

"What is that?" I gasped.

"Fernet Branca," he answered. "The Italian cure for everything. It's like your chicken soup. Now you'll be able to stay for lunch."

"No," I said, "I still have to get going. I have appointments with people."

And as I said it, my head got whirlier and whirlier, and I felt myself going down. I knew I was passing out and I wondered what had really been in that drink. They wouldn't poison me until they found out where the six million dollars was and whether I had left it in a will to somebody else. They wouldn't kill me after I had told them about Cibelli. They wouldn't kill me just like that. But then again, who knew what these people might do? Blood and pride were very important to them, and I might have offended on both accounts. So maybe I was passing out for good. The final indignity was that just before I lost consciousness, I realized I had also lost bladder control and was in the process of pissing my pants. The only consolation was that I knew there was nothing left to come out of the other end. A small consolation, but a consolation nevertheless as I passed into the great darkness.

6

There's a stock scene in television action dramas that probably ranks third to helicopter and car crashes. It has to do with getting knocked out. Or rather, with coming to. From unconscious to conscious, whether it's from being bonged on the head by a bad guy or having an operation and the anesthetist does the deed.

The camera takes the place of a person's eyes, and the angle is always straight up. It starts off blurry and then clears as the person supposedly returns from gagaland to the here and now.

The big scriptwriter in the sky brought me back in time-honored fashion because everything was blurry at first and then gradually cleared. The distorted object leaning over me turned out to be one of the most beautiful faces I had ever seen. The hair was a little too blond, which meant that her hairdresser lent a helping hand to the genes that had been literally laid down, but the various parts of the face had been highlighted into an incredible whole by only the tiniest bits of makeup here and there, just as frosting augments the tastiness of the cake. But at the same time you knew you could eat her cake plain and still think it was the best birthday you ever had.

"You're awake," she said. "How are you feeling?"

There's always something. Sofia's voice was as beautiful and sexy as her face was homely and her legs were thick. The work of art bending over me had a voice that was close to breaking glass. Not quite a nail drawn across a blackboard, but definitely one that you wouldn't want to spend the rest of your life listening to. Lovely to look at, probably delightful to know, but you prayed God she wouldn't sing.

"Where am I?" I asked. My mouth had not improved in taste since I had . . . since I had what? Drunk that infernal Branca. It all came back to me—the hot sausages, the visit to the Marcheses, the drinking of the potion, and the passing out.

"You're here," she said.

I figured right then that this lady's brain might match her voice. One step at a time.

"Where's that?"

"Here. At the Villa Marchese."

Jesus. Even in the Mafia you had yuppiness. The Villa Marchese. Did they have a guy named Villa buried on a hill somewhere? The Villa Marchese in Wackowick Heights. Next thing you knew they'd be mowing their lawn.

I moved my arms out from under the sheet and heard a rustle like a hundred snakes moving in the grass. Silk on silk. I was wearing purple silk pajamas and tucked in between silk sheets. One wrong move and I would slide all the way back to West Orange. Or maybe even California.

"Who tucked me in?" I asked, moving my head slightly to the left so that my breath had no chance of defiling that lovely face.

"I don't know," she said. "I've been in New York shopping and having my hair done, and Tomaselli just told me about you. He said you'd been unconscious for two days, so I thought I'd come and take a peek."

Two days! What the hell had they put in that drink? God, I was thirsty. Hot and thirsty. I put my hand up and felt the stubble on my cheek. The skin felt dry and warm. When I raised and lowered my lids, I could feel the grit on my eyeballs. They always felt like that when I had a fever. They had put bubonic plague in the drink. They were going to take me out with an exotic disease rather than pop five .22 slugs in the back of my head and dump me in a bog somewhere.

"Are you another daughter?" I asked. Sometimes it happened in families. There were the ugly sisters and Cinderella by the fireplace.

"What?"

"Are you Sofia's sister?"

She laughed. The laugh wasn't as bad as the speaking voice, but it was still shrill enough to put my furry teeth on edge.

"I'm her mother," she said.

I could only stare.

"Her stepmother, silly! I'm two years younger than my daughter. My stepdaughter."

One time when Cathy and I had been out to dinner and had drunk maybe three Scotches before we ate, and then had a half-bottle of white and a full bottle of red with the food and two cognacs afterward, and then had come home and had two more cognacs, we had become very giggly. Very, very giggly. And she had started babbling about this nobleman she knew back east, whom she called the Don.

"What his full name?" I had asked. "Don who?"

She had thought for a moment and then had smiled brilliantly at her own cleverness.

"He's a Spanish Don and his name," she had announced grandly, "is Fugaroun. Don Fugaroun." She had pronounced it very carefully so that I would get the joke, and from then on, sometimes when we were about to make love, she would stop, raise her head high, and say "Don Fugaroun." It always put her into the giggles even when she wasn't tiddly from drink, and quite often we would have to start the sex from scratch again. Or from rub or tickle. Literally.

It could be that she was thinking of Don Marchese at the time, and that the old son of a bitch had made a move on her when she was in residence. If he had the ego to be married to this piece of voluptuousness with the burden of his years and various terminal infirmities, he probably also believed he could get that six million dollars back from me one way or another. This had to be the source of the letter and the instrument of Wenker's death. Now they had me tied up in silk pajamas with nobody really knowing where the hell I was. Except maybe for Cibelli. My ultimate health probably rested with Cibelli. He had seemed like a smart cop, and he also seemed to like me despite my being a Yid. You didn't invite just anybody to your house for a home-cooked meal on first acquaintance, even a national hero like me. Or maybe you did. Of course, he could also be in the pay of the mob and have tried to kill me with the poisoned sausage. And when that hadn't quite worked, they had tried to finish the job off with the poisoned drink. The vessel with the pestle has the brew that is true. I tried to think of a label that the surgeon general could put on each of the Cibelli sausages. The beautiful face leaned down close to mine, and I wondered how ugly I could make it look if I just exhaled once in her direction.

"Do you want anything to eat or drink?" she asked. "Mama Maria could make you something tasty."

I swallowed experimentally to see if I could feel some reaction, and the result was a gurgle in the stomach area. The thought of food did not evoke nausea. I was weak and almost definitely dehydrated.

"Some orange juice?" I ventured. "A scrambled egg? Toast? Rye toast maybe?" Maybe I was a little hungry. The thought of rye toast had opened up my salivary glands a bit.

She laughed. "No rye toast in this house," she said. "It's Italian bread or nothing. You better like Italian bread and pasta if you're going to be around here awhile."

It made me wonder how long I was going to be around there. It also made me wonder how long I was going to be around. I was experimenting with sitting up to see how much strength there was in my body if I had to make a run for it, when a man came into the room.

He had a full beard to go with his bushy head of hair, so it took me a few seconds to figure him somewhere in his middle or late thirties. Like the lovely lady who had just left me, he didn't look Italian, even though his skin was tanned almost to the color of Tomaselli's skull. He was wearing dark glasses, khaki shirt and pants, and sandals.

"Hey," he said, "Elena just told me you'd come to. I was beginning to wonder if maybe you belonged in a hospital."

"Maybe I do," I told him. "I think I've got a fever and I'm sure I was poisoned by some bad sausage. What I'd like to do is get back to West Orange because I'm supposed to meet some people there. I told them and Lieutenant Cibelli that I was just coming out here for a couple of hours, and they must be wondering where I am."

"He called."

"What?"

"Cibelli called. He said he was calling because you'd checked out of your motel and he knew you were coming out here and he wanted to know if we'd seen you."

My heart sank into my troubled stomach. Yes, he was here, they'd told him, but then he left and we don't know where he is now.

"You told him I was sick?"

"I didn't talk to him. Sofia took the call and I guess she filled him in on what happened because he said he'd drop out to see how you were doing. The Don got pissed off at her something awful when she told him about Cibelli calling. Started yelling in Italian and she ended up crying, which is nothing unusual."

"What was he mad about?"

"I have no idea. The only word I know in Italian is 'vino.' It's like I was a little kid around here. Whenever they don't want me to know what they're talking about, they switch to Italian."

He sat down on the edge of the bed, pulled my wrist to him, and placed two fingers on the spot where my pulse was supposed to be.

"You a doctor?" I asked him.

He smiled and continued his hold for a couple of seconds more.

"They call me Doc," he said, standing up once again, "but I'm not a real doctor. Evaluation of controlled substances is my specialty."

A big old lady, pretty near six feet tall, dressed all in black except for a white apron tied around her waist, came into the room carrying a tray that had on it a plate with scrambled eggs and two toasted, heavily buttered, thick slices of Italian bread. There was also a mug that contained what looked and smelled like half coffee and half hot milk.

"Ah, Mama Maria," said Doc, "that looks like it would get anybody back on his feet." Then, turning to me, he said, "But I'd go easy and take small bites and chew carefully. Your pulse is still fast from the fever, and you're a couple of days from getting up."

"They say this is Caterina's husband," said the old lady, placing the tray on the lap I hastily assembled for the reception. She was looking at neither me nor the Doc, seemingly addressing the wall. Before anybody could answer, she spoke again.

"They say my Caterina's dead. *Morta!*"

Tears were running down her cheeks as she spread a linen napkin for me and adjusted the knife and fork, which had slipped under the plate. She still wasn't looking at anybody in particular, and she turned and left the room without speaking again or waiting to hear if there were answers to her questions.

"Who was that?" I asked. I knew it was Mama Maria but I wanted to know whose Mama Maria. She looked the right age to be the Don's wife, but I already had met the Don's wife. Was she the mother of the Don's wife?

"Mama Maria," said Doc, "was the mother of the Don's first wife, Celeste. I never knew the lady but they say that Sofia is the spitting image of her mother."

"So Mama Maria is the one who owns this place?"

"No, Don Marchese owns this place. Maria's husband, Ugly, left the estate to Celeste rather than to her mother or her brother because he felt that a man should run the family and its holdings."

"Wait a minute," I said, holding a forkful of egg in midair and watching it tremble because of the shakiness of my hand. "You said there was a brother. Is he dead too?"

"As far as the father was concerned he was," said Doc. "They tell me the old man always felt that his son Vincent had no balls, whereas his daughter's husband, the present Don, was all balls. I don't know how many notches the Don has on his pistol, but they say he was a real ball-buster in his day. So she got the farm, and when she died, she left it all to him."

"But who was Ugly? You mentioned an Ugly?"

The Doc laughed. He had a lot of laugh creases in his face. I thought maybe I might get to like him if circumstances were right.

"Umbriago," he said. "Umbriago 'Ugly' Merlino. In the Mafia, you have to have a nickname, and his was Ugly. And from the pictures I've seen, his was well-deserved."

There. He'd come right out and said it. Mafia. Yes, Virginia, there is a Mafia, and I was sitting in some kind of headquarters eating scrambled eggs and toast and wearing silk pajamas.

I don't know what turn the conversation would have taken after that, but Sofia came in before another word could be spoken.

"Who gave you that?" she asked, pointing at the food on my plate with a horrified look on her face. "You should be on a liquid diet until your bug goes away."

First things first.

"I understand Cibelli called," I said, "and he's coming out to see me."

"As soon as he can," she said.

"What does that mean?"

"He said that everybody in his family but his wife got sick as dogs the night you ate there and that he had gone back to work this morning, but it had come on him again, and the doctor had told him to go back to bed."

Mrs. Cibelli hadn't eaten any of her father-in-law's sausages. She said they were too spicy for her.

"I told him what had happened to you," she continued, "and that since you were Catherine's husband, you were also family, and that we would take care of you until you were back on your feet. He said he was sorry and he hoped you felt better than he did. Now give me that tray, and I will bring you a glass of cola. And then you must sleep. Shoo," she told the Doc. "This man must have rest."

So after two long sips of lukewarm cola because cold was supposed to be bad for a man in my condition, I was tucked in again by Sofia. The concern on her face made her look almost pretty in the dim light.

I had managed three forks of eggs and one whole piece of toast before she had come in, and they felt comforting in my belly, whose noises had quieted down to a soft rumble.

Family. She said I was family, I remembered as the drowsiness started taking over my body. As an only child, with a father who was as *meshuggah* as he was talented and a mother who was a classic Irish alcoholic, I had never known the comfort of the archetypal American family as described by Ronald Reagan when he addressed Pro-Life groups. It was something I had always yearned for in the secret recesses of my mind. And now I was being given a second chance. The lady had said I was "family." I wondered if that made all those Gambinos, Genoveses, Colombos, Luccheses, and Bonnanos my cousins. My last thought before I slipped into a dreamless sleep was that I should be getting some great presents on my birthday.

7

*D*o you remember those puzzles they used to have in the Sunday comic sections where there would be a half-page drawing of a bunch of trees and foliage, and the object was to find the faces that the artist had cleverly hidden among the limbs and branches and leaves and flowers?

It was only by chance that my eyes picked out the face of the little old lady who had poked her head barely around the corner of the doorjamb. She had to have been dressed all in black because her head seemed to be floating in space and her skin was almost as dark as that of Tomaselli and she couldn't have been more than four and a half feet tall and her eyes must have been all pupil with no white showing. I think it was the wrinkles that gave her away, the contrast where the light and dark crossed.

As soon as she saw that my eyes had stopped and focused on her, she was gone, and five minutes later a man appeared to replace her. Unlike the woman, who had obviously been his lookout, he didn't sneak around the corner but swaggered into the room. At least he thought he was swaggering. To me he just looked like a cocky little shit whose role model might have been Mussolini. The head was held at that peculiar angle affected by Il Duce, but his akimbo arms were too short to be impressive.

There was a scraggly mustache vaguely shaped like the one that adorned the Don, and the white suit could also have been a cheap imitation of that worn by the big boss. I had heard once that everybody who worked for

58

IBM dressed alike in dark suits and white shirts, and wondered if this was also the case in the Mafia. There was so much to learn that I shivered a little in anticipation. Now that I knew that Cibelli knew where I was, I felt a lot better about my health, and that had nothing to do with the bug that was giving me the fever. If you've got your health, my Jewish father used to say, you don't need anything else. Once, when he was looking at the twisted fingers that forced him to give up his life as a second violinist with the Boston Symphony, he said, "And even if you've got your health plan, you're not good for anything else either." That was a couple of weeks before he swallowed the eighteen pills with the help of a fifth of whiskey. Cibelli was my health plan. If I had Cibelli, I had my health. It suddenly occurred to me that the sausages might kill him off before he had a chance to tell anybody else where I was, and this gave me a momentary twinge, but I decided to think positive.

"So you're Catherine's husband," said the ugly little guy. His voice was somewhat strident, nervous, and his tone sounded like he was accusing me of being Catherine's husband rather than asking or stating a fact. I pushed myself into a sitting position and just looked at him. I couldn't stand the taste in my mouth, but he didn't look like anybody who would come up with a toothbrush and paste. His lips curled a bit and his teeth verified my supposition.

"Sofia's all excited about your being here," he sneered. "She hasn't done a goddamned thing to help me today. I carry the whole load of this place on my back, and she knows I don't know a fucking thing about how that computer works. We got all the payrolls to get out, and she's in the kitchen making you minestrone from scratch. She wants me to go into West Orange and get her some fresh escarole. How did you and Catherine get to be married?"

"We met, we fell in love, and we got married," I told him. "The magic was there."

"Yeah," he said. "The magic was also there for her

and Tullio Bandisi. And for her and Rocky Moritz. And
for her and Gidge De Fazie. You want some more
names? The list is as long as the fucking payroll that
Sofia ain't helping me with because she's got to make
soup."

I had used the word "magic" sarcastically because I
had taken an instant dislike to this guy, and I knew
there had never been any magic in his life. But he'd
turned it back on me with a vengeance. The knife had
been twisted out of my hands and into my gut. Catherine had turned out to be more than sexually proficient
when I met her, when, as a matter of fact, she had
picked me up in the bar that night. I had been involved
in a liquor-store shoot-out and had winged a guy in the
arm and was too revved up to go home. So we went to
her home. And that was the beginning. I knew she
wasn't a virgin just as I was by no means a virgin, but
she was dead now and it hurt to hear about a list as long
as a fucking payroll. It hurt bad and I almost used the
bug in my stomach as an excuse to double over. I
wasn't a male chauvinist pig; you could ask any female
cop on the force. I didn't expect my wife's past to be
any purer than mine, but there flashed through my
mind the picture of Angelo, the jeep driver, and I
wondered if all those guys who had been named, and
the ones unnamed, were stamped from the same mold.

"Who are you?" I asked, wanting to direct my hatred
toward a specific name rather than an ugly body.

"Me? I'm nobody, that's who I am. Mr. Nobody.
Vincent Nobody. The guy who keeps this whole place
going, who works his fingers to the bone, who gave up
his inheritance to his sister, may the angels guard over
her, so my brother-in-law can live in style and shower
the hooker he calls his wife with every luxury that my
money can buy. Catherine never told you about me?"

"Catherine never told me about anybody. That's why
I came here, to find out. You're Vinnie who?"

He came in and sat down on the leather chair against
the wall, all belligerence suddenly out of him. The

resemblance to Sofia was striking, both about five feet, seven inches tall, same bone structure in the face, maybe his a little more delicate, dark skin, big eyes, ears with large lobes, his hair thin on top, hers thick, he with a small potbelly, she the same circumference of stomach and hips.

"I'm Uncle Vinnie," he said. "I'm Sofia's Uncle Vinnie. Catherine used to call me Uncle Vinnie too. She never told you about all the presents Uncle Vinnie used to give her? Me and Hermie, we were thick. When they moved to their own house on the other side of the woodlot, I'd spend as much time there as I would here. Hermie took care of all the books then. He could do it faster and better than all the fucking computers in the world hooked together. He could fix books so that even the guys who make sure they don't cheat at the Oscar thing in Hollywood, even those guys wouldn't know they were looking at doctored books. But now, now it's all in the computer, and Sofia, she just knows how to do it straight. Sure, there are guys who know how to fix things even in the computer, but we can't afford guys like that. Guys like that cost money, and we're lucky if we clear enough from the pizza parlors and the bakeries and the laundry to keep the fucking Don Marchese and his whore in . . . Jesus, you're a cop."

He hadn't even remembered I was in the room after he started his complaint, but when he finally did remember, he remembered hard, and closed his mouth with a snap.

"They're all legitimate," he said defensively, looking down at the floor. "They're all legitimate businesses. Every dime that comes into this house now is clean money. Sofia and me, we work our fingers to the bone, and nobody appreciates it. I ain't putting Sofia down. Her only fault is she thinks her old man shits gelato even though he waited only eight months after her mother died to bring that whore into the house. Sofia says they really are married, that the Don is the kind of man who needs someone to take care of him. As if we all didn't take care of him when my sister was alive. All Elena takes care of is the spending of the money. You say that Catherine never mentioned me? Never mentioned her Uncle Vinnie?"

"You've got to be a Merlino," I said. "Vincent Merlino. Your father was Ug . . . was Umbriago and your sister was the Don's first wife."

"I don't blame her," he said excitedly. "I don't blame the dead. She always thought of the whole family owning this place and the businesses, and the will was just a formality. We didn't mind sending him the money to live in Miami because the weather was too cold for him here. But when he brought her back with him and they turned this whole place upside down, something's got to give. Just because he heard Bonnano and Valachi and those other guys got a million bucks for writing their stories, he thinks he's going to get the same. So he's scribbling away all day and all night, and he tells us he's writing a book. The son of a bitch never even finished high school. I at least finished high school, and Sofia went two years to junior college. Her and Catherine. We ain't never going to write no books. But he makes believe he's writing the inside story of the families. The families! He's lucky if they send him a truckload of waste once in a while to dump in the swamp. He's lucky if they . . ."

He stopped abruptly as it came through to him once more that he was talking to a cop. This guy was so frustrated he would have spilled his guts to the head of the FBI if he thought he was listening. There was a bit of froth on both sides of his mouth as he ranted on, and I thought that maybe he might also be a little crazy. He was out of the chair and out of the room before I could even blink at him.

Uncle Vinnie. Pizza parlors and bakeries and a laundry. Great drug fronts in the old days, but now if you bit into a pizza or a slice of bread, you were likely to break your tooth on an FBI bug. I smiled at the thought of the Mafia stuck with all those legitimate businesses and having to beat out the competition without being able to bomb storefronts or cripple somebody.

As soon as I realized I was smiling, I knew I was getting better. I pushed my stomach in with both hands, hard, and although it hurt, the pain was nothing compared to what it had been. The swelling in my belly had gone down. The smile cracked my face and opened my nostrils and I could smell how sour I was in those silk pajamas. There were two closed doors in the room besides the one that was open, and when I tried the one on the left, it turned out to be a nice tilted bathroom. The tub had sliding glass doors for the shower, and I turned it on just hot enough and lathered up and stood there in the warm steam, letting it run across my face and down my back, and I raised my arms and scrubbed my armpits until they hurt.

The towel was thick and soft and I wiped my body dry and then wrapped it around my waist. The other door turned out to be the closet, just as this detective had figured it out to be, and there were the clothes I had been wearing hanging neatly on the rod. Everything had been washed and pressed, including the tie, but I didn't feel like anything tight around my neck so I left that hanging.

My suitcase was on the floor and I rummaged through it until I found the toilet kit with the toothbrush and paste. I was in the middle of scrubbing up and down for the second time when it hit me, and I dropped the brush in the sink and whipped back to the closet. Pulling the suitcase into the room, I rummaged through it with my hands, and when that didn't work, I turned it over and dumped everything out on the floor. It wasn't there. The gun and the holster were gone.

I was still on my knees in front of the mess when Sofia came into the room.

"What are you doing?" she cried, dropping down beside me and taking me by the shoulders with both her hands. "Why aren't you in bed? Why are you dressed? You're a sick man. What are you doing?"

"My gun is gone," I told her. "Someone took my gun."

"What gun?"

"My gun! I'm a policeman. Someone took my gun."

"Don't worry about it," she said. "We'll find it. And if we don't, we'll get you another one. There are plenty of guns around here."

That got my attention and I turned my head to look into her eyes. No, she wasn't putting me on; she was serious. Guns weren't that big a deal with her. Everybody had one. Cops, crooks, everybody had one.

"You've got to go back to bed," she said. "I've brought you clean pajamas."

There on the floor, where she'd dropped them when she had fallen to her knees beside me, was a clean pair of silk pajamas, only this time they were pink. She stood up and pulled me to my feet, a strong girl, and suddenly I felt very weak and maybe sick again. She peeled off my jacket and unbuttoned my shirt and removed it, and sat me down on the bed. She knelt and pulled off my shoes and socks, loosened my belt and stripped down my pants as I raised my rear to give room.

But when she reached for my shorts, I caught hold of her hands.

"Hey," I said, "I can handle this from here. You go do what you have to."

She shook her head impatiently.

"You're Catherine's husband," she said, "and that's the same as being my husband."

She stripped them down and left me sitting on the bed naked as a jaybird as she reached to the floor for the pajamas. I looked down at my dick, which had been shriveled by the poison sausage into the weeniest of weenies. She was right. A nun could have looked at that thing without blushing.

I let her slip the bottoms up on me and button the top into place. Then she tucked me between the sheets again and I fell back exhausted.

"Tonight we've got to change these sheets," she said. "But right now you sleep."

Which I did immediately, and did not wake again until the aroma of hot minestrone hit my nostrils from the tray that was brought in by the little gnome who had been peeking through the door at me. She did not say one word as I pulled myself into a sitting position and made myself ready for the soup and the toasted Italian bread.

That minestrone was so good that I became hungrier with each spoonful. The broth had a richness I had never experienced in a soup, and there seemed to be every vegetable you could think of, including, as I stirred the bits of green with my spoon, fresh escarole.

The little old lady returned in about fifteen minutes with sheets over her arm, and changed the bed while I was in the bathroom. I took my time and even shaved, and when I came out, she was gone.

I crawled back into bed and lay there thinking about the questions I wanted to ask Sofia when she came back. But I fell asleep again, and when I woke, it was pitch black in the room. I was thirsty and thought about getting up for a drink, but I wasn't sure where the light switch on the lamp was situated, and before I could make any hard decisions, I knew I was slipping off to sleep again.

The last thing I thought of was Sofia saying, "You're Catherine's husband, and that's the same as being my husband."

What the hell did she mean by that? I took a course in religion once in the two-year college I attended in Boston because it was supposed to be a gut. And I remembered reading about the Jewish custom of the husband having to marry the sister of his dead wife. It had stayed in my mind because the footnote said that if the brother refused to marry the widow, she had the right in the presence of the elders to pull off his shoe and spit in his face. I had used that example in the exam but because I had spelled "Deuteronomy" wrong,

the fucking rabbi who taught the course had marked
the whole answer wrong. I think I had left the first E
out. But these people were Italian Catholics and not
Jewish. Sofia had a cross dangling between her huge
bezooms. The New Testament was second-semester and
I never got to that because I got a D in the Old
Testament and that cured me of religion forever. Was
there something in the New Testament about taking
over people's husbands? She was as homely as Cathy
had been pretty, but Cathy couldn't make homemade
soup for shit.

Who the hell had my gun?

8

I'm one of those people who can't sleep when there's any light in the room. Before she took sick, Cathy could have zonked in the middle of a prison yard with all the spotlights on her and the sirens wailing. But in her last month, I don't think she slept for a second because of the pain and maybe because of what was going through her mind. At first I would try to stay awake all the time in case she needed something or maybe just wanted to talk, but I eventually became so tired that I couldn't keep my eyes open, and it finally reached the point where my head would hit the pillow and I would be gone for six and sometimes eight hours of black, dreamless sleep. I was probably copping out on what was happening as much as sleeping, but I couldn't help it. I would feel so guilty when I woke up that I would have trouble getting out of the bed and walking around to where she could see me. The first couple of weeks she would smile to let me know she understood, and I would run around switching the IV bottles and washing her down with a cloth or changing the waste bag, but the guilt would sit in my stomach all day like a cold, hard ball and I would swear to myself that it would never happen again. But that same night off I would go to sleep like a rock again.

The last couple of weeks she was in too much pain to smile and I was too exhausted to feel guilty. But that morning at the Villa Marchese, when the light touched my eyelids, I woke thinking of Cathy, maybe because of what Sofia had said to me the night before, and for some reason the cold, hard ball of guilt was sitting there again right in the pit of the stomach. If I ever got married again, which at that moment I doubted, it wouldn't be to Sofia, no matter how big her heart and how good her soup. Even if I lost a shoe and got spit on my face. Duteronomy. Without the E. I don't think I forgot the E; I think that's how I thought it was spelled. But to mark me off for the whole question, that wasn't fair. Fucking rabbi bastard.

I opened my eyes and it happened so fast that I wasn't sure it had happened. That same little face of the woman who had brought my soup and made my bed the night before was stuck in the same place in the doorjamb. At least I had thought it was there, but it was gone before I could blink. Maybe her image was still on my retina someplace.

I went into the bathroom and washed my hands and face and brushed my teeth. From then on I was going to brush my teeth every chance I got. They still seemed a little furry but I felt I was getting down near the enamel. The white-coated tongue had at least a week to go.

When I came back into the room, there was a breakfast tray resting on the bed. Orange juice, scrambled eggs, some kind of fried meat that kind of looked like bacon but wasn't, toasted Italian bread, and a mug of coffee that was half hot milk. The female gnome had to be watching for me to wake up so she'd know to bring breakfast. I had really seen that face in the doorway. God, I was hungry, and the hot coffee dissolved the cold ball in my belly.

I brushed my teeth again, got dressed, including the tie, packed my bag, and went out looking for people to say good-bye to. It took me a while because I kept getting lost in back corridors or side halls or dead ends, but I finally heard voices in the distance and walked across a thick carpet to get to the doorway at the other end. But just as I almost reached there, I heard a sentence that stopped me dead in my tracks.

"Show me your tits," a male voice said.

I thought I recognized the voice that uttered the

words, but I was so surprised by what I had heard that I couldn't be sure.

"Why should I show them to you?" said a woman. It had to be Elena. "What are you going to do for me?"

"Nothing." It was Vinnie, Uncle Vinnie. The little high-pitched squeak.

"What if I showed you this?"

"Jesus! That might be different."

"How different?" she asked.

"What do you want?"

"I want to trade my car."

"It's only a year old."

"It's nearly two years old."

"How much you going to show?"

"All of it. I'll let you see all of it."

"Go ahead."

"Do I get the car?"

"Go ahead."

"There."

"Spread it. Spread it with your hands."

"Stop!" she said, and her voice was such that I stopped breathing for a moment, let alone moving. "You move one more step and I'll yell. The Don will kill you."

"Just let me touch it."

"No. That's it. I want blue this time. Royal blue."

"Sure."

"Are you going to keep your word, Vinnie? You gave me your word."

"Sure."

"When I get the car, I'll let you see it again. The whole thing. And the other too."

"The tits?"

"The whole schmear."

"Royal blue."

"That's what I want, royal blue."

I turned and retraced my steps, careful to keep my bag from banging into anything. Quite a household, I thought as I wandered down a long hall I hadn't seen before. Interesting set of rules. You could look but you couldn't touch. I wondered what rules Catherine played by when she lived among them.

You say that Catherine never mentioned me? Never mentioned her Uncle Vinnie? The list is as long as the fucking payroll.

It was time to get away from this cesspool. Never should have come in the first place. Stir-crazy. I had spent too many weeks alone in the apartment trying to come down off the high built up by the crazy bunch of churchers and the low of Cathy's death. It didn't matter a goddamn who had sent me the letter. They wanted the money, let them come and get it. No need for me to come looking for them. Which one of the denizens of the Villa Marchese had sent the letter? Or had it been all of them? Was Sofia in on it? Was she going to buy me a new car now that she'd seen my treasure? A subcompact maybe. The best thing was to get to California and draw up a will that split the six million among enough charities to make it impossible for these crooks to even dream of getting anything back. As far as I knew, there were no relatives on my father's side. My mother had mentioned two brothers in Ireland, and my father had sent them letters when she died, but they never answered. Probably couldn't bear it that their sister's name when she died was Freedman. Well, their bigotry was going to cost them six million bucks. Not that I would have left it all to them and theirs, but they would have gotten some of it.

I blundered into the kitchen, which was huge. The only visible pieces of flesh were a huge chunk of raw beef on a wooden butcher block in the center of the room, and my tiny little bearer of food trays and sheets, who was peeling potatoes in a corner by the giant restaurant-size stove and oven.

"Where's Sofia?" I asked. "The Don?"

She looked at me impassively and I wondered if she was deaf as well as a mute. I pointed at a door that was on the opposite wall of the one by which I had entered and looked at her inquiringly. Her expression didn't change. My only accomplishment was to stop her from peeling the potato she held in her hand.

Any door in a storm. I went through the one not yet taken, which entered another long hall and then a room and then a larger room and finally the front entrance hall. I wondered if a rat could have found his way out of the maze any faster than I had.

When I looked out one of the windows at the side of the front door, the only car I saw was a green Mercedes. What had they done with my rented Cadillac? Had it already been repainted and shipped to a Latin-American country? Or cut up into parts at a small used-car lot in Jersey City? Or was it garaged somewhere on the estate? Maybe I should hot-wire the Mercedes and try to bust my way through the front gate. I remembered how solid it looked and with what protest it had opened under the best of circumstances. I was only going to get out of there with the assistance of someone from the family. I had to find Sofia, my substitute wife.

Still carrying my suitcase, I retraced my original steps into the house and soon found myself in the Don's office, where he was sitting behind his paper-covered desk scribbling away with his gold pen. Today he was dressed all in blue. It might even have been royal blue. Sofia was sitting at a smaller desk, also covered with papers, and she was talking to somebody on the telephone. An ordinary Mafia morning.

The Don was the first to notice me, and today he did me the honor of standing despite his infirmities. He sure was a good-looking old man. Too bad that Sofia hadn't inherited his face and build. But when you marry a woman because she is the boss's daughter, you take what genes you can. And beauty was only skin deep anyway.

"Ah," he said, smiling and throwing his arms wide as if preparing to give me a big hug if I came within distance, "you are feeling better. You had us worried."

At the sound of his voice, Sofia turned to look at me, said something quickly into the phone, hung up, leapt to her feet, and ran over to my side.

"How do you feel?" she said anxiously. "Are you strong enough to be up? Did Marina bring you your breakfast?"

The mute had a name.

"I have to be getting back to California," I said. "They're expecting me back."

"But you can't do that," she exclaimed. "You just arrived here. We're just getting to know you. We want to hear all about Catherine, and I want to show you all the places she and I used to go. You can't leave now. Call them and say you are going to stay a few more days."

Call them! Right now only Cibelli knew where I was. Call them!

"It's long distance to California," I said.

The Don waved his hand in deprecation, and Sofia pulled me to the phone on her desk. I dialed the headquarters number and asked for the captain and they put me right through to him. He gave his usual grunt.

"It's Freedman," I said.

"Where the hell have you been?" he yelled.

"I'm in New Jersey," I said.

"We've been looking to hell and gone for you for two days."

"I'm not due back to work until the seventeenth," I said mildly, not wanting to emphasize that in front of Sofia and the Don.

"Somebody broke into your apartment and tore the shit out of it," said the captain. "Your cleaning lady reported it. It's a mess. It's worse than a mess. We thought maybe you'd been kidnapped or that one of those church people out on probation had fixed your clock."

"I'm all right," I said. "Has there been publicity?"

"No, we've kept it quiet. It's just in the department. We weren't sure about the church thing because it was done by pros. They even slit your toothpaste tube and every pillow in the joint. What the hell did they think you were hiding?"

"I have no idea. Listen," I said, "let me tell you where I am. I'm at the home of some people named Marchese at 1934 View Drive, Wackowick Heights, New Jersey. That's a suburb of West Orange, New Jersey. The phone number is . . ." I looked down at the number listed on the base and read it off to him. "I'm going to be here a few more days and then I'm coming back. If you don't reach me here, Lieutenant Cibelli of the West Orange police will know how to get hold of me. You got all that, Captain?"

As I emphasized the word "captain," I turned to look at their faces. There was nothing but polite interest there. They didn't seem the least perturbed that a captain of homicide knew exactly where I was, that if anything happened to me, that was the first place the police would look. What the hell was going on with these people? And why the hell had I decided to stay with them rather than go home? Because unknown parties were tearing my apartment to bits, and it was perhaps better to stay with a known quantity for the time being than to walk into an unknown situation? Probably.

They had not only not jumped at the word "captain"; they had also smiled with pleasure when I had said I was staying on for a few more days.

"I got it," the captain said. "I'll call off the hunt for you, but we'll keep working on what happened at the apartment. It doesn't smell right to me. There's something going on that I can't put my finger on. You'll be back for the mayor's ceremony, won't you? You've got a surprise coming."

Christ, how the captain had mellowed. There had been four years when I could have watched him bleed to death without even reaching for a Band-Aid, but since we had gone through the fire together with the church group, Tofutti wouldn't melt in his mouth.

"I'll be there," I told him. "And thanks for worrying about me."

"Fuck you," he said, and hung up.

Sofia clapped her hands together like a little kid, and the Don gave me a small punch on the shoulder.

"You know what I'm doing here?" he asked, pointing to all the papers scattered over his desk.

I shook my head.

"I'm writing my autobiography." He pronounced "autobiography" like he was saying the name of a woman he loved. *Autobiography*.

"This ain't going to be one of those 'written-with' or 'told-to' books. This is going to be the real McCoy. I knew them all, you know. I ran with those guys. The ones who run the show today, the guys the feds are running into the ground, they're nothing. They're dirt. They have no class. They don't appreciate the position I held when the Merlino family was something you had to deal with carefully, when the Merlino family got the respect it deserved. The drug money is too easy, too quick, too much. It's made them soft. I tell it all. I tell it like it was and how it is now. When my book comes out, we'll have to go to the mattress because they're going to put the kiss on me. And then they'll find that Marchese is still the old Marchese, that he's more than they can handle."

"Papa," said Sofia, "you're making yourself tired. If you want to write some more today, you've got to save your strength."

"I didn't sleep at all last night." He sighed. "I took two of those pills and I didn't sleep at all."

Sofia led him back to his chair and he sank into it. Picking up the gold pen, he started scribbling on the sheet where he had left off. I couldn't make out what any of his scrawling meant, whether it was being written in Italian or English. It seemed more like what I thought Sanskrit might be. All of the pages looked the same and I couldn't see any numbers or identification at the top to indicate which page went where. If he really had a story to tell, I figured they would have to bring in a "written-with" or "told-to" person.

Sofia's hand went around my right arm and squeezed me into looking at her.

"Look," she said, "I still have some calls to make and a payroll to get out. But if you're feeling stronger, we'll get a jeep this afternoon and I'll show you around the property. I'll show you where Catherine and Hermie lived and all the secret spots she and I used to hide in. Why don't you go rest for a while or go sit by the pool and get some sun on your face. Elena's around somewhere. Get her to show you something."

There was a crazy urge to tell her that I didn't like the prices Elena charged to show you something, but I held my tongue and politely settled for directions to the pool area.

The pool was a big one but it was littered with all kinds of crap. I spent five minutes skimming some of the larger pieces out, but finally gave it up as a bad job. The sun also proved too hot so I finally settled in a lounge chair under a nearby tree and tried to figure out who had taken my apartment apart. The people who had sent me the letter? The Marchese bunch had to be tied into it somewhere, but they sure were fooling the hell out of me.

I gave up thinking about the problem when Elena came out to sun herself fifteen minutes later. She was wearing a bikini small enough to garner her any kind of car she wanted, but all she gave me was a small smile before she lay flat on her back and closed her eyes. She didn't bother to ask me if I felt better. Remember, I reminded myself, you can look all you want, but for Christ's sake, don't touch! I was in the process of checking the headlights when I felt myself dozing off in the warm air. I wanted to go to sleep but something was holding me back. Ah, I said to myself as a ray of hot sun sneaked through the branches above me and heated the area of my crotch, remember that somebody stole your gun. And then I let myself fall asleep.

9

*T*he shadow across my eyelids turned out to be Sofia carrying a wicker picnic basket. I tried to hold on to whatever I had been dreaming, but it escaped the clutch of my mind and disappeared. It had been a pleasant dream, and I opened my eyes regretfully. Pleasant hadn't been that common of late. I stretched my arms out wide, then yanked my tie from around my sweating neck and flung it across my jacket on the back of the adjoining chair, and smiled up at the face that was smiling down at me.

"Did you have a good sleep?" she asked.

I looked over at the chaises by the side of the pool, but Elena was no longer there. How long had I been dreaming?

"What time is it?"

She looked at her wristwatch, whose jewels reflected brightly in the sun as she twisted her arm.

"Quarter past twelve. Are you hungry? We can eat right here. But if you'd just as soon wait, there's a beautiful spot up on the hill where you can sit on the pine needles and look at the mountains."

"Let's do that," I said, getting to my feet and scooping up my jacket and tie. I reached out to take the basket from her but she swung it away from my hand.

"The women do all the carrying in this family," she laughed. "You don't want the men to think you're not macho, do you?"

"Who's Doc?" I asked as we started to walk toward the rear of the house.

"Doc? He does stand out from the crowd, doesn't he?

Doc is Doc. He came here about a year ago because he was a friend of a friend and he needed a . . . Benny, I've got to know something."

She stopped and faced me and I faced her in turn.

"You're Catherine's husband," she said, "and that makes you a member of the family."

"But there's no blood tie," I broke in. "Catherine lived here and was your friend, but there's no blood tie."

"Oh, yes," she said quite vehemently. "There is a blood tie. Catherine's mother, Alicia, was a Merlino, a second cousin. Oh, there was a stink when she and Hermie ran away and got married, you can bet on that. But it smoothed out. Hermie was never really considered family, but Alicia and Catherine were. And Hermie was a key man in the business, which is sometimes almost as thick as blood. Blood is the most important, but business comes close."

"But you just met me," I said. "You don't really know me. I'm honored that you think of me as family, and I appreciate the care you've given me, but I don't expect anything special."

She reached out with her left hand and grabbed me by the right elbow.

"I can tell in my heart," she said. "You are a good man and you loved our Catherine. I want to be able to speak to you from the heart. I don't want to worry about you being a policeman, and I don't want you to worry about being a policeman. God brought you here for some reason, and we should not question that. All we want is for you to be part of us now that we have found each other. What is ours is yours."

And vice versa? I wondered. Six million vice versas?

"I am not here as a policeman," I told her. "I am here as Catherine's husband. If I see a crime being committed, or if I find out that the Don is plotting to murder somebody, then I will be a policeman because that is what I have sworn to do. But as far as your family goes, everything else I hear is personal family business."

"I won't try to make believe that we aren't what we are," she said. "My grandfather was a gangster, a crook in Sicily and part of the syndicate here. When I was a kid, he would take me into his bedroom and open bureau drawers that would be full of watches and jewelry, boxes of them. He would love to sit on the bed and watch me pin the jewels to my dress and drape the necklaces around my neck and laugh when the bracelets fell off my wrist. There would be forty or fifty men living on the place then, in the big house and the little houses all over, and my grandfather had a big black limo and there would be bodyguards, and at night you could hear cars and trucks coming and going.

"My own father is going to have to pay his debt in hell when he dies because of the things he did when he was younger. I know he's had to have killed men or had them killed, and that all the money that came in was from robberies and loan-sharking and prostitution and drugs. Maybe I'll end up in hell too, because these things put the food in my own mouth and the dresses on my back and paid for my convertible when I was seventeen, and even though I didn't think about it when I was young, I knew, I knew deep down that what was going on was bad. What do you do? Do you go to the police and say that your father is a thief and a murderer? What proof do you have? they would say. And I would have to tell them that I had no proof, that I just knew it in my heart. And what kind of a heart do you have, they would ask, that you would rat on your own father?"

She placed the basket on the ground and took hold of my other arm.

"Sometimes, when I was a kid, policemen would come here in uniform, sometimes driving police cars, and the men would put cases of whiskey in the trunks of the cars, and I would see my father give them a thick wad of money, and everybody would laugh, and I would laugh too, because the big policemen were my father's friends. That's how it was when I was a kid, and my grandmother never said anything, and my mother, may the angels guard her, never said anything, and I would never say anything.

"But it isn't that way anymore. They squeezed my father out. He wasn't even important enough for them to kill him. They just squeezed him out. They gave him the supreme insult. So he sits there every day writing down all that meaningless stuff that is supposedly going to bring him a million dollars. We could use a million dollars because the money comes hard for us. The only thing we have are those pizza shops and bakeries that were set up for drug distribution until the government broke that up, and the laundry, which barely breaks even because there's no crooked union anymore to make the hotels give us the business. Vinnie and I, we scrimp and work our fingers to the bone so that my family and the five soldiers who are left from all those men can eat and have clothes on their backs. You saw Angelo. There are four others like him wandering around the place. They still carry guns and they drive my father around and open the door for him and act like they're protecting his life from danger. They go through all the motions from the old days, but it's all meaningless.

"Oh, once in a while a truck comes from somewhere or a car in the middle of the night, and my father and Vinnie and a couple of the boys do something with those people. I'm sure it's illegal and maybe even dangerous, and the next day my father's got a wad of money stacked on the desk that he makes sure Elena and Nana and I should see. He's like a peacock the whole day, spreading his feathers out all over the place. I don't like it but there's nothing I can do about it because he is my father and I am his daughter. It's like I was born into a royal family and there's nothing I can do about my bloodline. You know all those royal families that live in exile somewhere and make believe that someday they'll go back and be kings again. That's the country we're stuck in, and there's nothing I can do about it."

I looked down at that sweet, earnest face pouring out all that stuff that had been choking her heart all those years, and I felt my body tremble in response to the heat of the hands that were holding me. Why had I been such a catalyst to all this? Because I was family and yet not family? The first person outside the circle who was supposedly within the circle? Poor Sofia had been waiting all these years for me to come along so that she could pour out all the guilty secrets that had been pinching her soul.

I leaned over her upturned face and kissed her softly on the lips. She both smelled and tasted good and what had been meant as a comforting gesture, a reassuring one, turned into something more as she closed her eyes and let her mouth relax into mine. Then I lifted my own arms and gently pushed her back.

"You don't have to worry about what you say to me," I told her. "Think of me as family."

She smiled and dropped her hands from my elbows.

"What I was going to tell you," she said, "is that Doc came to us about a year ago because somebody wanted him kept safe for a while. And he decided to stay on. He loves this place. He's got a giant vegetable garden and he's got all these plans he keeps trying to talk Papa into, like selling off some of the timber and making residential developments and that kind of thing. I think he has a ghost in his soul for some of the things he has done in the past, but this is kind of like a monastery for him, a retreat. I caught him on his knees in the woods once, and I think he was praying. But he won't go to church with me. Come on, I've got a lot to show you."

There was a garage with twelve stalls behind the house, seven of them filled with cars and pickup trucks of various vintages. Angelo was asleep behind the wheel of my rented Cadillac and did not wake up until Sofia gunned the jeep motor to back it out of its cubicle. He looked over at us with disinterest, barely awake, and I

wondered if he, too, had been given the word that I
was now to be considered famliy and of no lethal concern. I could probably get a job in the sideshow of a
circus, half-cop/half-mafioso. *He walks, he talks, he'll
shake you down and arrest you at the same time*.

Sofia certainly knew how to wheel a jeep. She headed
straight for a huge oak tree at the end of the garage and
at the last moment twisted the wheel to put us narrowly
between two saplings and onto a track that was just
wide enough for the small vehicle to squeeze through.
It couldn't have been used too often because it was
necessary to keep dodging branches, some of them big
enough to take your head off, that had overgrown the
trail. My right foot soon ached from jamming on the
brake that wasn't there.

Sofia drove with her lips parted into a slight smile,
leaning forward in the seat so that she could ride the
bumps and still shift up or down as the terrain demanded. The sun filtered through the thick trees, and
the noise of the engine drowned out all the natural
sounds of birds and beasts that had to inhabit this
wilderness. Once we frightened a deer into standing
still for a moment, a huge doe that gazed at us in
obvious indignation before bounding off to the left. It is
impossible to keep track of actual distance covered when
you are attempting to prevent a minimum of damage to
both your rear end and your head at the same time, but
just as I was beginning to wonder if we were anywhere
near Pennsylvania, we broke out into a clearing that
had a gigantic barn at the other end. Part of the building had fallen in, and it looked like the rest of it would
go if a stiff wind came up, but it sure was a hell of a lot
of building to be way out in the woods like this.

Sofia pulled up close and turned off the motor. The
sudden stillness was very loud. She pointed at the barn.

"This is where they stored the whiskey during Prohibition," she said. "Marina told me that sometimes the
cases would fill the whole building, thousands of them
piled up as high as the ceiling."

So Marina could talk. I doubted, however, that she would ever talk to me, adopted family son or not. Well, as long as she brought me food and clean sheets, I wouldn't complain.

"The floor is covered with broken glass," said Sofia. "When I was little, I would go in there and sort through the pieces looking for pretty shapes. The rest of the roof could go at any minute so it's not safe to do that now. Catherine used to go in there sometimes and yell to hear the echo, and I would stand out here and beg her to come out, and she would laugh and laugh at me, and I can still hear the echo of her laugh. She liked to do crazy things."

"Vincent said she had a lot of boyfriends here."

I said it as flatly as I could, but it came out somewhat strangled and Sofia looked over at me quickly. It had been at the top of my mind and tip of my tongue ever since the little creep had taunted me, and it was a wonder that I hadn't blurted it out sooner than this.

"There were still a lot of young guys around when we were in high school and college," she said, "and Catherine was very pretty. They'd even grab at me sometimes. They were all afraid of my father, but if they'd been here for several weeks without getting to town, and there weren't many bimbos shacked up at the cottages, they'd make a try. But they weren't boyfriends. You want the truth?"

She was looking at me so earnestly that her body trembled a bit, and I could see how white her hands were as they grasped the steering wheel.

Did I want the truth? A question like that implied that the truth wasn't something that would gladden my heart. Did I want to know if my dead wife had spread her legs for all these young punks who were stuck in the country with all that lead in their pants and nothing to shoot it into? Did I want the truth? What good would it do to know whether she had or had not? What difference could it make now? She had not told me the whole truth when she had married me. She had not told me about this whole family and the six million dollars she was leaving me from God knew where. She had not told me that the cancer was already in her belly when we got married. Did Sofia know the whole truth? Did the rest of her family? Was it their six million dollars and did they want it back? I hadn't mentioned it and they hadn't mentioned it, and there was all this sparring for position. Did they want the truth? Did I want the truth? It was probably the last thing I wanted to know.

I nodded my head yes.

"We never let anybody get very far," she said slowly. "It happened to Catherine a hundred times more than it happened to me, but we would always slap the hand away or crack somebody in the face or if they pushed too far, we would mention what my father would do and they would always back off. Except for one. The worst one of all. The best-looking and the worst one of all. Tullio. Tullio Bandisi. He was a pimp. Slime. He was staying here, I found out later, because he'd worked over one of his girls too hard and she'd died. Catherine never knew that. He was so good-looking. And she'd sneak out at night and they'd go to one of the cottages or maybe just the woods if the weather was right, and he taught her things no decent girl should ever know. He even brought her birth-control pills because he knew if he ever got her pregnant, he was a dead man. And she was crazy about him. He was so good-looking, the slime. So good-looking. And she was so happy that I didn't have the heart to do anything to stand in the way. All I did was worry. And then she started to talk about going away with him when he left. I'm sure that Tullio didn't know she was talking that way, or he would have quit in a minute. He was only tough with women; sometimes he would make Catherine do terrible things for him. But when she told me about going away, I knew I had to do something. So I went to my father the next day and told him that Tullio had grabbed me here"—she shoved her hand into her breast—"and I was afraid of him. He was gone that night. I don't know what happened, whether they shipped him out or he's buried somewhere on the place, but he was gone. And Catherine cried for three days, thinking he had run out on her. And I cried with her, mostly for what I had done to my friend, but I've never regretted it. He was the only one. There were no others while she was here all those years. I don't know what happened to Catherine after she and Hermie disappeared, but that was the only one here. That is the truth."

Her eyes had filled with tears as she had recited the litany of pain. The truth. She was so innocent in her way and so worldly-wise at the same time. *I don't know whether they shipped him out or he's buried somewhere on the place.*

She obviously knew this had been used as a burying place for elephants whose tusks were wanted by the Mafia. *So good-looking.* Catherine wasn't the only one attracted to Tullio's looks, and Sofia had probably lived vicariously through Catherine's actual experiences. *And then what did he do to you? Did that feel good?* I could picture the two of them giggling together when Catherine returned each dawn with her most recently acquired technique. The truth. Yes, the truth can hurt.

"What else do you have to show me in this jungle?" I asked brightly, not wanting to play the game anymore. She scraped the tears from her eyes, started the motor, shifted roughly into gear, and we were off again on the toad's wild ride.

There were all kinds of single-track roads through that wilderness, some big enough for a truck and some just barely wide enough for a jeep. Most of them obviously hadn't been used in years. Every once in a while we would come across a little house, sometimes of clapboard, sometimes of logs, sometimes in falling-down condition, and sometimes habitable. In one of them, two men came to the door as we drove up, both in their late fifties or early sixties, both needing a shave. Sofia didn't bother with introductions, just waved and kept going. They didn't wave back, their eyes never leaving my face. They were wearing sport shirts outside their pants, and I was sure they were carrying the obligatory guns in their waistbands. In a way it was like visiting one of those villages that have been built to represent the old west or a mining town or colonial Williamsburg, and I wondered about suggesting to the Don that he could recoup his fortunes legitimately by opening Old Mafia Village. He would probably regard it as an insult. I wasn't sure that Sofia would think it funny either, so I kept the joke to myself.

At this point she left the track and started climbing a hill, shifting the four-wheel-drive into low-low gear and bumping over half-rotted logs and fair-size boulders. We were at a pitch where I was getting nervous about tipping over backward, and I was poised for a quick leap out of the vehicle onto the ground when we went over a small hump and ended up on a grassy plateau. It wasn't a very large cleared area, and there were tall pines hemming it in on three sides, but to the north there was a vista that extended for miles and in the far distance you could see what looked like dark blue mountains in a thin haze.

Sofia slid out from under the wheel, pulled the basket of food from the floor in the rear, and walked to the center of the clearing, where she started to lay out the picnic on a blue tablecloth. I walked around the edges of the grass and then stood and gazed at the mountains in the distance. Maybe I was standing on one of the same spots that Catherine had once been standing on, looking at the same mountains. Mountains die too, I had once read; it just takes them longer. I was thirty-three years old. How many more years did I have? Less than the mountains, that was for sure. But more than the ant that was climbing over my shoe. I almost stepped on it with my other foot, but I philosophically stopped. Maybe somebody had a foot lifted over me somewhere.

"Hey," said Sofia, "do you like hot peppers? Mama

Maria's are guaranteed to make your whole body pucker
up."

There was a huge loaf of Italian bread, half of a
salami, two large chunks of different cheeses, the vaunted
peppers, a wicker-covered bottle of Chianti that was
in the process of being opened, peaches and nectarines.

"Are we expecting your father's bocce group to join
us?" I asked, pointing at the vast array of foodstuffs laid
out on the cloth.

"Start in," she said, indicating where I should sit.
"You'll be surprised at how much you can eat in the
open air. You'll also be surprised," she continued, slapping the right cheek of her more-than-ample rear end,
"how much I can eat in the open air."

I was thirsty as well as hungry and I drank down a
whole glass of the sharp-edged red wine before accept-
ing a plate with chunks of bread and cheese and salami
and peppers spread over it. Everything tasted so good
and I felt so good with the bug out of me and my
strength back and the hot sun shining down on us in
the middle of a clearing with the dark blue mountains
miles and miles away to the north. California seemed a
million rather than three thousand miles away at that
moment, and I wondered what it would be like if I
became like Doc and settled down here with my "family." Hell, I could end their financial worries in a minute with just a simple call to the Bay City Bank. By the
time I got through, Elena would be offering to show me
her treasures. I guess maybe I didn't like Elena much.

"What are you thinking?" asked Sofia through the
mouthful of bread and cheese she was chewing into
swallowable condition.

"I was thinking how nice it was here," I said, "how
beautiful."

"When Catherine and I were going through our horse-
riding stage, we would come up here all the time.
There are shortcuts you can take with a horse that will
get you here from the main house pretty quick. We had
all sorts of secret passageways through the woods and

the swamp, and hiding places. We were always talking of camping out, but we never would have had the guts to do it even if Papa would have let us."

"I'd like to see them."

"What?"

"The secret passageways, the hiding places. I'd like to see every place that Cathy used around here. Which was her bedroom in the house?"

"On the third floor. In the left tower. It's a small room, but she fixed it up nice, and I spent more time up there than we did in my room."

"How come she and her father moved into your house?"

"Her mama died. Hermie couldn't cook and she couldn't cook, and they started eating all their meals in the kitchen, and finally I asked Papa if they could move in because there was so much room. Besides, Hermie was always going off somewhere for three days or a week or even two weeks, and Catherine always stayed with me when he did that, so Papa said sure, why not?"

"Where would Hermie go?"

"We never asked questions. The women of the family never ask questions."

"What did Cathy's mother die from?"

"The cancer."

"What kind?"

"I think it was of the pancreas. Was that what . . .?"

I nodded. We looked away from each other.

"Hey," said Sofia, "your wineglass is empty. It's a good thing Papa isn't here or he'd be ashamed. 'You have committed an insult to my house,' he would say. 'You are no longer a daughter of mine.' "

Laughing, she filled my glass to the brim and I toasted her silently before taking a long swallow.

"What? Why are you looking at me like that?"

"Do you want to get out?" I asked her. "Do you ever want to leave this place, or is this where you want to spend the rest of your life?"

"What's wrong with it here?" The smile had left her face.

"Nothing. I wasn't talking about that. It's beautiful here. I mean, are you happy?"

"Happy? Sure, I'm happy. Why shouldn't I be happy? Do you think I'd want a husband, somebody who loved me better than anything else in the world? Do you think I'd want babies, little babies to hug and dress and feed and take care of and watch them grow? Why would I want any of those things?"

I stood up and walked around the tablecloth, dropped down beside her, and put my arms around her thick body. She was unyielding, her face granite. I could swear her skin had darkened three shades, and I was holding on to the equivalent of a Sicilian mountain. At that moment her blood had to be so thick that it barely ran through her veins.

"Sofia," I said, "I'm half Jewish and half Irish, and both races have a tendency to babble. And if you babble enough, you end up saying something that will hurt somebody. Somebody close sometimes. You were my Cathy's cousin and at the same time her sister, and she's been dead less than two months. You've been so good to me the three days I've been here, nursing me, feeding me, seeing to my every want, taking me into the heart of the family, making me feel that I've known you all my life. I babbled, that's for sure, but I guess I babbled because I sense something wrong, something that's eating at your insides, something that needs taking care of while you're so busy taking care of everybody else."

That did it. She turned and buried her face into the soft part of my right shoulder and let the tears flow to the point where I could feel the sogginess build up in my cotton shirt. I don't know how long it went on, but the wet spot was as round as a grapefruit by the time she pulled her head away and looked up at me with those huge brown eyes. And for the second time I leaned down and kissed those big soft lips, only this time they didn't relax into mine but stayed stiff until I finally realized she was poising them to say something as soon as I took my stupid mouth away. I did so immediately.

"I love Doc," she said.

This gave me pause, the information coming out of nowhere into left field. Before I could get to her problem, I had to solve mine. Why had I kissed this homely girl twice? This girl that I really didn't know too well despite all the talk of family. Was there something about her wide face, huge breasts, even huger hips, and thick legs that turned me on? My wife had been dead less than two months and I had already fornicated twice with a woman in California who was now also deceased. I had also been twice tempted by a hooker in California and had not followed through for some perverse or maybe sanitary reason. Now I might be extending my operations to the East Coast. Was I putting the make on my wife's cousin because I associated the two of them together or was I just being a horny son of a bitch? Had I been putting the make on her or was I just being compassionate? Were Tullio Bandisi, possibly the late Tullio Bandisi, and I slime of a feather? Had I drunk too much wine in the hot sun? There were obviously a lot of things I had to think through for myself, but right then I had to concentrate on the Doc. On the Doc and Sofia.

"Does he love you?" I asked.

"He loves Elena," she blurted, and buried her face in my shoulder again, a fresh rain of tears coming from somewhere inside the abundant wellspring of that body. I waited patiently while she sobbed her way through that part of her dilemma. The mixed aroma of garlic and cheese and hot peppers was wafting up from my shoulder area, some from Sofia's breath and maybe even some from the tears. Things were definitely starting to sour.

Sofia finally pulled her head away and started to wipe her eyes and cheeks with her napkin. One consolation

about her looks was that sadness and crying didn't make
her appear less attractive. There was a lovable suscepti-
bility to Sofia, one that caused you to know that here
was a person who would be sympathetic to your needs
and wants. She was also a mama bear or a tigress if
anyone threatened her family or her den, but basically
there was goodness in her soul, and I was pretty sure
that this was what I had responded to. Pretty sure. Not
convinced. But pretty sure.

"Do you want to talk about it?" I asked, careful now
not to overstep my bounds. No matter what happened
from then on, this was my wife's cousin and friend, and
any kisses would be on the cheek rather than the lips.

"There's nothing to talk about," she said, starting to
peel a nectarine so as to have something to do with her
hands.

"Does he know how you feel?"

"I've never said anything, and I'm sure he hasn't
noticed."

"What is going on between him and Elena?"

"Nothing."

"Does she know how he feels?"

"Oh, yes, she knows. And she knows how I feel. She
said if I didn't do something about it pretty soon, she
was going to. She was going to come right out and tell
him."

"Do you trust Elena?"

"Yes, I think so. When she first married Papa, I was
sure she had married him because she thought he was
rich and she didn't want to work in Vegas anymore. But
now I think she married him because he is Papa, because he dazzled her with the way he acts and talks.
He's a lot of man, my papa."

"So what are you going to do?"

"Do? I'm going to keep on doing what I've always
done. I'm going to work hard with my Uncle Vinnie
and keep the family going. And now I should be getting
back to my account books, and you should be taking a

nap. Just because you feel better doesn't mean you are well."

"Sofia?"

"Yes?" she said, starting to put the things in the basket.

"Will you take me out again tomorrow?"

"Where?"

"I want to go everywhere Catherine went."

I had never called her "Catherine," always "Cathy." And they had never called her "Cathy," always "Catherine." I wanted to find out about the secretive, beautiful woman I had been married to less than a year, who had left me six million dollars from somewhere, and a family. I wanted to know about Catherine so then maybe I could know about Cathy.

"Sure," she said, placing the basket in the jeep. "When you go back, I want you to take the Villa Marchese with you in your heart as well as your head. I think you've already got it a little in your heart. Tomorrow we'll go soak your head."

10

*S*upper, I was told, would be served at 6:30. When I was growing up, there had never been any regular mealtimes at our apartment, and most of the time I ate, usually standing up by a counter or the sink, whatever was in the refrigerator or in whichever cereal boxes might be in the cupboard. Both my parents became alcoholics, he when the Dupuytren's contractures started to twist his fingers to the point where he couldn't play the violin anymore, she from drinking sociably with him. She must have made a good beginning on the booze all the years she worked as a waitress and then a barmaid before they were married, but it was essentially my father's fingers did them both in.

Most of the people I hung with, both in Boston in my younger days and in California when I moved around as a cop in different cities, called it supper rather than dinner. But for some reason, maybe because they had dubbed themselves the Villa Marchese, I kind of expected Sofia to tell me we would be eating dinner rather than supper. I don't know why. I never knew any Italians who acted fancy no matter how much money they had, but this family was kind of a minor aristocracy, a Mafia fiefdom, who lived in this huge mansion and had servants and vassals of a sort, and "dinner" wouldn't have surprised me. But then again, "supper" didn't either, so it was basically a standoff.

When we returned from our jeep safari, I was both hot and sweaty, and decided to take a shower before I changed and wandered around some more. Despite the fact that both Cibelli and my captain knew where I was and who I was with, I was still somewhat nervous about being alone with this bunch. I was positive that there was no danger from Sofia, that she would defend me against the world, but the rest of them were still unknown quantities. If it could have been done without any fuss, I would have called the head of the FBI and the CIA and the president of the United States to tell them the situation, that I was alone among the Mafia and someone had lifted my piece, but I knew that would become terribly involved and ultimately unrewarding and really ridiculous so I discontented myself with those I had already contacted.

When I had finished undressing, the coolness of the room reached my body, and I thought I would just crawl between the sheets for a few minutes to rest a bit and then bathe. When I awoke and looked at my watch, it was ten minutes past six, and it was twenty-five minutes later before I had showered and changed and went looking for the dining room with my hair still damp and somewhat messy. Luckily, I blundered correctly and found the right place within five minutes.

I counted twenty chairs around the giant mahogany table, but only three were occupied—Sofia, Mama Maria, and Doc. Sofia patted the place beside her and I pulled back the chair and sat down. It really wasn't that simple. The chair must have weighed eighty pounds, and hauling it out was one thing, and then trying to pull it back with my ass in the seat and only my arms and legs for leverage was quite another. I wondered how the two women had managed. I knew Sofia was strong from the hugs she had given me, but Mama Maria must have had capacities far beyond her outward appearance.

"Elena talked Papa into taking her to town for dinner," said Sofia. "She gets restless when she has to sit still too long."

"He won't find food like we have here," sniffed Mama Maria. "And then tonight he'll have the *agita* and I'm the one who'll have to stay up with him. She'll kill him off yet."

Nobody said anything so I figured this was a subject that Mama had commented on before.

Vincent came into the room and he was so duded up and smiling that I wondered if this was some kind of special occasion that was yet to be revealed. He went to the head of the table, pulled out the huge chair that had another twenty pounds of arms attached to it, and settled himself in.

Mama Maria uttered a very audible sigh.

Vincent looked at her belligerently.

"This should be my rightful place all the time, Mama," he said. "Don't you go making faces at me. Because I deferred to my sister's welfare doesn't mean that I am not entitled to my rightful place."

It was obvious from the reaction of the others that this was something Uncle Vinnie did every time the Don was not present at the table. Nobody said anything further and we all just sat there until Marina brought in a soup tureen that was almost as big as she was. It was placed down near Mama Maria, who had a stack of soup plates in front of her, and as she ladled each bowl out, Marina would carry it around and place it in front of the person. I was served first, which indicated to me that I was not only a guest but an honored guest. Then Sofia, then Doc, and then one for Vinnie. Except that Marina didn't bring it to Vinnie at the head of the table. She placed it in front of a chair at the side of the table, two seats away from Doc.

Vinnie shoved back his chair, stood up and came around to where the soup was, and brought the plate back to his place at the head of the table. We all ate our soup.

This went on for every course. Pasta. Roast beef. Cooked vegetables. Pudding. Cheese. Fruit. Each time the little devil would put Vinnie's portion at the chair he supposedly sat in when Don Marchese was at table, and each time he would jump up and bring it to the spot he had selected and felt he was entitled to. It wasn't funny even in the deep recesses of my mind, and

I felt sorry for the little guy. I don't know why. For sure I didn't like him. Maybe it was because what he was doing was like the action of a stubborn little kid who was giving the baby-sitter a hard time when his folks were away.

I tried to eat only minimum amounts because I knew my stomach still had to be sore from the beating it had taken, but everything was cooked so beautifully and flavored so perfectly that I finished every portion that was placed before me. As a matter of fact, I was a little disappointed that Mama Maria didn't tell me *"Mangia! Mangia!"* in the classical tradition because there were a couple of things I would have enjoyed seconds on. Which was just as well, because my stomach was tight as a drum by the time we reached the espresso with the slivers of lemon peel. I had always considered Jewish food too heavy and greasy, and Irish food, what little I'd had because my mother could scarcely boil a potato, bland to the point of plastic reproductions, and I was happy for my late wife's Italian connections. But it had encouraged me to eat too much and I hoped it would not cause me to suffer a relapse of Cibellianotis.

After supper we all moved into a living room I had not seen before, leaving all the dishes on the table, presumably for the dwarf Marina to remove and wash. One whole corner of the room was taken up with a color television set that had the kind of giant screen that you usually see only in bars.

I commented on the size of it, and Vinnie grumbled about Elena having to have the biggest that was available. I wondered what she had shown him to make him come through with that.

Sofia read through the TV schedule so that everyone could hear what was available for programming that night, and everyone grumbled that there was nothing worth watching. So she put a videotape into the machine and we watched *The Godfather*. When the title was flashed on the screen, I looked around the room and there was Doc studying me with an ironic little grin on his face. I smiled enough to let him know I understood the joke, but I could hardly wait to check the titles of the other videos the Marcheses had in their library. How many of the Hollywood classics were considered training films? *Acneface*, starring Uncle Vinnie, Mama Merlino, and Elena Marchese, with special guest appearance by Sergeant Benjamin Freedman. See it at your local theater starting Friday. Hundreds of killings, beatings, and maimings. Gore galore. PG-13.

My face felt a little hot while we were sitting there in the subdued light with the screen flickering in the corner, but it felt more like sunburn from the jeep ride and the picnic than from fever, and I went into a semidoze as the real family in the room watched the fictional family on the tube. When Adam delved and Eve span, who was then the gentle-man? I thought of a Charles Addams cartoon I had seen once in which all the faces in the theater audience were horrified by what they were witnessing on the screen, while the classic little weird guy was laughing like crazy. What was "my" family's reaction to what they were seeing? Sofia's?

It suddenly occurred to me that I had meant to ask at the supper table who had taken my gun from my suitcase and if I could have it back, please, and I almost spoke up during the film, but I didn't want to interrupt their absorption. And then when it was over and everybody had refused an offer of something more to eat, and people were saying good night and going to bed, the question got lost in the shuffle. It came to me again just before I left the room, but as I was about to speak, I noticed that Sofia was maneuvering to stay behind with Doc while everybody departed, so I scooted out of there too. I owed her that much.

Despite the amount of food I had eaten, or maybe because of the amount of food I had eaten, I slept like a log, and did not wake up until Marina showed up with a reproduction of the breakfast I had eaten before. She didn't say a word to wake me, but she couldn't have been standing beside the bed too long because the food and coffee were still pretty hot when I dug in. It's good to be a king.

I brushed my teeth, shaved, and had just finished dressing when Sofia entered without knocking. She was dressed in dungarees, a man's shirt and sneakers, and she told me to change my pants into something more durable. I had running shoes and jeans in my bag, and I pulled them out and told her I could change in a minute. She didn't budge, just continued standing there talking to me about the problems of running a string of pizza parlors with help that stole you blind and didn't care about quality control and quit if anybody so much as looked cross-eyed at them.

I started to take the clothes into the bathroom but she tagged right along and held on to the handle of the door while she continued her speech. I finally said to hell with it and pulled my shoes and pants off. My three pairs of undershorts were dirty so I wasn't wearing any, and I don't know how much my shirttails covered front or rear, but she didn't seem to be paying that much attention so I sat down on the bed and pulled my pants on and tied the laces of the running shoes. It was one thing for her to consider me as her "husband," but she was acting like we had been married for a hundred years, and it was another thing for me to know she was in love with Doc, but I, for Christ's sake, was also a man, and deserved some respect. I started laughing when that flashed through my mind, and Sofia became a little indignant that I considered the pizza situation to be so funny.

"It's not that," I said. "It was just that I suddenly thought of something. I'm really very sorry for your problems."

"Hey"—she smiled—"everybody says I'm too serious all the time. And our problems are not your problems."

She reached out and grabbed me, gave me a tight hug, kissed me lightly on the lips, and stepped back. There was that good smell from her again, and I almost held on when she started to step back, but caught

myself in time. There was something so beautiful about
this very ugly girl that I felt my heart skip a beat, and I
very carefully folded my pants on the crease and hung
them up in the closet. *Simpatica,* I told myself, as I
tried to sort it out. She's *simpatica.*

Angelo was once again sitting behind the wheel of
the Cadillac when we went to get the jeep, and I
wondered what the hell was going on with him and my
rented car. I hoped it wasn't being used for any stick-
ups that were needed to augment the grosses of the
pizza parlors.

We drove out again on the track between the two
saplings, but we had hardly gone twenty feet into the
woods when Sofia applied the brakes and hopped out.

"Come on," she said, and I followed her in a semicircle until we came to a spot from which we could see the
front door of the house.

"Close your eyes and count to three and then open
them again," she said.

I did as ordered, and when I opened them, Sofia was
gone. It seemed impossible because I hadn't heard a
thing and the ground was covered with the kind of
brush that would have crackled. I looked in all directions and walked around in a small circle.

"Sofia?" I queried the emptiness, but all I could hear
was the breeze in the tops of the trees. Nothing. Nothing until she giggled. The sound was right by me somewhere, but I could see nothing.

"Sofia?"

Silence.

"I give up," I said softly.

A hand grabbed my right ankle and I tried to jump to
the sun, but I was held firmly, which caused me to
stumble. I looked down, and coming out from the base
of the large tree I was standing beside was the hairy
arm of Sofia. I dropped to my knees and peered into a
hole which seemed to go right into the roots of the tree.
Sofia's grinning face said "Come on in" and disappeared.

The hole was quite large and I quickly dropped in

beside her in a hollowed-out area that had just room enough for two people. Because of its coloring against the tree, it was perfect camouflage and you couldn't notice the hole from the outside unless you were really looking for it. But from inside you could see the house and the front door as large as life.

"Catherine and I found this when our ball rolled into the hole one day," she said, "and we used to hide here when we'd done something wrong and they were looking for us. We'd stay here until someone would come out and yell that we wouldn't be spanked if we came in, and then we'd creep out and go around and come from the other side. Sometimes they hit us anyway, but it was never more than a quick slap and it would always be followed by a kiss. I don't know how this hole got here, but it was our favorite."

We crawled out again, and I was amazed at how you didn't notice the opening from the outside.

"That's only one of our places," said Sofia, walking back to the jeep. "Come on, I'll show you the rest."

And show me she did. It took her all morning with the various stops we made, but she and Catherine had a kingdom of their own with trails through the cane-brakes and the swamp, which was a spooky, mosquito-infested maze even in daytime, and up through the hills and woods. Some of the paths were overgrown and we couldn't go through them, but it was amazing how many had stayed clear and open.

We ended up at the picnic spot after about four hours of driving and walking and crawling, and we threw ourselves down on the grass and let the sun dry out the sweat on our bodies.

"I didn't bring any lunch," said Sofia. "You hungry?"

"No. I'm a little thirsty, but I'm not hungry."

"That I can take care of," she said, and went to the jeep and returned with another bottle of Chianti and two plastic glasses.

"I brought two yesterday," she said, working on the cork, "and forgot to bring this one back to the house."

"God works in mysterious ways," I commented, draining the deep red wine down in a long gulp and then leaning back on the ground again.

Sofia suddenly leaned down and hugged me, her body lying across mine at an angle.

"I'm so happy that you found us," she said, and I could have sworn there was a little sob in her voice, "and I can't bear to think of you going away again."

I didn't know what to say. All the platitudes rushed to my tongue:

Oh, now that we've found each other, we'll visit often.

Oh, now you'll have to come out and visit me.

Oh, I think of all of you as my family and you as my sister.

Oh, bullshit.

I reached up and stroked her thick hair, saying nothing. The sweet odor was now mixed with her sweat but that made her even more . . . more . . . More what? What the hell was happening with me as far as this girl—this woman—was concerned? She let her weight sag on me even more. What was she trying to do? She had told me she loved Doc. Cried. Cried those tears that spurted out of the eyes rather than slipped down on the cheeks.

"Sofia?" I said.

Her voice was muffled in my chest. "Yes?"

"I need another glass of wine."

There was a pause and then she slowly pushed herself off my body and poured the wine without looking at me.

I drank it slowly because I really didn't want any more and it had lost its taste. I hadn't needed wine. I had needed time to think.

"Come on," she said, rising to her feet. "I'm hungry for lunch even if you aren't."

11

I decided maybe I could use a snack and followed Sofia into the kitchen when we returned to the house. Angelo and four other men were sitting at a long rectangular plastic-topped table eating bowls of spaghetti with some kind of white sauce on it, and Marina was stirring a big pot on the stove.

I knew that I must have seen two of the men outside the house Sofia and I had driven past the day before, but these old thugs looked like they had been stripped out of the same pea pod, and Angelo was the only one I could definitely identify. It didn't make any difference because none of them acknowledged our presence, mine or Sofia's. They just kept shoving the spaghetti down their throats and drinking from their water glasses of red wine. I had a feeling that none of these guys were into veggies.

Sofia bustled about getting together a platter of cheese and salami and bread, handed me two bottles of beer from the refrigerator and two glasses from the cupboard, and then led me out to a table by the pool, which had even more debris in it than the day before.

"Don't you people ever use the pool?" I asked her.

"Doc and I are the only ones who can swim," she said, "and we use the little pond I showed you yesterday. I suppose I should have somebody come and clean it out, but it's the kind of thing you never think about at the right time."

"What about those palookas?" I asked, jerking my thumb in the general direction of the kitchen.

She laughed.

"Hey," she said, "those are gunmen, killers, soldiers. Cleaning the pool is considered woman's work. These are specialists of the highest type. You want somebody killed, they're your men. But work? Are you kidding? They're half-smashed all the time on the cheap red wine we buy for them. They sit around or they stand around all day, and at night they play cards and watch television at one of their houses. The main reason we got the satellite antenna was that we wanted those guys to have something to do besides playing cards."

"They don't do anything?"

"Oh, they'll fill in as drivers when Angelo can't do it, or they'll run errands to town or they'll lift something that's too heavy for Marina, but mostly they eat, drink, and sleep. They all take long siestas."

"And you pay them?"

"Let's put it this way: they get an allowance each month. But they don't even use that up."

"Why do you keep them?"

"Why? They're family. Besides, the Don likes them around. It gives him the feeling that things haven't changed that much. It's almost funny when they take him to town to get a haircut or something. Except it's really sad. They jump out of the car and look around, and then the boss one gives a nod to show that it's safe, and one of them opens the door of the car and the Don gets out and goes into the barbershop. And then they reverse it when he comes out. They're getting old. Barbalunga has cataracts and Mafucci has prostate problems and DiStefano is so deaf that he farts right in front of you and thinks you can't hear."

"Is there a rest home for old Mafia men?" I asked her.

"Yeah," she said, "you're staying there."

After we had eaten, Sofia said she had some book-keeping to take care of, and I told her I would wander around a bit, which I did, checking out the hole by the tree once more. It was amazing. Then I went back to the pool and spent a half-hour skimming debris until I was sweating like a pig. So I went back and took a lukewarm shower, dried off, took a long look at the bed, said what the hell, and crawled in again. My body was soaking up sleep like it was one of those paper towels they hype on television. It was amazing what damage three relatively small sausages could wreak.

The dream was so real that when I sat bolt upright in the bed, I reached out my right hand and fanned it in the air to prove to myself that she wasn't really standing there. It had been the Cathy I had met, fallen in love with, and married, not the one who had literally wasted away into nothing. She hadn't been movie-star-beautiful, but there was such a delicacy to her face with that slightly olive skin that turned out to be an amalgam of Jewish and Italian that you couldn't stop looking at her whenever she was in a room. I couldn't believe it was happening the night she picked me up in that bar, that someone this attractive was coming on to me. I thought at first she was one of those five-hundred-dollar hookers who had lost her booking and was looking to make out with what she could, and I kept waiting for her to mention price after she bought me a drink.

I asked her about it afterward, unable to leave the question alone, and she said the electricity was coming off me that night like I was somebody from another planet. It was the second time I had shot anybody, the first time also happening during a liquor-store holdup, and I was still shaking from seeing the hole in that guy's shoulder when the paramedics were checking him out. I was so concerned that the other cops not see how nervous and shaking I was that it was like someone had tried to cork Mount Saint Helens the day of the big blast. There had to be smoke coming out of my ears when I went into that bar, and Cathy took me to her apartment and drained it all out of me. Courtesy of Tullio Bandisi, I suppose, but that didn't bother me at all. Not at all.

But I had not dreamed of her once since she had died. And here she had been standing before me with

her eyes staring straight into mine and her right arm
stretched out toward me. It made me think of Willie
Manchester, who had played the ghost of Hamlet's
father when we acted out the scene in the ninth grade.
He had funny pop eyes and he broke us up every time
he looked straight at us, until finally Miss Millet gave
detention to everybody in the play. Was my ghost
trying to warn me of something? Was she telling me to
get the hell out of that house? Was there something
rotten at the Villa Marchese?

Why was I staying on? What was keeping me there? I
was pretty sure that nobody from this place had sent
me that anonymous letter, that nobody from this place
knew about or wanted my six million dollars, that nobody from this place meant me harm. If I was wrong,
then I was the worst police detective in the world and
should get the hell out of the profession.

I shivered and sank back under the covers, feeling
the sweat evaporating on my skin. I had to get my gun
back from whoever had taken it. After all the years of
carrying a gun, I didn't feel right without one on my
body or somewhere close by me.

I crawled out of the bed, did fifty push-ups to check
out my strength, and took another shower, drying my
body as hard as I could with the big towel, but I
couldn't rub away the itchy feeling of something being
wrong. Maybe I should call Cibelli and find out how he
was feeling. I didn't know about him, but I thought it
would make me feel better to touch base again. It was
twenty-five minutes to seven, and I hurried out to the
big dining room, where everybody was already sitting
down, including the Don at the head of the table,
Elena at the opposite end, and Vinnie at the spot where
Marina had plunked down his dishes each time the
night before.

The Don kept complaining about having indigestion
from the restaurant meal of the night before, but I
noticed it didn't seem to hurt his appetite any. He
waded through the chicken broth with tortellini and the

pasta with pesto and the bracciolo and the salad and the
ice cream and the cheese and fruit, belching at appropriate intervals and tilting often enough in his chair to
indicate that the gas was available at either end. Slap a
pair of pantaloons and a doublet on him and he could
have been Machiavelli's cousin. No, not Machiavelli.
One of the minor dukes.

He was the one who started the quiz on Catherine,
how we had met and married and where we were
living. I learned more than I told because they got to
talking among themselves about the old days and how
surprised and upset they were when she and her father
had disappeared some five years before.

"Just like that," said the Don. "Gone. They couldn't
have taken more than a couple of suitcases because a lot
of their clothes were still in the closets."

"She left her dolls," said Sofia. "She didn't even take
one of her dolls. I've got them all in a big box in the
cellar."

"Pascaglia," said Vinnie. "I still think Pascaglia had
something to do with it."

"I asked Pascaglia," said the Don. "I asked him straight
out if Hermie was doing a job for him, but he denied he
knew anything about it. And then he kept calling to
hear if we knew anything. Why would he call like that if
he was the one had taken him away?"

"Hermie was doing a lot of things for him," said
Vinnie. "Toward the end he was going to Europe every
two, three months. I had the feeling Hermie was doing
Pascaglia's laundry for him."

"Hey," said the Don, "Pascaglia's got a dozen guys
doing his laundry for him. With what he takes in, he
should have automatic washing machines."

"You and Catherine didn't have time to make any
babies," said Mama Maria, and I could see that her
eyes were watering at the thought, and when I looked
over at Sofia, she was rubbing her right eye. "Your two
faces would have made nice babies, you and Catherine."

"We hadn't even gotten around to talking about babies," I said, as much to myself as to them. We were still feeling each other out, still discovering new layers, when she told me that the doctor had given her some bad news. I found out after she died that she had known about the cancer when she married me, and I was still puzzling over that one.

"Do you like being a policeman?" asked Doc.

The rest of the table looked startled for a moment. I think they were having a hard time remembering that I was a policeman, even Sofia, that it was something of a miracle for them to have a policeman in their midst, especially one that put on his pants one leg at a time.

"It all depends what you mean by 'like,' " I said, stalling for time.

"Do you enjoy it? Does it give you satisfaction? How did you get into it in the first place?"

"Well, my marks weren't very good in high school, but they would have been good enough to get into the University of Massachusetts, except that I didn't want to leave Boston. Being Jewish, being very Jewish, my father insisted that I had to go to college. So I enrolled in a junior college and just took courses that interested me. The easiest courses were in criminal justice, so I took a lot of those and I took literature courses so I could read novels and stuff like that. There were a lot of policemen who were taking the criminal subjects because they got more money if they built up credits. And I liked a lot of them and I would go to the gym and work out with them. So when my father died and I moved to California to get as far away as possible from Boston, I applied for a job as a policemen in the first city I stopped at and they accepted me. I found that I liked it."

"Why?"

Why? I had been a cop for eleven years now and I still liked it. Why?

"Well, I think part of it is being half Irish and half Jewish. I think it comes natural to the Irish to wear a uniform and be respected and a little feared and boss people around and do good."

"Hah!" said Vinnie. "You and I ain't met the same Irish, that's for sure."

"I know what you mean." I smiled. Under different circumstances I might have asked him what percentage of Italians were thieves and killers who lived off the worst characteristics of mankind. But at the moment I was eating their ripe peaches and sipping their potent espresso, and they were related to me by marriage. My smile was two-edged.

"You probably haven't met the kind of Jew who becomes a policeman," I continued. "My father was one of the 'never-again' Jews who would rant and rave that no Hitler better raise his hand against the chosen people this time around. He brought me up to step to the front of the line, to take no crap from anybody, and not to consider myself a minority citizen who should be grateful for whatever liberties he is allowed. Being a cop makes you a member of a special club. I work with guys who hate kikes and niggers and wops and whatever else there is that isn't exactly like they are. But when push comes to shove, you know that they will be with you all the way even against one of what they like to call their own kind. I like the security that goes with being a cop. Sometimes you let it go to your head a little and you do things that you're ashamed of later, but you also do good things and it more than evens out."

"Cops are different nowadays," said the Don, shaking his head in dismay. "But everything is different nowadays. Sometimes I think the whole world is crazy."

"Catherine and I majored in home economics at college," said Sofia, "and we both got our certificates. What was she working at when you met her?"

"She wasn't working."

"I had to pay for Hermie's funeral," said the Don. He raised his hand in a stop motion toward me, as if I had been about to say that I wanted to pay him back for my late father-in-law's funeral, even though I didn't know him or about him. I could have afforded it, that was for sure. "They told me he was living in a cheap rented room, and it cost me twenty-seven hundred dollars because I wanted him to have a nice casket. We couldn't bury him next to Alicia because it was consecrated ground, but he's in a nice spot in the city cemetery. I'd still like to know who called to tell us he was in the morgue. Somebody he was working with? A man doesn't disappear for five years and then fall off a building back into your lives."

"Did he fall?" I asked as casually as I could.

You could have sliced the silence just like the peach I was working on, it was that thick. And juicy. But not so sweet.

"You're a policeman," said Vinnie. "What do you think?"

"I'm a trained policeman," I said. "I don't draw any conclusions when I don't have any of the evidence. What did the New York police say?"

"Who asked them?" said Vinnie. "We didn't get involved. We hadn't seen Hermie in five years. We thought maybe he was already dead."

"I thought Catherine was dead," said Sofia, her face a frozen mask, the dark mole on the right side of her chin glistening almost black under the light from the chandelier. "Even as Benny was telling me, I knew she was dead."

"Did her father ever contact her while you were married?" asked Doc.

"Never that I knew of," I replied. "She told me both her parents were dead."

They all looked at one another, seeking clues from the other faces. I was tempted to tell them about the six million dollars—that Cathy had left me six million dollars from an unknown source. It would have brought things to a head one way or another. But all I did was pop the last slice of peach into my mouth and wipe my hands on the linen napkin.

"What do you say we watch *The Godfather* on the video?" said the Don, putting his feet together in preparation to pushing back his chair.

"We watched it last night," said Sofia.

"I'd like to see it again," said the Don decisively, getting to his feet just as Angelo entered the room and hurried over to him. Rather than rising, the rest of us sat and watched as Angelo placed his lips on the Don's ear and whispered rapidly in what seemed to be Italian to me.

"What?" said the Don out loud. "Here?"

Angelo whispered again.

"You're sure?" asked the Don.

Angelo didn't even bother to nod.

"Let them in," said the Don hurriedly. "Go back and let them in."

The Don's face had gotten pink and he seemed as excited as a fourteen-year-old on her first date, trying to look calm and sophisticated but about to jump out of the skin.

"It's Pascaglia," he said to his family. "Pascaglia's at the gate. Here we were talking about him and he's down there at the gate. Marina," he said to the little woman who had started to clear the table, and then he babbled at her in Italian. From the way he was pointing to what was left on the table, I figured he was telling her to bring more fruit and coffee.

He turned to look at Sofia and then at Vinnie.

"Pascaglia," he said again, his voice dropping with each syllable. "It's Pascaglia."

12

My mother used to say that all cats look alike in the dark, but since we never had a cat, I didn't have the experience to judge that either way. It would seem to me that if I owned a cat, if I were personally involved with one, I would be able to tell it from other cats even in the dark. My mother also did some weird things if she happened to put her underwear on inside out, part of which involved spitting lustily on the offending, or offended, garment and then whirling around several times. But she loved me and I can still feel a bit of the anger I experienced when she died on me when I was eleven years old.

What this whole cat dissertation involves is that I kind of expected Pascaglia to look like what I expected all Mafia cats to look like. Even though I had been a cop for eleven years and had arrested innumerable hoods who allegedly worked for the syndicate, my only experience with the bosses had been through newspaper writeups, television news, and most important of all, movies like *The Godfather*.

From the reaction of the Don and the rest of the people around the table, including the Doc, I figured Pascaglia to be a top mafioso, one of the guys who literally called the shots. The Don, with his rugged good looks, silvery hair, beautifully shaped mustache, and pseudo-courtly air, was my idea of what a Mafia boss should look like, and I guess I hoped that Pascaglia would be the Don tenfold, maybe a hundredfold, even a thousandfold.

He disappointed me.

He was a husky man, something around two hundred and twenty or thirty pounds on a five-foot-nine-inch frame with a round, hard belly that preceded him by maybe three or four inches. His wrinked gray suit was off the rack and his felt hat had a sweat stain over the band. The beefy face had red wine tracks on the nose, and stuck in the left side of the mouth was half a cigar, well-chewed. The eyes were small mean holes that were pink where you usually saw white. Do not fire until you see the pinks of their eyes. The hands were meaty, thick-fingered, with a huge diamond on the little finger of the left hand. I had a sudden vision of that hand meeting a face with the kind of open-handed slap that would jar your brains loose. I wondered just how big a boss he might be.

The four courtiers accompanying him were of various shapes and ages, but they had one thing in common— evil. You would not buy a used heat-seeking missile from any of them, but if you were a cement manufacturer, you would heed whatever instructions they brought regarding municipal bids.

One of them couldn't have been more than twenty years old, and he looked like a cobra who smelled mice. He had checked each one of the women lasciviously, including Mama Maria, and at the end his look came back to Elena in a way that made me squirm. He was a big guy, maybe six-feet-two, and lifting weights had given the top half of his body an awesome width at the shoulders. He balanced himself on the balls of his feet and his eyes were continually sweeping the room like he was a human radar machine. Whatever his cut of the action, he earned it.

The older bodyguards were squatter but menacing in their own way, and on two of them you could see the bulges of their shoulder holsters under the sport jackets. They were all wearing ties; this was a formal visit.

"Ah, Alfredo," said the Don, who had risen to his feet as soon as the men entered the room, "my house is honored by this visit. It has been too long since last we drank wine together."

Pascaglia moved forward and the two men embraced, their solid bellies preventing anything really intimate happening.

"You know my family," said the Don, the sweep of his hand including all of us. Pascaglia glanced and nodded, his attention somewhere in the depths of his mind rather than on us. He didn't bother acknowledging the identification of his own entourage.

"We were on our way back from Maryland," said Pascaglia, his voice a pleasant baritone, "and I was looking at the map and saw West Orange and got to thinking about the good times we had here in the old days when your sainted father-in-law and his wife"—he bowed slightly in the direction of Mama Maria—"made all their guests feel they had died and gone to heaven."

"Some of them probably had," said Doc.

Even I was somewhat shocked by the effrontery of the remark. The rest of them looked thunderstruck.

Pascaglia slowly turned until he was facing Doc directly. The cigar never moved while he was talking and it was like a magnet to my eyes.

"You never change, do you, Doc?" said Pascaglia. "And you never learn. I'm also here to learn if you're ready to go back to work and earn your pay."

"There hasn't been any pay the last six months," said Doc, his arms resting casually on the table, but I could see the tension in his shoulders. "I figured I had been fired and was a free agent."

The young mobster leaned forward on his toes a bit, like an attack dog waiting for the word to go. The sides of his mouth turned upward just a bit in the approximation of an anticipatory smile.

"Nobody ever gets fired," said Pascaglia pleasantly, "and nobody ever becomes a free agent. You're a talented man, Doc, and I'm a great respecter of talent. As a matter of fact, there's a job I can use you on right now. We've got room in the car and you can come along with us tonight."

"I've decided to retire," said Doc. "I like it here and right now I can't leave my vegetable garden."

The young punk was practically salivating at the thought of what he was going to do to Doc once the signal was given, but Pascaglia turned his glance to the Don, the business with Doc all settled as far as he was concerned. Doc opened his mouth a bit as if to reemphasize his position, but then he closed it tight, his lips pressing in on each other into one thin line. Whatever he was and whatever he'd done had taught him the score as far as Pascaglia was concerned, and I could see he had bowed to what he considered the inevitable.

"While I am here, Alessandro," said Pascaglia to the Don, "there is a small matter of business we have to discuss."

The women, all the women, including Sofia, immediately rose and pushed back their chairs. Keeping their faces inclined toward the floor, they left the room. It was almost like they were nuns participating in some religious ritual for which custom had laid down some very specific rules.

I had placed my feet together preparatory to shoving up and back, but I noticed that none of the men had moved. When it came to business, only the women were not allowed to participate or hear. The men of the family, even the minor members, could stay, and after all, for the past few days everybody had been telling me I was family. I decided not to call attention to my presence.

"Would you care to sit, have a glass of wine?" asked the Don, his hand including table and chairs.

"Not yet," said Pascaglia. "First things first."

The Don nodded his acquiescence. I could feel the sweat popping out of the pores of my body, and the menace in the room pushed down on the top of my head like a migraine. Up to that point I had been drifting along on the superficiality of the words that were being said, the elaborate politeness, the ritual of host and guest. It could be that I had not wanted to acknowledge the precariousness of my position among these people, Benny in the lion's den. But there they

were, the ultimate in criminal activity, a benchmark
group as far as lack of humanitarian feelings were concerned, and I was a cop trapped in their midst, a cop
without even his gun on him. Not that I would have
been able to whip the weapon out, go into the wide-
legged stance, yell "Freeze" in the time-honored tradition, and put them all under arrest. The four bodyguards,
especially the young tiger, would have blown my balls
off along with various other parts of my body. These
weren't Angelo and his cohorts; these were top-of-the-
line pros who kept in working condition through contin-
ual practice.

"I know you are aware," said Pascaglia, "of what
happened to Hermie Slotnick in the city a few weeks
ago."

"We paid for his funeral," said the Don. "It was the
honorable thing to do even though he left us more than
five years ago."

"I am aware of your fulfilling of your obligations,"
said Pascaglia, "and I commend you for your responsibility to your duties."

Even as I was squeezing my legs together to balance
out the pressure from my bladder that made me feel I
had to go to the bathroom and piss for half an hour, I
could not help but notice the formal cadence of the way
they talked. The Don had just the trace of a foreign
accent when he spoke, and I assumed he had been born
in Sicily and come to this country at a very early age.
Pascaglia's voice was strictly metropolitan New York, a
native son of America the Beautiful. But maybe because
of the men he had grown up with and dealt with all his
life, his tone had acquired a patina that echoed the old
country. It was possible that he only knew a few words
of Italian, but his speech was Italian in every way, just
as my father's had a Jewish tinge to it even though he
was born in Little Rock, Arkansas, and my mother had
a hint of brogue combined with her Boston A's and R's.
"You can change your noses but not your Moses," my
father was continually saying, and there had to be an
equivalent expression for the Italians.

"Hermie went to work for me full-time after he left here," said Pascaglia.

The Don nodded to show that this was what he had figured out for himself.

"I was doing a lot of things with the Bramini brothers in Boston then," said Pascaglia, "and Hermie was keeping the books on the deals to make sure that everybody got his fair cut. Hermie was a master with the books. I wish I had someone like him today. There is no honor anymore. They'll steal you blind every time."

The Don nodded his head in both acknowledgment and sorrow. I peeked at Doc to see if he was going to make any comment on the ironic situation that had just been laid before us, but he looked like he had his legs pressed together too, and I knew there would be no more flaunting of authority from his end. Death was speaking in that room, and nobody wanted to be caught looking into his eyes.

"Hermie was doing the Switzerland run," said Pascaglia, "him and Bandini. Making the deposits for me and for the Braminis, bringing back the slips. They were good slips. I don't know who they got to make up those slips for them over there, but they look as good or better than the real thing."

He shook his head in wonderment, a little bit of admiration mixed in with anger. *As good or better than the real thing.* Although I was too scared to work it out in my mind, the glimmer was beginning to come and the cold feeling in the pit of my stomach was getting heavier and colder by the second.

"It was a good year," said Pascaglia, "a very good year, and when Hermie and Bandini disappeared at the same time, we didn't make an immediate connection. Sometimes people take some days off for rest, relaxation. What the hell, you're in Switzerland, go down to the Riviera and soak up some sun for a few days, gamble in the casinos. It was the Braminis got nervous at first. So we put out some feelers, we made some calls. Nobody knows from nothing. I even thought maybe Hermie and his daughter had gone back to visit with you for a while, so I sent Vespucci to spend a few days with you."

I could see the Don thinking back to when that was and then nodding as he remembered the visit.

"He reported that you people knew nothing of what had happened, that you had no idea where Hermie could be, that you were still upset that they had taken off without saying good-bye."

Once again the Don nodded. You could see things clarifying in his head as Pascaglia told his tale. I looked over at Vinnie, who was frozen in his seat, sweat glistening on his face. He was too scared to even make connections in his mind. You could understand why Umbriago the Ugly had chosen to pass the kingdom on to his son-in-law rather than his son.

"I flew to Switzerland with the Braminis," said Pascaglia, "and we visited our Swiss banks to check the accounts. Twenty-five million. We were short twenty-five million. Hermie and Bandini had milked us of twenty-five million dollars. We showed the bankers the slips and they told us they were phonies. We asked them to check on where the money could be and they refused. They said it wasn't their table. The beauty of dealing with the Swiss bankers is that they fix it so nobody can check on you. But we found it works both ways. You can't check on anybody else either. The rule applies to you just as it does to them. And you can't put the squeeze on the Swiss either. You can't threaten to do things to their wives or daughters or to them because they just have to drop one word and you're dead in the water. They hold all the cards. If the good Lord would let me come back to this world one day, I want to come back as a Swiss banker."

"We had nothing to do with this," the Don started to protest, but Pascaglia waved him to silence.

"I know you had nothing to do with this," he said patiently. "We would have discussed the whole matter before this if I had thought you had anything to do with this. This was a Bandini operation all the way. My trusted Bandini. My flesh and blood. My second cousin on my mother's side. Hermie Slotnick would never have had the guts to work up an operation like this. The specialty of the little Jew was the books, and I don't know how Bandini convinced him to pull the con. I figure it was for the daughter, because Hermie's slice went to her. He was dead broke and on his ass when Bramini's people caught up with him. They were taken for fifteen million dollars and it was like it was blood from their veins. It makes no difference with the Braminis—fifteen million or fifteen cents—they never forget and they never forgive. They want their money back and your heart for interest."

Pascaglia was obviously not the strong, silent type. He enjoyed making speeches like other dictators before him—Hitler, Mussolini, the Russian bosses, Castro. He was telling a story, giving the state of his nation, and nobody ever had an audience paying closer attention.

"Ordinarily," he continued, "I would have been quite upset by their sending soldiers into my territory without requesting permission, but I can understand why they did it. They know they lost fifteen million dollars and that I told them I was ten million dollars short. But I had no way of proving to them that I had lost the ten million, and although they should take the word of a brother, you can understand why they would be careful. For all they knew, I might have taken their fifteen million and dumped Hermie and Bandini so they couldn't deny it was them. I admit I had my suspicions about the Braminis and my missing ten million. It's the same with me. You take me for ten million or just ten cents, I want it back and with your *coglioni* for interest. They found Hermie and they questioned him. He had a bad ticker and they had to have a doctor check him all the while they were putting him to the test, and he claimed it was all Bandini, that Bandini had taken all the money. But finally they got it out of him that there had been his own slice, that he had fixed it up for his daughter, and

they got the name of a bank upstate. But they couldn't
get any more, no matter what they did. He wouldn't
tell them where his daughter lived, no matter what
they did. Little Hermie. He did better than I would
have expected. And when they took him up on the roof
for a little more persuasion, he broke loose and jumped
off. They never figured him to do that. Little Hermie.
He broke loose and he jumped. So then they figured
they better bring me in on it, and they gave me the
name of the bank, and I sent the Crusher"—his hand
swept back to indicate his young tiger—"and Taormino
and the Creep upstate to find out what they could, and
they got hold of this bank guy and he told them what
they needed to know. He took some persuading but he
finally told them what they needed to know. And we
found out that the daughter had been living in California and was married to a cop. A cop! And she was dead
and had left all the money to her husband. Five million
bucks. To the cop! So I got permission to send a crew
out there, but the guy was gone. He'd been mixed up
in a whole crazy thing out there, you might have seen it
on the television, and he was gone. The boys tossed his
apartment, but they couldn't find a thing, not a thing.
We've got to find Bandini and we've got to find this cop
and put the screws on him to get the money back. The
Braminis are working on the Bandini end because they're
from Boston and Bandini's from Boston and there are
relatives there. But the cop belongs to me and we're
going to start from scratch and find him. I don't care
what it takes or how hard it is, we're going to find him."

"That's no problem," said the Don. "He's sitting
right there."

And he pointed at me.

So much for being a member of the family.

13

*I*s there a worse feeling in the world than suddenly realizing that you have been a sucker? Think about all the other things that can happen to you outside of physical damage, because I am not trying to claim that being foolish or stupid is worse than a spiral fracture or someone pounding a long nail into your ear. What I am talking about is the state of your mind and soul. If a woman you have the hots for tells you that she finds your friend Irving more attractive, if your boss drops word that his nephew is getting the promotion instead of you, if your mother tells you that she always liked your brother better, it does things to your mind that affect your whole body.

I don't know what I might have expected. Did I really think that I had been adopted into the Marchese-Merlino "family," that I was henceforth to be protected under the bylaws of the clan, that we would exchange gifts at Christmas? Does a leopard change his spots, a jackal his instincts, a thief and murderer his habits? I meant as much to Don Alessandro and Uncle Vinnie and Elena and Sofia—ah, there was the rub. What would Sofia have done and what was she going to do when she found out? What could she do? Because of her upbringing and her fierce sense of family loyalty, would she have simply gone along with what her father did to me? I was the new "relative" on the block. Which came first, the Don or the Benny?

And speaking of first things first—what was this son of a bitch who was approaching my chair about to do? Jumping up and trying to run for it would have been as

ridiculous as it was futile. Those punks of his were just
waiting to pounce. Also, like the mouse who is under
the eye of the cat, or the Jews who were being herded
into boxcars by the Nazis or the blacks in South Africa
who are being moved out of their squatters' towns by
the Afrikaaners, I was paralyzed. I don't know whether
it is fear or hopelessness or maybe hope of a miracle,
but I found out you just sit there and wait for fate to
grab you by the chin.

It was Pascaglia's meaty hand that came around my
chin rather than that of fate, but I'd had enough of that
shit and I yanked it back from under his hand and
shoved his fist away with my right arm. The Crusher
was halfway to us when his boss shut him off, stopped
him dead in his tracks with a slight shake of his head.
This guy was big Mafia all right; every little movement
had a meaning of its own.

He smiled down at me, and it was a real smile
because I was an unexpected cause of pleasure. Here
he'd been talking about a guy who had disappeared
three thousand miles away, and all of a sudden there I
was right in the grip of his hand.

"So you're . . . you're . . ."

"Freedman," I told him. "Benny Freedman. Catherine's husband. Hermie Slotnick's son-in-law. A policeman. A sergeant. And my presence in this house is
known by Lieutenant Aldo Cibelli of the West Orange
police department, who could walk into this room at
any moment, and by my own captain in California, who
could also be calling at any time to find out how I am
and exactly what plane he should meet when I go back
there."

Pascaglia looked over at Marchese, whose face had
become somewhat pinker than it had been a minute
before. The Don hesitated a moment and then gave a
slight nod.

"Who's Cibelli?" asked Pascaglia.

"He's a local cop," said the Don. "Been there a long
time."

"He on the payroll?"

There was a long-enough hesitation for Pascaglia to draw his own conclusion.

"You got a payroll anymore, Alessandro?" he asked with a touch of contempt. "You got anybody to help us out if we have to make any moves?"

"Things have been different the past couple of years," said the Don. "When was the last time we did any business? When was the last time we talked? It was as if we had a disease up here and nobody wanted to catch it. What was I to do?"

"The business has changed," said Pascaglia, anger twisting his features for the first time out of the mask of polite discourse. "The scum have been pushing us to the wall. The niggers. The South Americans. The Canadians. You read in the papers what they do? They wipe out whole families, women, little babies. They stick them into toilets. They scatter pieces of them over whole apartments. They do things that turn your stomach. You're suddenly dealing with people who are crazy, who care nothing for the traditions of business. We have had to change our operations, our ways. The money doesn't fall off the trees into our pockets. It is not that we no longer had any respect for you or didn't want to bring you into the deals that were being made. We have been fighting for our lives."

"I have nobody in West Orange who can help us with anything," said the Don, raising both his arms and then letting them fall again, "and it is true that Cibelli knows he is here and that Cibelli could come out to visit him at any time. It is also true that he spoke to his captain on the telephone because I heard the talk myself."

I thought for a moment in my relief and exultation that he was also going to admit that he had even paid for the call to California, but he stopped short of that. However, he had said enough to allow me to resume seminormal breathing and start considering the possibilities. Pascaglia was studying my face.

"So," he said, "you were Catherine's husband. Please

accept my sympathies on her death. Which gave you five million dollars of my money."

I couldn't be sure if he was being sarcastic. Who knows with these people? The crazy things that flash through your mind. I wondered what he would say if I told him that my money was not his but part of what the Braminis had lost and why didn't he let me settle it up with them at some future time.

"You got our letter, eh?" he asked.

I nodded.

"I thought it was stupid to send you that letter, that all it would do was put you on your guard, but my *consigliere* said it would give you something to think about, that it would make you do something foolish. And maybe he was right, because instead of us having to come to you, here you have come to us."

I thought back on the series of unfortunate actions on my part that had landed me in this dining room with these people, and it made me wonder what would have happened if the letter had not been sent. They would have had to go after me in my own territory, and that might have changed the odds somewhat. Here I had nothing but the odd chance that Cibelli might call or drop in if he wasn't dead from sausage poisoning. All I needed now was a call from Mrs. Cibelli inviting me to the funeral. At the same time I could invite her to mine.

"What happens to the money if you die?" asked Pascaglia.

My brain had never moved faster.

"I divided it up into five pieces," I said quickly. "A million goes to my cousin Doris in Dubuque. A million goes to the Policeman's Benevolent Fund. A million goes for cancer research because that's what killed Cathy. A million goes to a friend of mine named Dr. Everett Wallace. And a million goes for scholarships at my school, Cape Cod Community College."

Thinking up the last two had forced the sweat to clump under my armpits, and I had been cursing myself for not doubling the bequests in the first place. If you're going to have a make-believe list, make it short so you won't have trouble remembering what the hell it is. I repeated the five fake bequests in my mind three times. Cousin Doris in Dubuque! Suppose they asked me her last name and then checked with Information? That one wasn't too smart, but I was stuck with it. If God lets me out of this, I vowed, the first thing I am going to do is draw up a will. Even while all this was going on, I was thinking at the back of my mind who I should really leave the money to, because I had no relatives that I knew of, and I was damned if my mother's bunch in Ireland was going to get a dime.

"You an honest cop?" asked Pascaglia.

I didn't bother to answer, just looked at him.

"This money was stolen from me," he said. "From my business. If you're an honest cop, don't you think you should give it back?"

I straightened up in my chair and peered into his face. Was he kidding? Did this guy have enough of a sense of humor to be making a joke in the middle of all this? No, he wasn't kidding. I could tell that. Then he had to be stupid, because only a stupid man would think that I was going to turn over five million dollars to him just like that. Wenker had obviously told them only about the original bequest, not about the extra million that had piled up. They didn't squeeze anything out of him. But Pascaglia had a point about the money. It had been stolen from him and the vermin from Boston. But they had made the money in the first place by stealing, by drugs, by extortion, by prostitution, by loan-sharking, by every illegal means possible. This was the guy appealing to my sense of decency, fair play, honesty. Who did he think I was?

Well, who was I? How did I feel about inheriting six million dollars that had been made off the weaknesses and depravity of human beings? The descendants of the slave traders and robber barons didn't feel squeamish about where their money had come from. Why should

I? I could also spend it on humanitarian projects, make it up to new people with what had been taken from the flesh of the other people. I could use some of it for myself in the process because money never tells you where it has come from or what has been done to get it. Money is an end unto itself.

But what about Cathy? Wenker, the banker that Pascaglia's men had mashed into talking before sending his car into the tree, had told me the one time I met him that Cathy had taken almost nothing from the trust fund, that it had grown from the original five million to just over six million because she had told them she didn't want more than a few dollars at a time. She had bought her expensive apartment with the money and had given me clothes and presents that had cost a lot more than I had realized, but she had never done anything extravagant, never had told me or given me any indication that she was a millionaire six times over. If she hadn't died and left me the bundle, I still wouldn't know. Was this a lady who had been caught in a Mafia trap, who had kept her mouth shut because Hermie Slotnick, the crooked bookkeeper, money launderer, and thief from thieves was her father, her flesh and blood? Were she and Sofia sisters under the skin as well as cousins, or was Sofia just like her father, who had sold me down the river without a blink? Things were getting complicated. I had signed up for a philosophy course in college because the guidebook had made it sound like it was going to straighten me out on all the moral problems I would ever face in life, but all the professor had done was make jokes that would have embarrassed Henny Youngman. One day he told us that there were always several ways of looking at things, that nothing was black and white. "If I tell you my girl's a vision and yours is a sight," he said, "it doesn't mean the same thing even though the words can mean the same thing." I shifted to a course in "Criminal Behavior" that same day.

But here I was stuck with six million dollars in crooked

money, and I considered myself a fairly honest person. This was something I would have to work out if I lived. *If I lived!* That was the problem I was going to have to work out first.

Pascaglia hadn't expected an answer to his question because he had moved away right after he had asked it and was pacing up and down by the side of the table. He came to a decision.

"You got a phone in here?" he asked the Don, who pointed to a wireless one on the sideboard against the wall.

"You dial one for long distance?" he wanted to know, and again the Don nodded. He punched the numbers and waited. From the time it took and the expression on his face, you could tell that somebody was supposed to be sitting right there, to answer on the very first ring.

"Where the fuck you been?" he asked the lucky answerer. He listened impatiently to the reply.

"Listen!" he shouted. He fished in his pocket and pulled out a crumpled piece of paper, which he painfully unfolded while trying to hold on to the telephone. "Listen!" he yelled again. "You tell number two to go to number four. Fifteen minutes. Number two at number four. Shut up!"

He walked back to the sideboard, banged the receiver into the charger, and turned to the Don.

"This is one of the things you have to put up with nowadays," he shouted. "You can't even talk on the telephone. You have to number pay phones on a list and change them every week to new locations or they'll have bugs in them as sure as your mother was a saint. Fucking feds can stick a bug in anything nowadays. You take a shit and look down, they got a bug in your turd. You can't talk in your house, you can't talk in your car, you can't talk on the street. They got remotes that can pick up a fly farting in the next block. You ask me why I didn't return your calls? Because you can't make any calls anymore. Maffucci told me his teenagers were driving him nuts so he put in a children's phone, and they even bugged that. They bugged the kids' phone. Go ahead, Alessandro, tell me about your troubles. But I could use some coffee. You got some coffee?"

Vinnie scurried out of the room in the direction of the kitchen, and everybody sat still and quiet for the next ten minutes while Pascaglia paced up and down beside the table.

Sofia brought the tray with the coffee and cakes into the room and set it down on the table. She gave me a quick glance but then was very careful not to look at me again. I couldn't believe that she would have betrayed me, and I hoped she was thinking of something that might be done. Maybe she would call Cibelli. If there was only some way I could get across to her that the only way to get me out of this was to call Cibelli. If she wanted to get me out of this. She left the room, and Pascaglia noisily drank a cup of coffee before returning to the phone. Three of his men also had a cup and some cake, but the young one called the Crusher just stood there with his eyes fixed mainly on me. He occasionally checked everything else out, but the eyes always came back to me.

Pascaglia pulled the piece of paper out of his pocket and dialed one of the numbers written there, whatever the hell was designated as four for that week.

"Hey," he said, "I'm at Marchese's in Jersey. Our California pigeon is here. Yeah, that's the one. Never mind how. Just listen. I want you should get up here and bring some people with you. Ten. Twelve. Whatever. Yeah, you gotta come. Never mind about that now. I need you here. Now. Get moving."

He hung up the phone, walked over to the table, and ate a piece of cake. Then he poured himself another cup of coffee. Nobody said anything or moved.

"Alessandro," he said, "you still got those rooms down there that we used to use once in a while?"

"Nothing's changed," said the Don. "It's all the same."

"The metal one. That's still there?"

"I haven't been in it in a long time," said the Don, "but it's still there."

"Why don't we put our boy in there for now," said Pascaglia, "keep him safe until Brachi and my people get here."

"Whatever you say," said the Don.

"Vinnie," said Pascaglia, "why don't you go with Crusher and Pietro and our friend here and show them where to put him in. Then maybe we'll drink a little wine and eat a little more of this very good cake and talk about old times."

So there I was ten minutes later, sitting on an old kitchen chair in a room in the cellar that had tin nailed all over the walls and ceiling in a way that reminded me of a giant humidor. I figured it had been originally built to store something, but it made about as good a jail cell as anything you could devise, or an interrogation room whose echoes could drive some poor son of a bitch right out of his mind. The Crusher had his chance at bringing me down, because the grip on my arm had decreased my biceps size by about an inch. He had also entered me into the room the way you might launch a rocket, and I had banged into one of the four chairs and knocked it over. My hip still ached from that, but it had not lessened my attention to my sore arm muscle.

There was one light hanging down from the ceiling with one of those transparent bulbs that were common at one time but can only be bought now in specialty stores. The illumination was dim.

And so were my thoughts as I sat there in the chair with only depression for company. Vinnie had not looked at me once all the way down and had not said a word. He had pulled the bolt on the heavy wooden door, gone in and turned on the light, and then come out again. After he had thrown me in, the Crusher had come in for a moment to check out the place. Quickly satisfied, as he should have been, he had gone out, slammed the door, and shot the bolt. I couldn't hear their footsteps as they left.

Pascaglia wanted his money back and he was going to make me unhappy until he got it one way or another. Very unhappy. Very, very unhappy.

I dropped to the floor and did a hundred push-ups, but I was just as tense when I finished as when I started.

If I'd had an Anthony Cibelli hot sausage hidden on me, I would have eaten it then and there.

14

Policemen as a whole consider themselves psychological experts when it comes to dealing both with criminals and with the public. Sometimes the two categories get mixed up, and innocent citizens are caught in the crossfire. A uniform, a badge, and a gun are formidable weapons in the psychological arsenal. People tend to do what they're told when faced by any one of the three. I myself once gained great satisfaction when involved in a fender-bender with a very belligerent young man. I moved my jacket just enough for him to see the butt of the gun and he turned into the proverbial putty. The accident was my fault so I let him off with a warning.

There are various ways to cow a prisoner, of course, and isolation is one of them. You can also fill a room with shouting cops who swear and carry on and argue with each other and act so crazy that the prisoner fears the moment when they remember why they're in there and all turn on him. But I have always felt that a good dose of isolation is the best. It gives their imagination time to do your work for you. I had a course once where the lecturer, a lawyer from Boston University, described some of the techniques used by the Russians and the Chinese to break people's minds into little pieces, and it upset me for two days. And then when I became a cop, I found I was using some of those very techniques without thinking about it twice.

The quickest way, to be sure, is a club or a rubber hose or a sock with sand in it or sticking needles under fingernails and all those other little beauties that have been thought up by sick minds over the centuries. You can only do this, of course, when you don't have to worry about damaged goods. We still had cops on our force who would sneak in the quick kidney or stomach punch or cut somebody's air off for a minute or two or even grab a guy by the balls and squeeze until his eyes popped. There were one or two occasions during interrogations when I did something in anger that bothered me after I had calmed down. Right now the wheel was grinding full circle on my own imagination. Like a doctor who comes down with a disease or has a heart attack, I knew too much for my own good.

It was somewhere around nine P.M. when they dumped me into durance vile, and for ten minutes I just sat on that rickety old kitchen chair in a funk, my body operating without benefit of mind. When the brain did begin to function again, it didn't improve things because the first emotion I felt was despair. There was no chance that Cibelli would visit or even call at this time of night. There was also this terrible feeling in the pit of my belly that his father's sausage had killed him, and there was no likelihood of John Wayne and that cavalry troop appearing on the brow of the hill.

It was a little after six P.M. in California and the captain was on the way home to whatever conglomeration of cholesterol his wife had boiled down during the afternoon. He wasn't expecting me until the day before the mayor's ceremony, when I was to get the city medal for surviving in the church camp, and he was not the type to spend the department's money on a three-thousand-mile phone call in the first place. I was pretty sure they were going to name me a lieutenant at the mayor's ceremony, that was the surprise he was talking about, and all I had to do was be there. That's all. Be there. I became very depressed.

It's amazing how even when you think somebody is going to kill you or at the very least maim you, there still are minor matters that can upset you on top of the fear. I wondered how I was going to sleep under my present circumstances with only the crummy chairs and no bedclothes and no place to wash up or brush my teeth or go to the bathroom. My subconscious must have been trying to break through on that one because the moment it passed through my mind I realized how bad I had to go, and I stood right up and walked over and pounded on the heavy wooden door with my fist.

The bolt was immediately pulled back and the door opened. One thing was for sure: I couldn't complain about the service. Standing there was the goon that Pascaglia had designated as the Crusher, and right behind him were Sofia and Marina, their arms loaded with blankets and baskets with all kinds of bottles and plastic-wrapped objects.

"Whaddaya want?" asked the Crusher, shoving me back into the room with the flat of his right hand. Sofia and Marina came in and started to place their burdens upon the chairs.

"I need to use a bathroom," I told him.

He considered that for a moment, then nodded to himself before turning to Sofia and asking if there was a bathroom close by.

"There's a toilet out by the laundry machine back over there," she said, pointing out to the left.

"Come on," said the Crusher, motioning for me to precede him out of the room. I knew he had a gun on him somewhere, but such was his confidence in his strength and quickness that he wasn't even considering its use in his control over me. And although I worked out in a gym four times a week and had studied the martial arts with the two black belts of our department, I also had complete confidence in the Crusher's strength and quickness and was not about to put him to the test.

We found the toilet without any problem, and I was a little surprised when he crowded into the tiny room with me, but such was my need that I did not quibble or plead modesty. I just hauled out and let it flow.

"Hey," he said, watching my stream, "you're hung pretty good."

I had one cold moment in the pit of my stomach before realizing that this was straight man talk, sincere admiration. I didn't acknowledge but continued doing my business.

"The boss told me that Hermie said to him that the Jews were the most optimistic people in the world because they cut off ten percent before they even knew how long it was going to be," said the Crusher.

"They send the tips to Sicily, where they plant them and they grow up to be Mafia men," I said, shaking off and flushing. He wanted old jokes, I'd give him old jokes. There was no washbasin in the room, only the toilet. I thought how it would feel to be standing under a warm shower and rinsing off the sweat that had dried on my skin. The night before, it had been straight luxury in my room on the second floor; tonight it was the tin box.

When we got back to my cell, Sofia and Marina were just finishing placing the top blanket on the floor with a pillow at one end. There were two bottles of water and a shiny pail and some bread and cheese and a basket of fruit. Honest to God, a basket of fruit. There was even a giant Hershey bar stuck between a peach and a nectarine in the basket. My toilet kit was placed by the pillow, and my pajamas were neatly folded on the blanket.

"Okay," said the Crusher, "let's go," and Marina started out of the room.

"I want to talk to him," said Sofia, standing by the makeshift bed.

"Out!" he commanded, moving toward her, and I started moving toward him. He stopped and looked at me with relish, savoring for a moment what kind of damage he would inflict.

"You get out," she told the Crusher, "and let me talk to him."

"No way," he said, starting forward again.

"You put one finger on me," she said hotly, "and you're a dead man. I'm Don Marchese's daughter and don't you forget it. Your *padrone* won't forget it either. Now, get out."

You know how they say anger can make a woman beautiful. Well, even that didn't work for Sofia, but she sure was a commanding figure with her eyes flashing and her body drawn up to where she was practically standing on her toes, and no palooka was going to question that kind of authority. He moved backward to the door and stepped just outside into the darkness of the cellar. She turned to me, standing close, and the clean, sweet smell rose up from her hair.

"All this time we've had together and we still don't know each other," she said. "I don't want anything to happen to my father, but I also don't want anything to happen to you. It's all mixed up. Don't do anything crazy."

"I don't think you should be talking like this," said the Crusher from the doorway. "That's enough."

She had spoken too softly for him to hear, and it had bothered him to the point where he was going to break it up, at least for now, until he could check with his boss on what was allowed and what wasn't.

"Don't worry about me," I told her. "Call Cibelli," I whispered.

"That's enough," said the Crusher, coming into the room and taking her by the arm.

She yanked it away from him, but stepped back from me and turned to walk out. Had she heard me? If she had heard me, would she do it? If Cibelli came out on his own, they could hide my car and tell him I'd left. Would he call California to check on it or just let it slide until it was too late? It would take a call from her to alert him to my situation. Once the ball started rolling, however, it could roll right over her father. The charge right now could be kidnapping, and these people were as aware of the law as any district attorney. Just with

what had already happened, their plans for me had to be
terminal. I shivered in the tin room.

Sofia stopped at the door and turned slightly toward
me.

"Be sure and eat your Hershey bar," she said, and
walked out into the dimness. The door was slammed
behind her.

I was still shivering a little bit and I thought of
picking up one of the blankets and wrapping it around
my shoulders, but Marina had made the bed so neatly
that it would have felt wrong to disturb it. So I sat
down in the chair again and listened to my heart beat
for a while, which seemed to be increasing its speed
with each second. I tried the breathing we had learned
in the stress-management course they had made everybody in the department take the year before, and I
tried blanking out my mind, and I even tried to recall
unique sexual experiences I had enjoyed in my adult
years, but nothing stopped the shivering.

So when the bolt was suddenly drawn and the door
yanked open again, I jumped off the chair and twisted
in the air to come down with my feet spread and my
hands in the ready position. When Pascaglia saw what I
looked like, he stopped still and considered me carefully. In addition to everything else that was crowding
through my mind, I felt foolish and straightened up
quickly. I was so screwed up that I'm surprised I didn't
offer him a welcoming smile to show him that to me
this whole situation was a piece of cake that I could cut
into pieces whenever I wanted and eat with a glass of
milk.

"Hey," he said, looking around the room at my bed
and the bread and cheese and basket of fruit, "they've
got you fixed up pretty good here."

I knew he hadn't come down to see if I was comfortable, so I didn't bother to answer.

He walked over to the bed and moved the blanket a
bit with the toe of his right foot, leaned over and prod-

ded a peach with his finger to test its ripeness, pulled the Hershey bar out a way and then shoved it back in.

"All the comforts of home," he remarked cheerfully, and moved back to the center of the room. I caught the glimpse of a movement with the corner of my eye and looked at the open door, where somebody was standing just outside the circle of pale light cast by the bulb. There were a few lights in the corridor outside but essentially you couldn't make out more than dim shadows. Under their present circumstances, the Marcheses had probably tried to keep their electric bills as low as possible.

"Shut the door," Pascaglia called out to whichever bodyguard was standing out there, and the order was immediately carried out.

"Sit down," he instructed me, and I sank into the chair nearest me while he took the one that was under the light.

"What's going on with you and Sofia?" he asked conversationally in a man-to-man tone. "She acted like a crazy woman when she found out you were down here. Started yelling at her father and then at me, until finally Vinnie had to put a hand over her mouth. A couple of days here and you're hitting on her, huh? Hermie's daughter's dead how long, and you're already hitting on Sofia, huh?" There might have been a bit of admiration in his voice rather than reproof. I couldn't be sure.

"You've got that wrong," I told him. "She and my wife were real tight, cousins who grew up together, and she feels responsibility toward me. That's all there is to it."

"They were close," he mused. "Always together. They always walked with their arms around each other when they were kids. Hermie's daughter was a looker. Even then. I never even saw her once when they moved to the city after he came full-time with me. They had an apartment in Manhattan because Hermie said she liked to go to shows and things, but I never saw her then. But quite a looker. Not like Sofia. Sofia's built to have kids, she's got the hips and the ass, but you'd have to put a bag over her head. Alessandro was telling me how he'd like to have grandchildren, but you'd have to put a bag over her head. Now, Elena, I could understand your trying to move in on that. Jesus Christ, that old son of a bitch is twenty years older than me and he's got something looks like that. I can buy stuff that looks like that when I go to Vegas, but he went and married one. Imagine going to bed every night with a thousand-dollar hooker. And the son of a bitch is not only alive but he looks good."

He reached into his back pocket, pulled out a wallet, and thumbed through until he came up with a color photograph.

"That's my wife and kids," he said proudly. "We took that last Easter after church."

The woman was not as homely as Sofia, but her face had a hardness to it that made her ten times as ugly. The boy and girl were somewhere in their early twenties, she a younger version of her mother, he a fairly good-looking slim guy just under six feet tall. I didn't know what to do. Was I expected to say "nice family"? Or comment on the loveliness of the wife and daughter or the good looks of the son? Fuck him! Fuck them all. I handed him the picture without a word and he tucked it back in the wallet and replaced it in his pocket.

"We've got to work out something on the money," he said, getting down to the meat of his visit. "My deal with the Braminis is that we split three for two on everything we get back because they lost fifteen to my ten, so we've got to figure that in, but I'm willing to give you some lagniappe if you cooperate. Ten percent. You sign over four-point-five mil and we let you keep five hundred thousand. Now, the Braminis are going to want your cut out of my slice, but that will be between me and them. Once we catch up with Bandini like we did with Hermie, we'll get the rest no matter where it's stashed, but your case is special and we've got to bend a little. We could keep you here or somewhere else and squeeze your pecker until we got the whole thing back, but we'd have to do it a piece at a time because of the bank setup, and I don't want to wait that long. The Braminis are convinced that Bandini's holed up somewhere in Boston, and they'll eventually find out where, but a bird in the hand is what you are and that's good enough for me right now. So, you can make it easy or tough on yourself, makes no difference to me."

"I'm a cop," I told him.

"I know you're a cop. I didn't know it when Marchese let me spill my guts in front of you, but he said he knew you weren't going anywhere and he wanted to find out if you'd do or say anything."

"What guarantees do I get? How do I know you don't squeeze me almost dry and then waste me to keep my mouth shut and kiss off the final five hundred thousand?"

"Hey," he said, lifting his hands in the air in that classic Italian gesture, "you're a cop with five million bucks' worth of organization money. If someone blows the whistle on you, how you gonna explain that? They ain't got nothing on us they ain't already got. But you have your whole life ahead of you, and it would be better to have a half-million that you don't have to explain to everybody. It's lousy all around, but we've got to work together to make the best of the situation. It's like Sofia's been yelling up there: you're family."

"I don't know," I told him.

"This is all off the top of my head," said Pascaglia, standing up. "We'll wait for Brachi to get here. He's a lawyer and he'll figure out the way to do it. But I just wanted you to know that I'm willing to make a deal, that I'm willing to work it out. You get a night's sleep and think on it. For the sake of your own health, think on it."

He banged once on the door, it opened, and he was gone.

Think on it, the man had said. What the hell else was there to do in the tin room? They were probably all up there watching *The Godfather* on the VCR, drinking grappa, and talking about old times when Umbriago could afford to have policemen on the payroll. Would Pascaglia keep his word, give me the half-million, and forget about it? I would also have the extra million that they didn't even know about. And then what was I supposed to do? Go back to being a cop and forget about it too? That would be the same as putting me on the payroll. I'd taken some free meals in my time, coffee, discounts on various things. There was that old joke about the guy asking the woman if she'd put out for a million bucks and she said she would. Then he asked her if she would put out for two bucks and she got highly insulted and said, "What do you think I am?" And he said, "We've already established that; now we're arguing about price."

It was one thing to accept a free meal and quite another to take the five hundred thousand and the extra million and my life and shut up about it. My life. Would they really let me live? And if they did, would I let them exist? If I went to Cibelli or the FBI with my story, what would I have to back it up? And what would happen to me when the whole story came out? I wouldn't have a dime of the money and eventually I would be out of a job because there was no way I could continue being a cop. And let's face it, I liked being a cop. Deep down, there had never been any doubt that I wanted to keep doing what I was doing, six million or no six million. I wanted to stay a cop. A good cop. Why the hell hadn't Cathy been just like what she seemed to be, a beautiful woman with no family and no money? That would have been enough, and I could have mourned her and then gone on with my life. But now she had given me a fortune and a family to go with it. Some family!

Sleep on it, he had said. Think about it and sleep on it. I got one of the bottles of water and the pail and my toothbrush and paste and brushed my teeth and spit in the pail. I thought about getting into bed with my clothes on, but then I said what the hell and undressed and put on the pajamas, turned out the light, and crawled in between the blankets. It was hard but it wasn't bad. Just like being back in summer camp. Except Marina hadn't short-sheeted my bed. That Sofia was something. Up there fighting for me against her own father and all that scum. From what Pascaglia had said, I knew I could at least count on her.

Be sure and eat your Hershey bar.

I sat bolt upright in the dark, scrambled out of the covers, and stumbled around until I found the light cord. I reached into the basket and pulled out the giant Hershey bar. Was there a key hidden in there? A key? The goddamned door had a bolt on it, not a keyhole. A file like in all the old prison movies? There weren't any barred windows in this room. There weren't even any windows. The only air came from the cracks around the door.

My hands were trembling so that I could barely slide the bar from the wrapper. A piece of paper fluttered to the ground. I picked it up and looked at it. Nothing. Turned it over. One word was written there—"plastique." What the hell! I tore off the foil and there was nothing there but chocolate, which I broke into pieces, but nothing fell out. I carefully bit into a chunk and it tasted good but there was nothing else in it.

Plastique! Christ, that was the explosive that the French developed. We had studied it at the police academy during the safe-robbing lecture. You slapped it on and then used a triggering device. But where the hell was it?

I pawed through the basket with the bread and cheese. Nothing. The only thing left was the fruit basket, and I took the pieces out one at a time and laid them on the blanket. At the bottom was a whitish-gray ball shaped like an apple. I pushed with my finger and it gave like putty. Near the bottom was a black plastic thing stuck in the side, and when I lifted out the "apple," I saw that the black thing was a triggering device. Push down the little plunger and stand back. I stuck another square of chocolate on top of my tongue and chewed, the saliva slipping out of the side of my mouth.

I ran over to the door and looked at the wide cracks around the frame. Cover the right area and you could probably blow the whole fucking bolt off. Then down the hall past where the toilet was and out that back door. To where? To anywhere. When? When everybody was asleep. Then what? Out! Out to Cibelli or any other cop or the FBI or the Army or the Navy or anybody at all as long as it was out. Face whatever consequences that came after that, but the primary thing was out.

I thought I heard a noise and my heart stopped. I sprang into action, putting the plastique ball back in the bottom of the basket and covering it with fruit. I ate more chocolate, cramming it into my mouth as fast as I could. Then I drank half the bottle of water. Then I brushed my teeth again. Then I did fifty push-ups. Then I put my clothes back on. Then I put out the light and got back into bed. I had to wait. Three o'clock. I would do it at three o'clock in the morning. When the night was darkest before the dawn. I wondered if there was a moon and if it would still be up. One thing at a time. Face the problems one at a time.

Twice I got up to put on the light to see what time it was and once to piss in the bucket. I'd had to do that a lot when I was trapped in the canyon with the church bunch. I'd thought my bucket-pissing days were over forever, and here I was doing it again barely six weeks later.

At a little after midnight, the bolt was slid back and the door opened. I sat up in the dark and looked at the doorway, where I could see the shadows of the two figures in the dim light from the corridor.

"You there, cop?" a hoarse voice asked.

"I'm here," I said, and the door slammed shut again and the bolt was shot.

I got up and put on the light and that's how I saw it was a little after midnight. I thought of getting back in the bed and resting until three, but I was afraid I would fall asleep and go right through to the morning. There was small chance of that happening the way I was shaking, but there was still a chance. So I ate the rest of the chocolate bar, which made me feel a little sick to my stomach, and then I made a package of the food and one of the bottles of water and wrapped it in a blanket, and then I put out the light and sat down on top of the remaining blanket with the pillow behind my back and waited for the time to come. I remembered a poem or a story or something I had read in which it was "always three o'clock in the morning." No, it was a song my mother used to sing. "It's three o'clock in the morning, Mother, may I go out?"

I was sure as hell going out of there at three o'clock in the morning, and all those mothers upstairs were damned well going to know it.

15

One of the things you really have to work at in order to be a good policeman is learning how to wait. Dumb people are better at it than smart people because their minds don't churn away while they are sitting or standing for long periods, which puts your brain in conflict with your body. Poor people take it for granted that they are going to have to wait, whether it be for unemployment compensation or welfare or free cheese, and after a while, even if they aren't dumb, they get into the habit and they're programmed for the rest of their lives. You can wait forever if you're lying down because your whole body can be relaxed that way, but if you're sitting or standing, waiting can be a real problem.

I never walked a beat when I became a cop because in California you do everything in a car. You take your car to cross the street. When it wasn't my turn to drive the police car, I would sometimes get terribly restless on quiet nights when all we did was cruise around. And then when I made detective, there were all those stakeouts, most of them meaningless, where you had to stay in one place for what seemed eternity and quite often was. I even went as far as taking a course in yoga, thinking that I could do a facsimile lotus position that would get me through the long waits without my partner thinking I had gone bonkers. But after I had taken five sessions, I was sitting there one night with my legs crossed and my hands together and the guru up front wearing a turban and clanging little bells together when I suddenly realized that what I was doing was exactly

what I had been forced to do in class from the first
through the sixth grades. Yoga and all that Eastern
philosophy crap were nothing more than elementary
school for adults. I finally reached the point where I
could keep myself from rushing into a situation where I
might get my head blown off or could sit in a car or the
back of a store with my eye glued to a peephole without
my heart getting all fluttery, but it still came hard.

What I'm saying is that it was tough as hell to wait for
three A.M. to roll around. I had decided that it would be
best to hold off until the last minute before puttying the
cracks in the door with the plastique because if I did it
too early and they came down to check me again, the
whole deal was blown.

I tried lying down on the bed and couldn't stay still.
Sitting up against the wall was lousy, as was plunking
down on a chair. I unrolled the blanket and rearranged
the bread and the cheese and the fruit, then rolled it up
again and forced it into one of the wicker baskets.
Christ, I was going to run out of there like Little Red
Riding Hood off to visit her grandmother, but if I had
to hide in the woods somewhere for any length of time,
I didn't want to take any chances on being cold or
hungry. I was so proud of myself for thinking ahead in
this manner that it was frustrating not to be able to tell
somebody about it.

The other thing I tried to think ahead on was whether
to have the light on or off when I blew the door. With
the light on, it would be easier to see what was going
on from inside the room, but then when I ran out into
the dim corridor, I would have trouble seeing while my
eyes shifted, and that could be a problem.

But if I put the light out before I triggered the
mechanism and waited for my pupils to adjust to the
dark, then I would be able to see fairly well in the
cellar and could zoom through to the back door. But
that would mean putting out the light and then waiting
about ten minutes before feeling my way to the door,
pushing the plunger, and retreating quickly to the cor-

ner to be out of the way of the blast. The problem was that I could screw up in the dark with both the plunger and getting out of the way. It was a puzzlement.

I finally decided to go with the dark and take my chances on the plunger and getting back to the corner. My watch showed twenty minutes to three and that was good enough as far as I was concerned. It took about ten minutes to get the stuff jammed into the doorway, and then I made a thick wad in the middle where I figured the bolt to be on the opposite side and stuck in the plunger. I took my provisions basket in my left hand and put out the light, felt my way to the door, and began to count, starting with a thousand and one. I didn't want to fool myself into thinking that my eyes were ready for the dark before they really were, so I figured on counting for ten minutes, which seemed like ten hours by the time I reached the right number.

My hand had found the trigger mechanism, and just as it was about to press down, I stopped to wonder where the hell Sofia had gotten this stuff, trigger and all. Was she part of the family burglary ring? What the hell difference did it make that she happened to have a wad of explosive putty around? I asked myself, and pushed down firmly until I heard it click. I had no idea how many seconds I had before the thing went off, but I felt my way carefully to the corner to the left, crouched down, and pushed my head into the tinned V of the walls.

It must have been a thirty-second timer because it didn't seem to take that long before there was this loud bang and I saw pink through my closed eyelids. I can't imagine what the noise sounded like upstairs, but in the tin room the pain in my eardrums was tremendous and that's when I went deaf for a while without realizing it. With all my planning ahead, I hadn't thought to stuff something in my ears.

I stood up and felt my way to the right until I ran into the door. It had been busted loose and was open about three feet, with jagged splinters sticking out along the sides. I went around it and out into the corridor. The only bulb that was lit was the one down near the toilet and I ran toward it and the door beyond. I couldn't hear anything from upstairs and was wondering if the thick walls and beams had muffled the sound. If I'd known I was deaf from the blast, I would have been a lot more scared about it, but it wouldn't have changed anything anyway.

I reached the back door and pulled it open. It had never occurred to me that it might have been locked or barred or whatever, and I don't know what I would have done if it had been, but it was no problem. There were concrete steps leading up to the yard, and I tore up them, catching my foot on the last one and sprawling flat on my face in the stones, but never loosening my grip on the basket.

I was just to the side of the garage and I ran around behind it and to the left. There was no moon and it was dark as hell out there and I would run into trees and stumble and fall and jump up and run and bump into something again. This wouldn't do, so I stopped still to catch hold of my breath and my mind. I took a quick look at the house and saw lights go on in two different windows. Everything was so silent.

My impulse was to go straight into the woods as far as I could and as long as I could and then figure out something when it got light. But who knew how far I could get in the dark or what I might fall into or where I might end up. For all I knew, I could be running in a circle and end up at the front door just in time for them to scoop me up.

The front door!

I got my bearings by the garage and moved around in a circle toward the front. Out of the corner of my eye I could see more and more lights going on in the house, casting illumination through the windows on the ground outside, but I was well outside where they fell. I finally reached the front and moved a little deeper into the woods until I came across the giant tree, dropped down to my knees, and fanned around with my hands. There it was. My heart gave such a leap that I thought it was going right out of my chest. The hole. Sofia and Cathy's secret hiding place. I swiveled my body around on the ground and scurried backward until I dropped into it. The bushes swung back into place and as I sank down on my butt, I could have sworn I could smell the sweet clean aroma that came off Sofia's hair.

She'd gotten me out of there and now she had me snug as a bug in a rug where those bastards couldn't get at me. I saw the reflection of light through the bushes and lifted my head high enough to peek through the lower branches. The house was loaded with lights now, and someone had put on spotlights on the front of the house. I could see men running around, some with guns in their hands, but I still couldn't hear anything and it took me a minute to figure out what my problem was. I hoped it wasn't permanent, but my relief was such that I didn't take time to worry about it.

I pulled the blanket out of the basket and unrolled it to get at the bottle of water. I drank just enough to slake my thirst because I didn't know how long I'd have to be in that hole before I would be able to make a run for it. And I didn't care. I pulled the blanket around my shoulders because the sweat was evaporating off my body and making me cold. The blanket was mohair and felt soft against my skin. She'd given me a mohair blanket. Before I married Cathy, I had thought I was in love two times, once with a girl I went to school with in Boston and once with a married lady in California. Cathy was a whole new experience and I realized that before I had only thought I was in love. With her I knew I was in love.

When Sofia had told me that if I had been Cathy's husband, I was her husband too, I had been somewhat embarrassed and somewhat annoyed. But now I knew what she was talking about. My wife was dead but I still had a wife to love me and take care of me. And that comforting thought was enough to put me to sleep with all that had happened and all those guys running around with guns in their hands ready to blow my balls off. They were probably yelling around there all night with Pascaglia on their ass. But I was deaf to all of it, stone deaf.

16

The sounds of the birds establishing their turf just before dawn was what brought me out of my doze or daze, whichever it was, and it took me a few seconds to establish where I was and how I got there. Then came the realization that I could hear again, which was good. Then I started wondering how I was going to get out of there, which was bad.

All the lights in the house were still on, but I couldn't see any people, and I sank back against the dirt feeling exhausted despite my short rest. It was time, as the captain always said when we were hopelessly bogged down in a case, to assess the situation.

The main objective, of course, was to get the hell out. O-u-t. But the gate was the only way I knew and that was not only closed and locked but most certainly watched at this stage of the game. The fence was too high for me without a ladder, and all those spikes and glass at the top would make it that much tougher. The only alternative was to strike out through the woods and hope to blunder my way to one of the other estates, where a simple phone call would solve the problem. Assuming, of course, that the neighbors were law-abiding citizens and this wasn't Mafia CondoLand East.

But that was wild country out there and it would be a matter of luck to keep from going deeper and deeper into the woods and reaching nowhere. A toss of the coin to decide between ending up alive and ending up dead. At the moment, it was more likely to decide between dead and dead. And on top of that, Pascaglia's men could be roaming the woods in hopes of picking up my trail.

The only thing I had in my favor against these guys was summer camp. When I was a kid, my father was still playing second violin for the Boston Symphony Orchestra, and each summer we would go to the Berkshires for the Tanglewood music festival. Most of the time he would enroll me at a sports day camp, but one summer I was pissed off about something and decided that sports day camp was something I would draw the line on. Instead of starting the argument I had hoped for, all it did was get me enrolled in the local Audubon camp, where I learned about the bees and the birds and the flowers and beavers. The high point of the session was the final thirty-six hours, when we were supposedly left alone in a marked-out area and had to build our own shelter and subsist on raisins and nuts and whatever melted candy bars we'd sneaked in our pockets. We didn't know that the counselors had us under pretty close observation all the time, and that whole following winter in Boston I lived with the glow of having survived ALONE in the wilderness, like I'd been a commando in the war or something equally hazardous.

I was pretty sure that none of Pascaglia's men had any kind of experience in the woods unless a couple of them had been Fresh Air kids in their substandard youths. So they would be both leery and sloppy if they had to go thrashing around looking for me in the forest primeval. It could be that Marchese's soldiers were a different story because they had lived in this place a long time, and that was something I would have to take into consideration. But when nighttime came around again, I would have to sneak down along the driveway and see what was going on at the gate. If that wouldn't work, I would have to go along the wall both ways to check if there was a break somewhere or another way of getting over or through. Or maybe I could write a message on a piece of paper or cloth, attach it to a rock, and heave it over the wall in hopes it would land on the road and a passing motorist or hiker would pick it up.

Christ, I couldn't believe this was happening to me.
But it was. In a lot of ways it was like when I was held
by the church people and then busted loose. But they
were people who at least thought they were doing
right. Pascaglia and his people were all wrong. And
goddamned good at it, too.

I ate some bread and cheese and a peach, saving the
water. Despite the plastic wrap, both the bread and the
cheese tasted stale. I didn't drink any water because I
didn't want to piss inside the hole if I could help it. It
would be bad enough for me to be in there with it, but
it would be even worse if somebody walking by smelled
it and followed their nose right to me. Why the Christ
couldn't Sofia have put a gun into the basket along with
the explosive? I'd have felt a hell of a lot better.

I felt my mouth twist as I rethought what I'd just
thought. She would have put a gun in the basket if she
could have, for Christ's sake. What the hell did I want
from the poor girl? It made me think of the old Danny
Thomas joke about the guy who gets the flat tire in the
middle of the night, and while he's walking to find a
house where he can get help, he starts thinking about
all the negative things the guy might say when he
comes to the door at that hour, and by the time he
reaches the place and the guy answers, he tells him to
stick the tire jack up his ass. Here I was telling Sofia to
stick the plastique, and it was only because of her that I
was sitting free rather than in the tin room with the
Crusher with his arm around my throat asking if I was
going to cooperate with Mr. Pascaglia.

At 10 A.M. a long black limo and a big station wagon
rolled up the driveway to the front door and several
guys got out of the two cars. Twelve altogether. They
stood around stretching their arms and talking to each
other, and then Pascaglia came out the front door with
the Crusher, and he hugged an old fat ugly guy and
shook hands with one of the other men and nodded and
smiled at the group in general.

They were of all shapes and sizes, and I would say

that most of them were in their late thirties or early
forties. The reserve troops had moved in. I wondered
how big Pascaglia's army might be. He couldn't call in
everybody because you needed people to carry on the
day-to-day operations, but there were now seventeen
genuine syndicate members gathered in my honor. Five
million bucks was nothing to sneeze at, and I could
imagine what their reaction had been when they found
out that they had been taken for twenty-five million.
How much the hell could they have stashed away in
those Swiss banks and how much did they gross in a
year? It could be that business beneath the counter
throughout the world was as big as or bigger than
business over the counter. But I guess I couldn't complain. Without crooks you wouldn't need cops. How big
a business was the one that fought crime? In the last
ten years the narcs alone had become a major corpora-
tion. How would all those guys feel if somebody suddenly did away with drugs? They'd have to go out and
get real jobs.

Pascaglia pointed to the back of the house, and the two
drivers slid behind their wheels and moved their vehicles to the garage area. Then everybody went into the
house. Marchese's grocery and liquor bills were going
to be something this month. I pulled the blanket around
me and stretched back against the dirt again. It was
going to be a long day.

At noon, four of them appeared from the back of the
house carrying a body. I could tell that the guy was
dead from the way they were hauling him and the way
he fell when they dumped him on the stones of the
driveway. They stood there chatting and two of them lit
up cigarettes, and one of them got very excited and
started waving his arms around, and then all of a sudden pulled back his leg and gave the body a tremendous kick in the stomach area. Two of the other guys
thought this was funny as hell and almost doubled up
with laughter, but the one who had delivered the kick
was still angry and shouted loud enough for me to hear

that the two who were laughing could go fuck themselves. The fourth one kept peering down the driveway as if he was expecting something, and two minutes later Angelo drove up from that direction in the jeep.

He stopped right beside them and stalled the motor dead, causing the vehicle to make a jump and almost hit the guy who had kicked the body. This made him so mad that I thought for a second he was either going to kick the jeep or to haul Angelo out of his seat and kick his ass to West Orange. But he finally calmed down a bit and started a conversation with him instead. In answer, Angelo pointed off to his left toward the swamp where Sofia had taken me the day before.

The kicker then gave some instructions to two of the other men, and they lifted the body and threw it in the back of the jeep. Although the face was battered almost to a point beyond recognition, in the moment they held the body up in the air, I recognized the Doc. My stomach churned and I pushed my face forward into the dirt at the base of the bushes concealing the hole. It was only for a moment, but by the time I had lifted my head again, the body was on the floor of the back of the jeep and two of the men had clambered into the seat with their feet resting on the flesh beneath them.

Angelo got out of the driver's seat and walked around the house to the garage area. He was back in a few minutes carrying two long-handled shovels, which he handed to one of the men in the back. The third man got into the front seat, and Angelo started up again and went lurching off in the direction toward which he had pointed for the head honcho. The guy stood there for a minute looking after them and then went back into the house through the front door.

I had never really gotten to know the Doc, and I had the feeling that there was a time in his life when he had done despicable things that were going to send him straight to hell now, if the information was correct in the Bible. But Sofia had said she loved him, and that was a big point in his favor. I also had the feeling that

the Doc had become a born-again human being in the
time he had spent with the Marcheses, and had truly
repented whatever he had done in the past and that all
he wanted for the rest of his life was to live and let live.

But I remembered what Pascaglia had said to him in
the dining room.

*Nobody ever gets fired and nobody ever becomes a
free agent.*

Well, they had fired him from being alive, and now
he was free of them. A tough way to do it, but his
problems were over. I still had a way to go. I ate a
nectarine and kept the pit in my mouth so I'd have
something to worry with my teeth. My legs became
cramped so I moved back in the hole against the wall
and stretched them out. For the next four hours I kept
dozing off and waking up, shifting position up and down,
from one side to the other, back and forth. It was hot
outside and I could see the heat waves shimmering off
the driveway, but it was pleasantly cool in the hole,
sometimes too cool and I would pull the blanket around
me for a while. Twice I ate pieces of cheese and bread,
not so much because I was hungry as for something to
do, and then I ate a nectarine because I found ants
crawling over it and I didn't want to share.

I must have dozed off again because I was suddenly
wakened by the noise of a lot of people chattering
away in the driveway, and when I moved to the front of
the hole, I saw about a dozen of the mobsters fanning
out into a semicircle, and as the cleared space opened,
there was Pascaglia with the little fat man who had
come in the limo, and the Crusher holding Sofia by her
right arm. He was as much holding her up as he was
holding her prisoner, and even from this distance I
could see that her face was swollen and bruised.

A feeling of sadness went over me like when you're
told that somebody you love has died. That has only
happened to me three times in my life. No, really
twice. I was eleven when my mother gave up her
ghost, and in her last two years she was practically a

basket case, someone who was there but not really
there. The doctor put her in the hospital the week
before she went and my father only took me twice to
see her, so when they told me she was dead, I became
angry rather than sad. I knew I'd been deprived of
something, but I didn't really know what it was at the
time. It was only years later that I began to remember
the period when she had been my real mother when I
was very small, the hugs and kisses and tickles and the
feedings in the high chair. The years that the vodka
bottle had been her baby had blocked all that out until
I became old enough to fight my way through it. But
there had been too many other things to crowd out the
sadness, so I couldn't count that.

When my father committed suicide, it was different
because nutty as he was and as exasperated as I would
become with the crazy things he would do and say, we
had developed a relationship, an understanding, after
my mother's death, and I knew that the loss was going
to affect my whole life. That's why I had moved all the
way to California; I didn't want to be reminded of
anything that was Boston.

And then Cathy. The sadness was still sitting there in
my belly, a constant ache, a perpetual reminder that
something vital was missing.

So when I saw Sofia there in the middle of all those
men, one lone lady and all those sons of bitches, the
sadness that went through me was so overwhelming
that it was like a fire in my heart. The situation was so
hopeless that I couldn't work up even a vestige of
anger, and once again I put my forehead down on the
cool earth just as I had when I had recognized Doc. He
was now buried somewhere in that swamp, and in my
gut I knew that this was where Sofia was now headed.

"Benny," Pascaglia shouted, and my head came up
with a jerk. Had he seen me right through the bushes
and in the hole? My muscles tensed, ready to jump out
and run. Run, run, run. Run where?

No, he hadn't seen me. He wasn't even looking in
my direction. He was yelling in all directions.

"Benny," he yelled again. "Benny, I know you're out there and can hear me. I've got your friend here, your Sofia. I want you to come in here, Benny. I want you to come back to the house so we can sit down and work out a deal. I'm raising my offer. Fifteen percent. Fifteen percent, Benny, and everybody walks away clean and healthy. That's my final offer. If you don't take it, if you don't come in, the deal's off. And if you don't come in, you get the girl out there. A piece at a time. A piece at a time, Benny. Her left tit first. Then her right. Then the fingers and the toes and the rest. One at a time."

He said something to one of the men in the circle and the guy came out and stood next to him. He said something else and the guy raised his hand, and I could see the sun reflecting off the big butcher knife he was holding. The cheese and the bread and the nectarine came partway up my throat, and I gagged loud enough for somebody standing close by to have heard me, but they were too far away. Too far and too close.

I looked at all the faces in the semicircle and they were all set in that hard look of men whose stomachs can take anything where cruelty is concerned. There would be no gagging in this bunch. They would stand there and watch Sofia carved up without a blink, and if Pascaglia so ordered, they would cut off their own chunks of her as indicated.

How the hell did he know whether I was really out there or not? He didn't. He couldn't. The important thing was, he didn't care. This was an idea he had come up with and he would carry it through. If I wasn't there or if I chose not to come in, he would shrug it off, cut her up, and then try something else. Sofia would be dead, multilated, would have suffered untold agony, but so what? So what?

It's the kind of thing you see on television thrillers all the time. The bad guy gets cornered and puts a gun or knife to the head or throat of the beautiful girl, and then the good guys put down their weapons and the

bad guy starts to back away, only something always
goes wrong for him and he ends up in the shit.

But the only thing I had to drop was me, and I knew
that if I gave myself up, they would probably still cut
Sofia to pieces and then add parts of me to the pile. The
best thing would be to let them do to her what they
were going to do anyway and continue trying to get
away, and if the miracle should happen, make sure that
these guys paid in spades for what they had done.

Even as I was thinking that, I was crawling out of the
hole into the bushes and around to the back of the tree.
I got up on my hands and knees, and moving as slowly
and quietly as I could, I worked my way to the far side
of the circle so I could come out at a spot far removed
from my hiding place.

In the couple of minutes it took to do this, the
Crusher had ripped down the front of Sofia's blouse and
the guy with the knife had cut the front of her bra in
half so that her breasts were almost fully exposed, the
big brown circles of her nipples standing out through
the ripped cloth. Even as I was stepping forward out
from behind the tree, I noticed that some of the men in
the circle around her had small smiles on their faces
and one was wetting his lips. I could feel the anger
fighting its way through my sadness.

It wasn't one of those last-second reprieves, because
Pascaglia hadn't even raised his hand for the guy to
begin the slicing when I was first noticed and somebody
shouted and three of the men started to run toward me.

"Don't touch him," yelled Pascaglia, and they stopped
dead, confused as to what they were supposed to do.

"Come in, Benny, come in," said Pascaglia in a conversational tone, and I turned to walk toward him. The
Crusher dropped his hand from Sofia's arm and she
clutched the material together in front of her to cover
her nakedness. As I drew closer, I could see that her
eyes were filled with tears and her swollen cheeks had
rounded out her face to the contour of a small pumpkin.
She was shaking with fear and pain, and I would have

given anything, all the money, anything, if I could have taken her in my arms and comforted her and assured her that she would be safe. But I couldn't. It was all I could do to put one foot in front of the other and keep moving forward.

"Good boy, Benny," said Pascaglia, "good boy. Now we can finish our business. Brachi"—and he turned to indicate that the little fat man was Brachi—"has come up with the answers to our problem."

Despite all those sons of bitches being there and looking on, I stepped up to Sofia and put both my hands softly on her cheeks, careful not to squeeze, and leaned forward to kiss her on her damp forehead. Pascaglia smiled at this like one of us was his child and we had just announced our troth.

"Take the girl to her room," he told one of the men, "and take Benny to the other place in the cellar," he told the Crusher. "Be careful with him," he admonished. "He's got a lot of papers to sign."

So five minutes later I was sitting on an old couch in another room in the cellar, this one with stone rather than tin walls, and furnished like a small sitting room with chairs and a table. Only this time I was not alone because they had a big guy sitting in with me, a personal guard whose breath was so bad that it almost cast a glow around his head.

I wondered if they'd let me take a shower and change my clothes. I also wondered how long they were going to let me live. Chances were about the same on either of them.

17

*T*he guard and I didn't exchange one word for the four hours we sat together in that room. I had nothing to say to him, and he obviously had nothing to say to me. Which was just as well, because I probably would have fainted if he'd pushed air from his mouth in my direction.

Meanwhile, Pascaglia and Brachi were probably working out the fine points and how they were going to remove the five million from my trust fund, and when they had dotted all the I's and crossed all the T's, they would be down with the papers for me to sign. By then they would also have thought of a way to remove me. They obviously still didn't know that the fund had grown to six million bucks or they would have mentioned it. Oh, how they would have mentioned it. Pascaglia had sweetened the ante to fifteen percent. They were going to let me keep seven hundred and fifty thousand dollars if I cooperated. They were also going to let the cow jump over the moon and convince Reagan to sign a disarmament pact with the Russians and convert Khomeini to Orthodox Judaism. The best that I could hope for was that I would be dead when they shoveled the dirt over my face.

A relief guard came on a little after seven P.M. who was even bigger than the guy who had been baby-sitting me for the afternoon. He was bigger but he didn't smell as bad, which was a case of thanking God for small favors. They didn't bother to exchange any words either. When the new guy came in, my companion shoved himself to his feet and walked out the door.

Whereupon the new guy sat down in the same chair the other guy had been warming. It was as good a time as any to break the ice.

"I have to go to the toilet," I told him.

I could see his mind actively working on the problem.

"Which one ya gotta do?" he asked.

I thought of giving him a typical Hawkeye response to a question like that, but he was big enough to mash me flat so I played it straight.

"Number two," I told him.

This required further thought. When he had resolved it in his mind, he stood up, reached under his shirt to pull out a .38 caliber and let it hang down by his right side.

"Let's go," he said, motioning with his chin for me to lead the way. I walked down the corridor to the toilet I had used before, pulled the light chain for illumination, turned, and closed the door with him standing on the outside. I waited a second but there was no protest, so I lowered my pants and did what I had to. When I was through and had flushed and all, I unrolled some sheets of toilet paper, folded them neatly, and stuck the wad in my pocket. Strictly a squirrel reflex. You never knew when someone might whisper in your ear a method of constructing a nuclear device from toilet paper. In case of that unlikely event or something similar, I was going to be ready.

When we returned to the room, we resumed our former positions and sat there quietly. My mind was blank even of old jokes and I had the feeling that his was blank most of the time.

The appearance of Brachi was almost welcome relief. He bustled through the door without knocking, confident that everything was as it should be and that asking entrance was beneath his status. In his right hand was a beat-up briefcase of some synthetic material, and in his left one of those sugared pieces of deep-fried dough that Italians like to eat for dessert. The sugar had drifted all over his wrinkled blue suit, but you could tell that sartorial splendor was not one of Brachi's priorities.

He dropped the case on the table, took a minute to finish his zeppole, and then fished a stack of papers into the open.

"This is a complicated business," he informed me, "especially because we have to work fast. What do you know about the trust-fund setup?"

"Nothing," I told him. "I let the bankers handle all the details."

He nodded as if this was exactly as he had expected. He probably spent most of his time with guys like the one who was guarding me, and the best they could manage was an understanding of criminal charges. Bosses like Pascaglia were undoubtedly somewhat smarter, but their success was due more to lack of moral integrity and conscience than sharpness in business dealings. They furnished the nerve and the muscle and depended on legal scum like Brachi to figure out the angles.

"I gave the guys who squeezed the banker a list of questions I wanted answered," said Brachi, "and they got him to do them into a tape recorder, but there are still some holes that have to be filled in."

I had a quick nightmare vision of poor Wenker with a pair of pliers on his fingers or the point of a knife sticking into his throat while he tried to speak into a tape recorder the answers to the questions that were being laboriously read to him by some thug. It was best that Mrs. Wenker believe her husband had died in a simple car crash rather than ever knowing what really happened. I hoped she had dismissed my implications as stabs in the dark to try to kill off my own ghosts. The remembrance of those tuna-fish sandwiches made me realize that I was hungry.

"I haven't had anything to eat," I told Brachi.

He looked at me impatiently for a moment, then reconsidered.

"Giuseppe," he began, turning to the giant sitting in the chair, "go tell . . ."

He stopped and thought about the order he had been about to give, and then decided that he didn't want to be alone in the room with me while Giuseppe went on the errand. Uttering a big sigh, he turned and walked out the door and didn't return until about five minutes later.

"They'll bring you something," he said, and started pawing through the papers on the table. "What we have to do," he continued, "is set up a transfer of the trust so that we can move the whole fucking thing to a bank we know, and then we can take it from there. It isn't going to be easy because it's all going to have to be done by letters and phone calls and people with your power of attorney. The quickest and best way would be if you could go there in person, but too many things could go wrong with that. You came in for Sofia this time, but that doesn't mean you wouldn't change your mind once you smelled the air outside again. If only you had a mother or a sister or something, but you don't have anybody except that cousin you mentioned in Dubuque and I doubt you give a real shit about her."

"Do you have a wife and kids?" I asked him.

He looked at me shrewdly. This was a smart man and he knew what was coming. He nodded anyway.

"What would you do if our positions were changed and I had your wife and kids?"

"The wife you could have." He laughed. "The kids we might talk about."

There was a slight knock on the door, and it was pushed open to reveal the tiny Marina carrying a tray with what looked like a ham sandwich on thick Italian bread, a dish piled high with the hot peppers, and a tall glass of a carbonated cola drink.

Brachi started to push his papers to the side so she could place the stuff on the table, but instead of coming to me, she walked over to the big guard sitting in the chair and held the tray up before him, almost as high as his chin. His face showed annoyance and he started to raise his hand to show her where the food and drink were supposed to go when she brought her right hand down from under the tray and shoved her whole body forward.

The guy let out a soft whoosh from his mouth and his face froze into an unbelieving stare, the eyes bulging out a bit from their sockets. I knew the old lady had done something drastic, but her body concealed his stomach and it was impossible to tell. Brachi was still concentrating on moving the papers and didn't notice anything for the moment.

But as the old woman stepped back, I could see the handle of a knife sticking out from the center of the big brute's belly, and the size of the handle was such that I figured he had at least twelve inches of steel inside him. He tried to get up but couldn't move, and his mouth worked in his beet-red face as he tried to talk or yell or maybe even just moan. But the lungs no longer had the power.

It was still enough of a sound to get Brachi's attention and he looked over to see what had caused it and opened his own mouth to yell, when I smashed the side of my hand down across his neck in the soft spot between the throat and the shoulder where all those nerves lie, and he fell to the floor like a pile of oily rags.

The guard managed to stagger to his feet and to grab the handle of the knife with both his hands, but then like a giant tree that poises for a long moment when the chain saw has bitten all the way through, he turned to the side and fell over with a thud, his right shoulder hitting first, his head bobbing in the air and then coming down with a thunk on the concrete floor. He was still alive, you could tell he was still alive, but he was also dead.

The old lady carefully placed the tray down on the spot Brachi had cleared for her on the table, reached under her apron and from who knows what secret area brought out my neatly wrapped gun and holster and harness and handed them to me.

"Where's Sofia?" I asked her as I buckled on the gun.

She responded in a torrent of babble, and it took me a few seconds to realize she was talking Italian.

"Capisce inglese?" I ventured.

She shook her head. That was all the Italian I could come up with, so that was it as far as communication was concerned. I could feel the change in me with the gun strapped on. I know all the reasons we should have gun control in this country, probably in the whole world, but you can never take away the fact that a gun is the great equalizer. Before the gun it was the big bastards of the world who ran the show. If you didn't do what they said, they would break your bones or choke the life out of you or take away all your possessions or make you a slave or whatever. But once the gun came along, the little guy had an equalizer. He could tell the behemoths to fuck off. With the gun, little guys like Napoleon could come into their own. Which is why, I suppose, we should have gun control after all.

Of course, the little old lady hadn't done too badly with the knife. Surprise can be more than half the battle. She was just standing there with no expression on her face, waiting to see what I wanted her to do. She wasn't even looking down at the guy gasping his life out at her feet. I had an idea that to her he was just one of the scum who had dishonored her Sofia, and she was ready to stick a knife into every one of the men who had been present at that little exhibition.

I took another minute to think things through a bit; then I reached down and lifted the gun from Giuseppe's waistband. His breathing had quieted down and I pulled him by the shoulder until I had him on his back. His right pocket yielded a box of bullets. Two guns and bullets. I couldn't take my eyes off the handle of the knife. You never knew when you might need a knife. I pushed all the air out of my lungs, grabbed the handle with both hands, and tried to ease it out, but it wouldn't move. Standing up, I spread my legs wide, reached down, and yanked with all my strength this time. At first it was like when NASA is sending up a rocket—

during the first few seconds of burn, nothing seems to be moving; but then I heard this sucking noise and the knife slid out. The guy didn't move or make a sound. I grabbed the ends of his shirt and wiped off the blade the best I could. There was a paper napkin on the tray on the table and I used that to finish the job. It looked like the same kind of knife that the guy was going to use on Sofia. Looking at the old lady, I wondered if it was the same knife.

She had her eyes nailed on me, and I put my right hand on her back and pushed her gently toward the door. "*Grazie. Grazie,*" I said, using up the rest of my Italian. She didn't say a word in return, but looked down for the first time at the guy lying on the floor, bent her head and made a spitting noise in his direction, and then went out the door, presumably to return to the kitchen as if nothing had happened.

I was going to have to go out the back door as I had done the day before, but all this would result in would be Pascaglia taking Sofia out in the driveway in the morning and again threatening to cut her tits off. I needed more leverage than my two guns.

Leverage! I looked down at the little fat man on the floor, picked up the glass of cola, and threw it in his face. He groaned. I reached down and pulled him into a sitting position, shaking him hard enough to catch his groggy attention. He moaned, a good loud moan. I took the knife and stuck it in his throat a little ways, deep enough to cut. He tried to pull away but I clamped my hand on the back of his skull and held him tight.

"Listen, you little fat shit," I said, "you and I are going out of here through the back door, and if while we're doing it, you make one sound, your throat is cut and you are dead. You see him down there; that's what you will be."

He took a peek at Giuseppe and a look of horror took possession of his face. He tried to lick his lips but his mouth was too dry.

"Listen," he croaked, "we can work something—"

"We can work nothing out," I told him. "You fucked with the wrong guy this time. We're going out of here my way, and if you so much as breathe more than I think you should, you're going to die hard. Hard!"

I shoved the knife in the left-hand side of my belt and Giuseppe's gun in the right side. I was more comfortable with my own gun in hand, knowing exactly how it shot and at what distance I could be accurate with it. Which was basically not very far. I hauled Brachi to his feet and shoved him toward the door. He was holding his left arm in such a way that I thought I might have broken something on him with the karate chop. Too bad. I took a quick look around the room before I followed him out, saw the sandwich on the plate, and grabbed it with my left hand. Despite what had happened or maybe because of what had happened, I was hungrier than ever. I even took a big bite as I followed Brachi down the dim corridor, and was chewing fiercely as we went up the cellar stairs to the outside.

I shoved the remainder of the sandwich inside my shirt and used my left hand to guide Brachi around behind the garage. There were all kinds of lights on in the house and I could hear music coming through an open window somewhere. I couldn't understand why these guys didn't have lookouts posted. I figured maybe they weren't used to being in the country like this and they probably didn't know how to handle it. It was one thing to skulk in doorways or follow a car down a highway or bar an entrance with four locks and a steel chain, but what the hell did you do with a tree? For whatever reason, I was grateful they all stayed in the house because we weren't really that quiet and it was almost impossible to see where we were going.

When I got Brachi behind the garage, I made him stop, took his handkerchief out of his pocket, and blindfolded him.

"What's that for?" he asked, and I whacked him on the head with the flat of my hand.

"No talking," I whispered, "or I cut your tongue out.

Not one more word. And just move slow where I push you."

I took him a little deeper into the woods, bore right and then left, turned him completely around, walked back into the woods, and then led him to the tree where the hole was. It took more time than I wanted and I kept looking back at the house to see when all hell might break loose, but I think I had him fairly well disoriented and nobody came running out.

When we reached the hole, I made him get down and slide in backward. I gave him a little shove when his feet touched and he fell back and banged his head against the dirt, making a small moan. I slid in beside him and pricked his throat with the tip of the knife again.

"You made a noise," I told him, "And it should have been your last one, but I'm going to give you one more chance. Now shut up."

I moved the basket with the blanket and what was left of the bread and cheese and fruit so that I would have room to sit down too. I felt little things crawling over the peach and nectarine that were left so I threw them out of the hole. Bugs bother me. Which reminded me that there could also be snakes, and snakes scare me shitless. I didn't know whether New Jersey had poisonous snakes. It so upset me that I almost asked Brachi if he knew, but concluded that he probably knew less about it than me. Maybe human snakes, but not the kind I was concerned about at the moment. I pulled the sandwich out of my shirt and ate it, then took a drink from the stale water in the bottle. Brachi was being careful not to even breathe too loud. He was probably thinking about Giuseppe lying on the floor with his guts oozing out.

"Take off your belt and your suspenders and your shoes," I told him quietly.

"What?"

I gave him a good jab with the knife in the throat,

enough to make him start moaning softly. I could tell he didn't want to utter a sound but he couldn't help it.

"Do it."

He removed the pieces and laid them down on the dirt as softly as possible. He was finally thinking quiet. I used the belt to bind his hands together at the wrists and the suspenders to tie his legs together, pulling the elastic as tight as I could so there would be no give to it. Then I used the shoelaces to cinch down the belt and the suspenders, and was pretty sure that this would hold a fat man in his condition.

They had Sofia and I had Brachi. The problem was how to work the trade. Once I had her out of there, the leverage wouldn't be so tough. They could take the Don and Elena out in the front yard and cut them up an inch at a time, and I wouldn't make a move. Marina they wouldn't even think to bother with, even though I would have some second thoughts about her. She'd gotten me out of there, but I was sure that it was because Sofia had told her to. What she had done was for Sofia, not for me. Not that I wasn't grateful, but basically she was not my table. But the point was moot, I hoped, because to Pascaglia she was just an old woman who brought food and cleared up. I shivered a little as I recalled the thrust she had made with the knife. Never again would I turn my back on the littlest of the little old ladies that cops have to deal with all the time.

It sounded like a pack of wild horses and I moved my head to the front of the hole to see four guys come tearing around the side of the house to the front, where they ran around in circles yelling to each other in the dim light cast by the fixtures on each side of the front door. They must have discovered Giuseppe and someone had sent them boiling up the cellar stairs into the backyard, and they had kept right on coming to the front. I wished I could be more objective about what was happening because it would have been funny if nobody's life was at stake, but all I could do was watch and shiver a little. I didn't know what Brachi was hear-

ing, so I took some of the toilet paper out of my pocket,
made little wads, and stuck them in his ears. Just
before I put the second one in I said, "One sound and
you're dead this time. Just one sound will do it." He
nodded his head slightly to show he understood, and I
realized I was finally getting through to him. How was I
going to trade this little tub for my Sofia?

I looked down at the toilet paper and then out at the
men, who had quieted down and were just walking
around now, not knowing what to do next and nobody
giving them orders.

A message. I would leave them a message about the
trade of Brachi for Sofia. I would leave the message
under the windshield wiper of the limo that was parked
in the driveway and they would find it in the morning.
But first I had to think through how it could be done
safely and what I wanted to say in the message. I
assumed they would all eventually go back inside, and
then it would be safe to sneak over to the car and
decorate it with the toilet paper. The medium is the
message, that guy had said. Which guy was that? I
knew he was a Canadian but I couldn't pull his name
out of the hat. In any case, toilet paper was the right
method of communication with the Pascaglias of the
world.

A pen. I needed a pen. Brachi had two in his shirt
pocket, a ball-point and a felt-tip. The ball-point ripped
the thin paper and the felt point made blobs, but the
blobs were distinguishable if I used short words. So
help me, I started off with "Dear Mr. Pascaglia" and it
wasn't until I looked at it that I realized how ridiculous
it was. One thing about toilet paper was that it ripped
off easily.

"Pascaglia," I finally decided on. "If you want . . ." I
stopped and thought about it. Might as well have it
right.

"How do you spell your name?" I asked Brachi. He
didn't answer and I felt the rage building up in me until

I realized he thought I was trying to trap him into talking, making noise.

"Just tell me softly," I advised him. "I won't use the knife."

"B-r-a-c-h-i," he whispered like it was going to be our big secret.

"Okay," I told him. "Now don't talk anymore."

". . . Brachi," I continued, "you'll have to give me Sofia. Let her come out the front door alone. Tell her I said to meet me at the picnic spot. Don't ask her any questions. Just tell her what I said. If she is hurt, if anybody is hurt, you get Brachi back one piece at a time. Let her out at seven P.M. just before dark. You get Brachi back once I am sure she is clear. You will then have one hour to get out before the police come. One hour. Do not fuck up or Brachi is a dead man and anybody else who gets in the way."

It was almost impossible to write in such a faint light coming from the driveway and a little from the moon, but I wrote carefully and big, using the wicker basket under the wad of paper, unfolding one sheet at a time. I would have liked to read it over, maybe make it clearer, or tougher, but it was too dark for that, and I was sure I had covered the essentials.

Three guys came out the front door and joined the four who were already there and who had relaxed enough by this time to be smoking cigarettes and chatting. I assumed they had figured that I was long gone, either with Brachi in tow or that they would find his body nearby in the morning. Either possibility didn't seem to bother them too much because every once in a while one or two of them would burst into laughter.

I suddenly felt very tired and sank back in the hole beside Brachi.

"You want a drink of water?" I asked him softly, and he nodded his head. I held the bottle to his lips and tipped it carefully so he could swallow without choking. He finished what was left and I almost asked him if he wanted some from the other bottle, but then I figured he'd had enough and to hell with it. This squat little man who looked like a squab the way I had trussed him would probably have watched his people pour gasoline down my throat and then lit a match for them, and I couldn't afford to let what he looked like now affect my judgment.

My father used to harangue me about that all the time when I was a kid. "The Jews are famous for looking at both sides of the question, all the questions," he would yell. "And while they're looking and asking should it be this or should it be that, the other people are shoving them into concentration camps or mass graves. The Israelis have learned. They shoot first and then ask if there are any questions. Do you have any questions about that?"

And he would look at me fiercely until I shook my head to show that I didn't have any questions. There was no question in my mind that there would be only one way to deal with Pascaglia or Brachi or any of their hero sandwiches. So I blanked from my mind any questions about whether I had tied Brachi up too tight or whether he had enough water to drink or whether he was going to live or die. Me or them. And I picked me.

I pulled my own handkerchief from my pocket, grabbed the corners and rolled them tight and then made a makeshift gag for Brachi's mouth. In case any of those punks should take a stroll near us, I didn't want a sudden yell to change the whole picture. Then I leaned my body against him so I would feel any movement, and fell asleep. I had only intended to rest my eyes and body a little, but they decided on their own to take it all the way.

Waking in the pitch black of a hole in the ground at the base of a tree while sitting next to a fat little crooked lawyer that you didn't remember was there in the first place can be quite disorienting. If I hadn't had all those years of training and discipline as a police officer, I am sure I would have yelled out loud. As it was, I gave a pretty good grunt, enough to cause Brachi's body to stiffen in terror.

I moved forward and looked out the front of the hole and could see that the driveway was deserted. A couple of lights were shining through windows from the front of the house, but there didn't seem to be any noticeable movement. It was impossible to read my watch in the dark, but it felt like it was late, real late. Cathy had bought me a very expensive watch with a luminous dial and had been quite hurt when I didn't wear it, but I explained to her that there were too many occasions when the last thing in the world a cop wanted was to glow in the dark. One time in bed she had used it to circle a very private area.

"Now," she had said, "I am going to prove to you that glowing in the dark can also be very rewarding to a policeman."

"Don't you move or breathe too loud," I whispered in Brachi's ear. "I'm going to be right outside where I can hear you."

I crawled forward to the point where I could read my watch from the lights in the driveway, and it was ten minutes past three. Everything felt damp and moldy and when I went to slip the toilet paper under one of the windshield wipers, I felt the heavy dew on the glass. The tissue paper would disintegrate before morning and they wouldn't even know what it had been or was meant to be.

I crouched down behind the car and tried to think it through. I could maybe leave it on the seat, but there would be the noise of the door opening and the dome light would also come on. Either of those things could alert somebody. But what the hell else was there to do? I had to chance it.

I picked up a stone from the side of the driveway and held it on top of the toilet paper in my left hand. I held my gun in my right hand. As quickly and quietly as I could, I scurried to the front porch and up the steps, laid down the paper with the rock on top of it far enough in so that the roof would protect it from the damp. I kept expecting a shout or people to come pouring out of the house or from around the back, but there was only the noise of the crickets and the peepers rubbing their legs together or whatever the hell it was they did. Moving backward like a crab, I retreated once again behind the big car, breathed deeply a few times, and then made my way back to the hole, which I dropped into like it was a luxurious suite in a fine hotel. There's no place like home. Brachi looked like he had been careful not to breathe too loudly, and I settled back against him once again.

I wondered if he had to go to the bathroom. I almost asked him if he had to do number one or number two. Then I thought of Wenker and all the guys before Wenker who had answers to the questions this man wanted asked.

Let him drown or choke in it. I settled back to wait for the dawn.

18

*I*t's amazing how necessary even the smallest habits can become when they are suddenly beyond your reach. I sat in that hole the next morning running my tongue over my slightly furry teeth and going against the stubble on my cheek with the backs of my fingers. My armpits felt like the flesh on either side was stuck together and the individual hairs on my head were like fine wires filled with little jolts of electricity.

I had no idea what course Pascaglia might decide to take. He had to be getting somewhat jumpy about Cibelli or any cop suddenly showing up, and his men would maybe feel a little nervous this far from their home turf and nothing but trees around them. I hadn't seen anybody take any suitcases from the cars, and although they weren't hiding in the dirty roots of a tree, they had to be getting a little gamy themselves. From what I had seen, that wouldn't bother these guys as much as it would a maiden schoolteacher, or even me for that matter, but being dirty and not having a change of clothes had to be detrimental to morale.

My mouth approximated a small grin as I thought of one Mafia general discussing troop morale with another. And what about Pascaglia? The loneliness of command. How much was my five million worth to him?

From where I was I couldn't really see the rock-topped paper I had left on the porch and I worried that the wind might have blown some of it away or an animal might have gotten to it or that somebody would come out and just dump it as trash. There was plenty of time to worry about it because nobody came out of the house until nearly a quarter to nine.

Just before that, Pascaglia's big station wagon careened from the garage area with Angelo at the wheel and another man beside him who looked too young to be one of Marchese's troopers. They wobbled down the driveway toward the gate.

The guy who came out on the front porch was also one of Pascaglia's men, and the way he stretched and shuffled about indicated that he was just there to sniff the breeze. He walked about four steps forward and then leaned slightly over before coming to the front of the porch and bending over where the message was placed. When he stood up again, he had the paper in his hand and seemed to be reading it. Then he turned and went quickly into the house, banging the door behind him.

I sat back and studied Brachi beside me, who had not stirred one millimeter and was breathing so carefully that I leaned over to hear if he was breathing at all. This was a man who wanted to live, and who had probably been thinking of nothing else since I had taken over control of his life. The only other thought that could possibly have been going through his mind was what he would do or have done to me if I ever again became under his power.

"The Jews always put themselves in the victims' place," my father used to say, "even if the victims were once the oppressors. So even when they win, they lose."

I wondered what I would have been like if my mother had been the major influence in my life, if she had been the one with the dominant personality and drive. And if she had lived longer than she did. The Irish genes were in me, lying dormant or doggo somewhere. Would they ever burst forth or even show themselves in some way? Someday I would go to Ireland to seek my roots. I didn't have to go to Israel, that was for sure. And Cathy. Cathy had been half Jewish and half Italian, much to my surprise. There had been a Slavic tilt and maybe tint to her face, but mostly her beauty had been neutral. Our kids would have been something with all those mixtures in them. We had never discussed having children and it had never even crossed my mind even when I thought she was as healthy as a Clydesdale. When you looked at Sofia, you thought of children, lots of bambinos and her bouncing them in her arms and on her knees. But with Cathy, you just thought of Cathy.

Three guys came out of the house, walked down the stairs, and looked off at the woods in various directions. One of them seemed to be looking straight at where I was, but you couldn't see the hole when you were standing right next to it, let alone that far away. Even though I knew this to be true, I still felt naked crouching there and drew back a little into the comforting darkness of the tiny haven.

Pascaglia came out the door, followed by two of his bodyguards, and conferred with the three who had been looking around. They were maybe discussing bringing out the full force and scouring the estate, and I comforted myself in being a needle in a haystack. The six of them pointed this way and that way in all directions, and I could tell from the way they were doing it that they had no idea in hell where I might be.

Pascaglia sent one of the men into the house again, and he returned five minutes later with the Don, who seemed in normal shape and spirit, and after listening to Pascaglia for a few minutes, he too pointed in various directions, which indicated that they were no better off than they had been before his sage advice. They all went back into the house.

Brachi made a small noise through his gag. I pricked his neck with the knife and then loosened the cloth a little so that he could talk. He whispered, which indicated he was still very aware that the knife that had pricked could also plunge. It's amazing how much more effective a knife is at close range than a gun. Somehow you feel that a person won't really shoot you, maybe because it would involve a loud explosion and a hole in

a body and blood and guts and bone and sinew and be
so definite. You can poke a gun into somebody without
really hurting him. But if you slip a knife in even for an
inch, it can cause terrible pain and damage. And there
is the silence. A knife is so silent. Silence is probably
the most fearful thing there is.

"I can't hold it no more," whispered Brachi. "I got to
go."

I knew what he meant so I unzipped him and slipped
his little thing into the neck of the empty water bottle
and held it carefully while the warmth filled the lower
third of the glass. Then I screwed the top back on the
bottle, tidied Brachi up, gave him a drink from the
second bottle, and replaced the gag. There, I thought,
my housekeeping should be done for the day.

Just before noon, the station wagon returned, seemingly piled high with bags and boxes of groceries and
cases of beer. The garrison was replenishing its sup-
plies, which indicated that Pascaglia was not that worried about the police descending on him. Either Cibelli
was still sick or dead or had forgotten about me. For
the time being, at least, I was on my own.

The rest of the day went interminably. I would doze
off against Brachi, or sit forward with my chin resting
on the dirt and my eyes focused on the house. Men
came out a couple of times, but mainly to wander
around a bit or just stretch in the air. These guys sure
did a lot of stretching. I had the feeling that this was
the extent of their exercise program. You couldn't tell
what was going on behind the house in the garage area,
and only once did I hear a vehicle start up and drive
away, but it didn't come out the front and I had no idea
where it might have gone.

Just as the twilight was descending, a little bit after
seven, the front door opened and the Crusher came out
with Sofia and two men behind him. She was wearing a
blouse and light slacks, and looked much better than
the day before, the puffiness having receded from her
face.

They stood there a couple of minutes with the men talking among themselves and Sofia off by herself a few feet from them, her face set in a mask. Then the Crusher turned toward her and said something harsh, the bark of his voice reaching all the way to where I was even though I couldn't make out what he was saying. She looked at him for a moment, then turned and went out at an unhurried pace into the trees along the track on which we had returned from our jaunt two days before. Was it two days or two hundred years? In ten seconds she had disappeared.

The men stayed out there a few more minutes, getting dimmer in the fading light, and then returned to the house. The Crusher dragged behind the others, reluctant to give up the turf, but finally even he had to admit to himself that the field right then was mine. Pascaglia wanted Brachi back, and was willing to pay the immediate price.

I waited a few minutes to see if there would be a sudden surprise rush of men from the house, but nothing happened. I untied Brachi's feet.

"Listen," I whispered in his ear, "we're going out of here, and if you don't screw up, I'm going to let you go so that you can return to the house."

I could tell he didn't trust what he was hearing. How many times had he reassured somebody that everything was going to be all right, knowing that in the near future the person was going to be dead? But the game was being played by my rules and he had no other choice. He mumbled something into the gag and I loosened it again.

"I can't move," he said. "I got no feeling in my legs."

I massaged him until the tingles returned and then had him move them up and down.

"Remember," I told him, retying the gag before helping him from the hole, "one little screw-up and you're gone."

I got him out of the hole, made him crawl a little ways deeper into the woods, and then had him stand up and walk. We cut across through the brush until we hit the track that Sofia had taken. It was almost completely dark by then, and I took the blindfold off his eyes but left the gag where it was. I turned him so that he was facing in the right direction to reach the house.

"You go that way," I told him. "Look to the tops of the trees and stay between them and you'll be in the middle of the road. Take your time and don't panic. I'm going to be close behind you most of the way so I don't want you to yell or make any sound until you reach the house. Then you can yell for them to come out and get you. If you do make a noise before that, I'll put a bullet in your back and that will be the end of it. Tell Pascaglia that Sofia and I are going for the police, and if he isn't out of here like I said, his balls are in the wringer. Tell him I kept my end of the bargain and he's got you back alive. Tell him I always keep my end of the bargain. And tell him that he's on my list. And you're on my list. So maybe you all better go back to the old country while there's still time."

Even as I was handing him this bullshit, my heart was contracting with fear. Pascaglia was not going to sit still until I was dead, and he had the money and the contacts to bring in killers from wherever. But that was something that would have to be handled in the future, maybe with my disappearing with my six million bucks to parts unknown for the rest of my life. At the moment I had to take care of right now.

I gave him a little shove to get him started and didn't wait to see that he kept going, but turned and started down the track slowly and carefully, my gun in my right hand.

After I had moved a little ways and when I was sure that Brachi couldn't hear me from wherever he had made it to, I started calling out softly, "Sofia. Sofia. Sofia."

I don't know how far I went or how long it took in the absolute blackness that I was stumbling through, but all of a sudden a body leapt out of nowhere and fastened itself to me in a grip of death. My hand had foolishly been on the trigger of the gun and the surprise almost made me pull, but the aroma of Sofia filled my nostrils and stopped the reflex action.

She was hugging me and kissing my face and crying all at the same time, and I spread my legs a little for balance and squeezed her back.

"Benny," she was burbling, her thick thighs plastered solidly against me. "Benny, Benny, Benny."

More for something to say than for any other reason, I asked the stupid question. "You okay?"

She didn't try to answer through her tears, just moved her head up and down against my neck.

"We're going to have to hide somewhere for the night," I told her, "somewhere safe. We can't do anything in the dark. Do you know a place you can take us where there will be no chance of them coming across us by accident? We can't go very far in this kind of dark, but we've got to be off all the tracks."

She pushed away from me but held on to my left hand with both of hers. The sky around us glowed from the stars shining down all those billions of miles away, and all the tensions seemed to melt away that had been squeezing my heart the past two days. The fear had been like a pool of water in which one is continually being dipped and then pulled out—wet, dry, wet, dry, wet, wet, wet—and it felt so good to be all dry again, even when I knew it could end at any moment. I've never really known how much guts I had or whether I really had any guts at all because both my body and my mind reacted at such a fever pitch whenever I was in a jam. And maybe it didn't make that much difference as long as nobody else knew what was going on inside me. But I always knew, that was for sure.

"I think I can find it," said Sofia, and I had to stop myself from clamping a hand over her mouth when she spoke out loud. I listened as hard as I could for a moment, but there was nothing. If he hadn't fallen down, Brachi was probably back at the house by now, but they wouldn't have come into the woods in the dark. They could have done it in the jeep with the headlights on, but we would have seen or heard them. Even so, I thought I had better caution Sofia about speaking in whispers.

She held on to my hand and led me slowly down the roadway. We stumbled a few times but managed surprisingly well considering the circumstances and terrain. Sofia obviously knew the whole estate like the back of her hand and maneuvered incredibly in the dark. About a quarter-mile down the road, she stopped and felt around to the left for a bit, grunted happily, and pulled me off through what seemed like solid woods but had to be a slight footpath. There was moonlight now and you could see where you were going except when we were in patches of trees that closed off the light.

Sofia stopped again and then led me off to the right. Stopped again and then to the left. We entered the tiniest of clearings, which we crossed, and then Sofia dropped to her knees and started banging against the small bank with her hand. I heard a clunk as she hit metal. She pulled backward and there was a groan of metal leaving metal.

"Do you have a match?" she asked.

"No," I told her, and wished to hell for the first time in my life that I was a smoker.

"Wait," she commanded, and I could hear her crawl into the side of the bank. Another secret hole? Another hiding place that she and Cathy had frequented as children? The estate had to be honeycombed with places used to hide whiskey during Prohibition, bodies when necessary, and whatever contraband was in vogue at the time. The Villa Marchese could just as easily have been called Pirate's Lair or Brigand's Booty or some other equally significant criminal nickname.

"Ah," I heard Sofia exclaim with satisfaction. "Benny, crawl in here."

I put out my hand and moved it around until it banged into a round metal door that was sticking out from the mound. Further exploration revealed the hole which the door had blocked. I crawled through, banging my knee on the metal threshold, and found myself on a concrete floor of some kind. Sofia reached around me in the darkness, crawled over the back of my legs, and pulled the metal door shut with a clang. Then I felt her lean back off my legs and settle on her bottom with a slight thump. There was a scratching sound and then a flare of light as she held up a wooden match.

"Look for a lantern," she said, and I saw one right near her just before the light went out.

"To your left," I said as she struck a second match, and she reached over, pulled up the glass, and touched the match to the wick. It caught in a second, she dropped the glass back, trimmed the wick carefully, and we had light.

We were in a small concrete blockhouse that had some wooden shelves built along the wall and another lantern on the floor, but nothing else. It was dry and comfortably warm inside and there seemed to be fresh air from some source because the light was flickering slightly in the kerosene lantern.

"Imagine," said Sofia, "after all these years the matches work and there's still kerosene in the lanterns."

"What was this used for?" I asked, starting to open the cabinet closest to me.

"I have no idea," she replied. "Tullio showed it to Cathy, and she showed it to me after he was gone."

I had an instant picture in my mind of what they had used it for, but the cabinet door swung out and I purposely concentrated on what was in there. There was a big leather gun case of some kind with straps closing it down. I unbuckled the straps and folded back the cover. Inside was a tommy gun, a Thompson submachine gun just like the ones you would see in the gangster movies of the 1930's, blazing out of the open touring cars as the vehicles careened around corners. For a moment I felt like the guy who uncovered King Tut's tomb, and I pulled the gun out of the case with a feeling close to reverence. It was heavy as hell, and the oil that had been spread all over it glinted in the lantern light. The boxes contained six more magazines, all fully loaded with .45-caliber bullets and all equally well oiled. This place had probably been built to store Umbriago's arsenal, and this was one of the remaining items.

The next cabinet yielded another gun case, this one with a sixteen-gauge shotgun and boxes of shells, most of which looked like they might have deteriorated into uselessness. I wondered if the tommy gun was in working order. Shades of Elliott Ness.

"Benny," said Sofia, and I turned to look where she was still sitting in her original position. There were huge circles under her eyes and such a look of exhaustion on her face that I caught my breath.

"Are you all right, Benny?" she asked.

I nodded.

"Are you all right, Sofia?" I asked in turn.

She nodded gravely.

"But I'm very tired," she said. "Very, very tired."

"Is the family all right?" I asked.

"At least for now," she said.

"Should we stay here for tonight?" I wanted to know.

"It's as good a place as any. Nobody else knows about this, not even my father."

"Okay."

"Benny, I want to sleep now. Will you hold me for a while until I am asleep? I won't sleep too long, but I have to sleep."

I looked at my watch, which showed 8:35 P.M. I don't know whether it was due to my dozing off for most of the day or the adrenaline that had been pumping while we had stumbled through the woods, but I couldn't have closed my eyes or my mind if my life depended on it.

I held out my arms and she moved over until she was leaning into me with her back against my chest and her head just under my chin. She smelled a little bit sweaty rather than her usual fresh, sweet aroma, but I inhaled deeply to get as much of her odor as possible inside me. Within a minute her breathing went into the metronome cadence that showed she was in deep sleep. I had the feeling that she hadn't had a moment's rest since this whole thing had begun. One of my guns was digging into my side with painful insistence, but nothing would have made me move an inch no matter what. Not an inch. We had a hell of a long way to go, the two of us, a hell of a long way. But right then I felt content. Incredibly content.

19

*S*ofia snored—little growling sounds that could have been two puppies going at each other in the midst of a thick blanket. I'm a light sleeper and I thought how impossible it would be to lie in bed beside that noise each night. Right then I wouldn't have begrudged her the trumpeting of elephants, but as the minutes passed, her noises increased in intensity if not in volume.

We all have limits in what we will sustain or undergo even for our most loved ones. I hadn't loved that many people in my life, and even then there had been those selfish times when I wished I was all alone, that I had only myself to think of and take care of and do for. When the cirrhosis had my mother down to practically nothing, I didn't want to visit her in the hospital even when my father said she was asking for me and made me go with him. Later on, I explained this away, and it was amazing how often it passed through my mind and had to be explained away over and over again, by telling myself that I was a kid at the time, that I didn't know any better when I shrank away whenever she reached out to me.

And even with Cathy, whom I loved more than mother or father, there had been times during the last few weeks of her life when I sat looking at her and wishing that she would give it up, let go, die. I told myself that it was to spare her further pain and misery the two times I let it come to the front of my mind, but I knew that it was because I had undergone enough, that I wanted no more, that it was my peace of mind I was thinking of.

When Sofia leaned against me to sleep, I was convinced that I would sit there forever if need be so as not to disturb her, that the Spartan kid with the fox gnawing at him was a whiner compared to my own determination and fortitude. But I doubt it took more than fifteen minutes for me to wake her slightly while I moved the offending gun out of my rib, and then I kept flexing my arms to keep them from falling asleep and shifting my legs and rolling my buttocks as the discomfort grew proportionately to the time that had elapsed.

It's amazing that she managed to sleep as long as she did, some ninety-five minutes, with the way I was rolling around. She had to have been exhausted to the final inch of her body.

When she did awake, I had both my arms clasped around her large breasts, for whose comfort I am not sure. The first indication she gave was by placing both her hands over mine and squeezing in so that I felt her flesh bulge all around the backs of my fingers.

"What time is it?" she asked.

I slowly unfolded my arms and looked at my watch.

"It's ten minutes past ten."

"Morning?"

"No, it's still night. You only slept an hour and a half. Do you feel all right?"

She nodded her head vigorously, leaned forward, and slid around so she could look right at me. Then she took my right hand in both of hers and squeezed hard, so hard that her eyes filled with tears.

"They killed Doc," she said. "They took him away to the cellar and then he was dead. They knew that he was the only one who would have the explosive."

"Doc sent me the plastique?" I asked in wonder.

"He gave it to me for you," she said. "He's the one thought of the bowl of fruit, and he gave me the explosive and told me what to write in the note. I never saw him after they took him to the cellar, but my father told me they killed him."

She was sobbing now, her body shaking with each

exhalation, the tears coursing down the dark brown skin and fading into the thin sheen of perspiration that glistened in the hollow of her neck.

"He loved you," I said. Even as the words were coming out of my mouth, I moved my tongue up to stop them but it was too late. What the hell was I trying to do? Pay her back a little for what she had done for me? Try to make her grief a little less, her happiness a little more, her present situation somewhat bearable? Whatever it was, I had said it, and now I would have to carry through or destroy everything.

The shock had stopped her crying, even her tears. She couldn't speak. I had to fill the void.

"He told me that afternoon before Pascaglia came," I said. "He told me that he never wanted to leave here, that this place and you were all he wanted out of life now, that everything else was behind him."

"But Elena . . ."

"He said Elena was beautiful and he admired her for being exactly that, but she was your father's wife and he respected that, and this was when he told me how he felt about you."

"But why didn't he ever say anything, why didn't he . . . ?"

"He was almost at that point, I think. This could have been the very week he would have been ready to say something. Doc obviously had a lot to work out in his mind, but I think this might have been the week when he would have said something. I had the feeling he would have said something just before I was going to leave, because I think he liked me, too."

"He did, he did!" she exclaimed. "He said we must save you because you were a good man and you still had the capacity to do good for others. He told you he loved me?"

I nodded vigorously at her, and she almost smiled at the thought of what nearly was hers. Gods of liars, protect me, I told myself, because she is going to want to hear the whole thing over again and I've got to keep the story as straight as though she were four years old and this was her nightly bedtime tale.

"What has happened at the house?" I asked her, as much to change the subject as find out what was going down. "Is your family all right?"

"Papa and Elena and Mama Maria are staying in their bedrooms," she said. "Uncle Vinnie has made me sick the way he has kissed Pascaglia's ass, and when I told him so, he said he was only doing it to protect the family, but he has made me sick. Tomaselli grabbed at one of the men who tried to put a hand on Elena as she was walking past, and the man threw him against the wall and broke something in him. He is in bed and needs a doctor, but Pascaglia wouldn't let me call. Marina is working herself to death waiting on everybody. He wants nobody from the outside near here, and has men down at the gate and along the wall all the time."

"Can we walk to another house and call the police from there?" I asked.

"It would take us hours, and Pascaglia keeps saying that if anybody comes near the place, anybody at all, he is going to kill Papa and Elena and Mama Maria and me. He said it right in front of Vincent, and Vincent didn't say a word. Marina has more *coglioni* than he has."

"Thank you for sending her to save my life."

"Who?"

"Marina."

"I brought the bowl of fruit. Marina didn't know the explosive was in there."

"No, the second time. When she came with the knife and gave me the gun."

"I know nothing about that. I didn't send her."

"You didn't send her to help me get out?"

"I didn't know how you got out. They have made me stay up in my father's bedroom with them."

"Marina helped me on her own?"

"No, Marina wouldn't do that. Somebody would have to tell her."

"But who would that be if it wasn't you?"

She thought for a moment, her brow furrowed.

"It had to be Papa. He is the only one who could give her such an order."

It was my turn to furrow my brow. Why would Marchese do a thing like that? He was the one who had fingered me to Pascaglia! Was he thinking that far ahead at the time? Was he trying to assuage Pascaglia's suspicions in advance? Sicilian shrewd. Was he playing both sides against the middle, hoping to have points which-ever side came out on top? Whatever it was, at least I was here in a gangster's bunker rather than down in that cellar room signing my fortune and life away. Jesus Christ! Was I now responsible for Marchese and his clan as well as for Sofia? The son of a bitch wasn't playing fair.

"Pascaglia is very angry," said Sofia. "He and my father have been having big arguments, and when you took Brachi, he seemed to go crazy. He slapped one of his own men in the face just because he was standing there. He keeps calling New York and Boston, and he fell down on his knees one time and pledged to God that he would cut up Bandini and eat the pieces an ounce at a time. Papa said he thinks the Boston people have told Pascaglia they are holding him responsible for the money that was taken from them, the whole fifteen million dollars."

"He can't hang around here forever," I told her. "There are too many things that can go wrong. Cibelli could show up here at any time, or if there is any shooting, someone will complain to the cops."

"Cibelli hasn't been out here in years," she said wearily. "The people over on that side of us have a rifle range, and the people on the other side have a skeet range. Sometimes when the wind is right, you can hear them shooting, and it sounds like a world war. I think you could have a world war here without anybody hearing it, or if they did, thinking it was anything but target practice."

I stared into the flame of the lantern, watching the thin wisp of smoke drift out of the glass chimney. This was like being marooned on a strange planet without being able to tell Scotty to beam you up. What could this girl and I do against all those mobsters at the house? The only sane solution would be to hike out as soon as daylight came and get the police. But Pascaglia had said he would kill Sofia's family, and he was probably in enough of a rage to carry that out even though it could mean his own doom. He was caught between the Boston people and his own greed. My five million dollars was looming bigger and bigger to his eyes. Suppose I offered to turn it over to him if he would pack up and go away? Would that be sufficient? Would he keep his word and go away, or would he kill everybody first? I knew in both my heart and my mind that once I signed those papers I was a dead man. And there was another thing: I didn't want to give up the five million. I was finally hooked on the idea of having five million— no, six million—dollars. My history teacher in high school had told us a story about Abraham Lincoln, which he said was probably apocryphal. I remember the story because none of us knew what "apocryphal" meant and after we found out how to spell it and looked it up, I used it on every occasion I could from then on. Once when I was walking a beat, I used it at the morning roll call, and the sergeant told me to watch my mouth because there were female officers present. I wondered if he was putting me on, but I don't think so. Anyway, these arms manufacturers were trying to sell the government bad rifles and Lincoln blew the whistle on them. A delegation visited him and offered him five thousand dollars if he would okay the deal. He kept saying no as they kept raising the offer a thousand bucks at a crack. They finally reached ten thousand dollars, which the teacher noted was quite a sum in those days.

"Stop right there, gentlemen," Lincoln said. "You're getting near my price."

My price was obviously five million dollars. I wondered how low it would have to get before I would voluntarily give it up to save somebody's ass or my own soul. I wasn't sure I wanted to know.

"Is there any chance of them coming out of the house and trying to track us down?" I asked Sofia.

She shrugged.

"Then maybe we'll have to go there in the morning and see if we can blast them out of here," I said.

"I don't want anything to happen to my family."

"I don't think he'll do anything if there are no cops involved," I told her. "If it's just you and me, he won't be too worried. But if we can keep picking off his men or kill him, then the rest of them may get the hell out."

"I can shoot the shotgun," said Sofia. "I've done it many times at the Richardsons' skeet range."

"I don't know if any of these shells are still good," I told her. "We'll have to go through them and pick out the ones that look like they might work."

"We're going to do this in the morning?" she asked.

"No, I think it might be best to wait a day, make them wonder what we're up to, get them a little nervous. We can drink water out of one of the brooks, but we may go a little hungry."

"Oh no," said Sofia. "We can go to Doc's garden in the morning. He's got all kinds of vegetables and we even had some melons out of there last week. Doc was so proud of his garden."

Even though she wasn't making any noise, the tears were pouring out of her eyes and running down her face. No matter what the Doc had done in his life, this lady had already beatified him into sainthood and only God knew how many candles were going to be lighted in his honor if I kept her alive through all this. If I kept myself alive. All of a sudden I felt terribly sad and lonely because there was no one in the world who would shed tears over my death. There were people I worked with who would be upset for a short period, although there were also a hell of a lot of others who wouldn't even bother to shrug. Sofia might shed a few tears over me, but nothing like she was pouring out for Doc. I didn't know whether to try to take her in my arms again or just leave her alone until she cried herself out. I left her alone. And even then I was wondering whether it was because I thought it was best for her or I didn't want to be caught in a situation where my arms would go to sleep again. You've got to be more Irish, I told myself. There's too much Jewish going on in your mind.

So while Sofia was going through her *shiva*, I busied myself with the tommy gun, checking out the parts and sliding the mechanisms, removing the magazine and replacing it again, and trying to decide if it could be depended upon to work if and when it was needed. I supposed I could try a short burst the next day in an area far removed from the house, but I worried that some of Pascaglia's men could be out looking and jump us or kill us.

I also sorted through the shotgun shells, some of which looked in pretty good shape. I thought it might be okay to try one blast, but then again, even if one particular shell worked, the next one might not. Heads we lose, tails we lose.

The air started getting a little close in the bunker, and I worried about the lantern using up the oxygen.

"I think we should put out the light and try to get some sleep," I told Sofia.

There was no life in her eyes as she looked over at me.

"Use this gun case as a pillow," I told her, "and try to get some more rest. The next couple of days might be pretty rugged. But don't worry. We'll get your family out and everything will be okay."

I arranged the leather gun case as best I could and Sofia lay down without saying anything. I fixed the shotgun case for my own headrest, blew out the lantern, and lay down in the dark. I thought of moving over and holding Sofia for a while to comfort her, but then I wondered if I was the one who needed comforting.

As I lay there, I could feel my heart beating faster than it should have been and there was a tightness in my chest and through my shoulders that made me feel scared. I thought about it for a second and concluded that I didn't feel scared—I *was* scared. What the hell were this woman and I going to do against those fucking thugs the next day? Here we were just outside of West Orange, New Jersey, in the United States of America, and we might as well have been in El Salvador or Nicaragua or Afghanistan as far as law and order or even civilization were concerned.

This is a crazy world, I told myself, and with that brilliant observation I felt the tenseness slide out of my body and sleep move in to replace it. The rest was darkness.

20

You know how it is when you have to get up real early in the morning to do something special, like maybe catch a plane or keep an important appointment. You're always worried that the clock radio won't work, so you dig out from the back of a drawer an old alarm whose ticking is the equivalent of drops of water falling on your head and you set your digital watch to make those little ping sounds at the time you want to get up and then you lie awake all night in fear that none of them will work. The neon brightness of the digital numbers on the radio burns through your eyelids, and the ticking of the alarm clock across the room is like that of a bomb getting ready to blow you away, and you keep picking up the watch from the bed table and pressing the tiny button on the side, but the light it generates isn't enough for you to make out whether or not it reads the same as the radio clock.

Finally, maybe fifteen minutes before you're supposed to wake up, you fall into an exhausted sleep, and when all your alarm systems sound off within a minute of each other, your body jumps away from your heart and leaves it unprotected and alone on the bed, banging its way to terminal fibrillation.

I had convinced myself in my mind that the only thing we were going to do the next day was stay away from the house and any of Pascaglia's men who might be out looking for us. I didn't know how we were going to handle the problem of Pascaglia when the time came, so I put my mind, and with it all my fears, on hold. Consequently, in the darkness and quiet of the concrete shelter, I let myself go and slept, it turned out, something near ten hours.

When you wake up in complete darkness like that, it takes a while for you to catch up with not only where you are but also a little bit of who you might be. I lay there with my eyes open, and some seconds later I picked up the sound of Sofia's breathing. It wasn't the smooth in-and-out whooshing of sleep so I called out softly, just a touch above a whisper, "Sofia?"

"Yes?"

"Are you awake?"

There are so many people in the world who would have given me a middle-finger answer to that question. "No, dummy, I'm in a catatonic fit," or something equally as clever.

But Sofia being Sofia, she said, "Yes."

I moved my hand around on the floor until I found the box of wooden matches, and struck a light. My watch showed ten minutes past ten.

"Hey!" I exclaimed. "I must have been really pooped to sleep this long."

"You snored the whole night," said Sofia. "Once you got so loud that I thought they would hear you through the walls."

"I never snore," I said. "Nobody's ever told me that I snore."

She barked what could have been a sound of derision or laughter; you couldn't tell in the dark without seeing the face that uttered it.

"Should we light the lantern?" she asked.

"No. Why don't we just go outside and have something to drink and then go to Doc's . . . and then go to the vegetable garden and get something to eat."

I moved up to the wall and felt around for the latch to the door, pulled it back slowly, and then eased the round ball of metal out about half an inch. There was just the barest hint of noise, and a slash of light entered the room through the thin opening. I didn't want to make any sound getting the door open, and it was also going to take a little while for our eyes to become adjusted to the bright sunlight of the outdoors. Slowly I pushed the door all the way and then stuck my head out carefully to see if any inhumans might be there looking to do us damage. There was nothing extraordinary to see or hear, and I slithered through the opening, my gun at the ready.

"Bring the shotgun with you," I instructed Sofia, and she came out bearing arms.

"It's loaded," I told her as she moved her legs over the threshold. "Keep your finger off the trigger."

I closed the door behind her and we sat in the warming sun, blinking away at each other and smelling the freshness of the air after the night of staleness.

"First we have to get some water in our bodies," I told her.

"First I have to do just the opposite," she said, laying the shotgun on the ground and moving off toward the bushes on the right.

"Sofia," I called softly to her. She stopped and looked back, impatience darkening her face.

"Here," I said, digging out of my pocket what was left of the wad of toilet paper. "All modern conveniences." She shrugged, came back and took it, and then disappeared.

When she returned, she stopped at the edge of the little clearing and motioned for me to come toward her. She led me into the woods a ways, turned right and then left up a small hill, and there just over the crest was a small brook splashing down toward the swamp area. I had no idea where we were on the estate or even on which side of the swamp we had driven around a few days before, but my thirst dropped me to my knees and my face straight into the water. It was ice cold and I gulped great amounts down my throat, nearly choking at one point when both mouth and nose were involved. Then I splashed large handfuls over my face and head, and moved back up on my haunches so the sun could dry off what was left.

Sofia was still drinking beside me and as I leaned back, the mound of her huge rear was looming alongside, and I couldn't help but give it a love tap with the flat of my hand. The face came out of the water like a trout rising to a fly, and the look was so baleful that I could feel my eyes widen in surprise.

"You keep your hands to yourself," she said sternly. I wanted to think she was joking but she was obviously not.

"I'm sorry," I mumbled, but she pushed herself up and walked away a couple of steps, not looking at me. I tried to convince myself that the pat had been the same as banging someone on the shoulder, but an ass is an ass, and a woman's ass especially is not the equivalent of a shoulder. Here the man she had loved was barely beginning to molder in whatever section of this swamp they had buried him, and I was making a move on her heinie. Nice guy, Freedman. A little insensitive to other people's feelings maybe, somewhat crude and impulsive perhaps, a bit of an ass-grabber, but basically a nice guy. How long has his own wife been dead? A little over two months, you say? But a nice guy? Yeah. I'd say he was a nice guy. At least, I think he means well.

I don't know how long she would have stood there gazing off into nothing, but I needed to break the ice barrier for myself if not for her.

"Hey," I said, "how about that food we were going for?"

She turned and faced me, and I was relieved to see that her eyes were dry and her mouth wasn't in a tight line. She moved off without saying anything, and I followed where she led, up small hills, through ravines, on old paths that had grown almost completely over, until finally we came to a track that had obviously been used quite a bit, presumably by the jeep because of the roughness.

We listened carefully and then like good children looked both ways before stepping out on the makeshift

road. I was carrying the shotgun as well as the two
pistols and the knife, and the sweat was beginning to
dampen my armpits.

The road ended suddenly at the gate of a tightly
fenced enclosure, and through the strands of wire I
could see one of the most beautiful vegetable gardens I
had ever encountered, something like a color picture in
a slick magazine.

Sofia unlatched the gate, and as we entered, I became somewhat uneasy.

"I don't think we should stay in here too long," I told
her. "We're caged if someone comes down that road or
out through the trees. Let's take what we need and get
out."

"We haven't got anything to carry the stuff," she
said.

I thought for a second, placed the shotgun on the
ground, and unbuttoned my shirt.

"We can use this for a bag," I said, knotting the
sleeves and holding the edges. Sofia looked at what I
had done and quickly unbuttoned her own shirt and
turned it into a cloth sack. We picked tomatoes, peppers, and cucumbers and pulled carrots, and I took out
the knife and cut off a cauliflower and a small cabbage.
The radishes were all wormy and we gathered only a
few green beans, which had begun to shrivel on the
vine.

Sofia was tapping the ends of some small cantaloupes
and finally tore the stem off three of them and slipped
them into the bottom of her shirt. I stood there eating
leaves of gritty lettuce while she made her choices. We
must have been a sight, and I would have liked a
picture to look at years later if we lived through the
whole mess. There I was with one gun in the shoulder
holster, another stuck in one side of my pants and the
knife in the other, the shotgun balanced in my left hand
and the sack of vegetables in the right.

Sofia looked like a peasant woman from another planet
with the bra concealing only half of her huge breasts

and the heavily loaded shirt swung over her shoulder. She had tried to carry it in her hands, but the cantaloupes must have weighed a lot, and she couldn't manage it. The problem was that much of the stuff was quite fragile and squashy, and she had to be careful not to jounce it into V-8 juice.

"Are we going back to the bunker?" I asked as she cut off from the road into the woods at a different spot from the one by which we had entered.

"No," she said, puffing a bit in the heat and humidity. "There's a place Catherine and I used to go to for sunbathing. Nobody would ever find it, and we'll be safe there. Maybe tonight we'll go back to the other place."

It was a long journey, and by the time we broke through a dense thicket on the side of a hill and reached a round grassy spot that faced west, I was covered with sweat and what felt like insect bites. I itched all over but I had nothing free to use for scratching. When we reached the grassy spot and Sofia carefully laid down her burden, I fell to my knees so it would be easier to unload all the stuff I was carrying.

"I'm boiling," I told her. "I'm on fire."

"There's a little water hole right through there," she said, pointing between two spruce trees, "and the sun warms the water this time of year."

I walked through where she had pointed and there was another grassy little spot with a pool the size of maybe ten bathtubs. It looked like it might have been dug out by hand at one time, but you could see the silt bottom about four feet down. I put my hand in the water and was amazed at how warm it was. I picked up a double handful and dipped my face into it. There were red welts on my arms and chest where whatever the devil they were had taken small bites. My shirt was already off. To hell with it. I quickly pulled off my shoes and socks, pants and undershorts, and slipped into the water.

I have had some physical pleasures in my life, but I

doubt there was ever anything to match those few moments when the warm-cool water stopped the itch and cleansed my pores of all that greasy sweat. With my eyes closed, I scrubbed with both hands under my armpits and then between my legs. My movements were stirring up muck from the bottom, but even that felt soft and silky on the soles of my feet.

"Catherine and I used to come here all the time," Sofia's voice said softly in my ear.

I opened my eyes and she was right in front of me in the pool, her large breasts floating on both sides of my chin, the big round brown eyes with the incredibly thick eyebrows focused on mine. Behind her I could see her clothes stacked neatly beside the ones I had torn off and thrown down. Over the trees the sky was that incredible blue of a late-August day with a few slight clouds on the horizon and the sunlight making the air shimmer in tune with the noises of the insects. We could have been Adam and Eve at the dawn of history, and it wouldn't have shaken me a bit if a loud voice had come down from the sky and ordered us to go forth and multiply, but easy on the apples.

I placed my hands on both sides of her waist to steady myself and felt the warm soft skin in contrast with the cool water. A small distance through those woods a gang of men waited to do us harm, perhaps take our lives, but here all was tranquil, easy, inevitable.

I pulled ever so slightly with my hands and Sofia moved into me, her breasts melding into my chest, my erection sliding between her legs, our lips coming together so tightly that I felt my teeth scrape against hers and the tip of my tongue exploring all the secrets of her mouth.

I knew it was too late to stop what we had started so I released her body and turned to lead her to the shore, our feet making sucking sounds as we pushed our way to the bank. At first I thought the noises were those that we were making, but as they became louder and more staccato, I realized that it was a motor vehicle I was hearing and it seemed to be coming straight up the hill toward us.

We were still in the water up to our knees so I turned and pushed hard against Sofia's chest, moving her backward as I surged forward until we were once more in the middle of the little pond. And just as the front of the jeep broke through the brush, I pushed down so that she went under the water with me on top of her. We sank to the bottom and I went down on my knees, my arms across Sofia's chest to anchor her beside me. I didn't know whether she'd had time to take a breath as we were going under, but she wasn't struggling or pushing, just lying there quietly. You couldn't see anything through the silt, and it was as if we were suspended in wet, timeless dark, almost like another world. I don't know how long I stayed beyond what I thought possible, but finally I had to go up and I slowly moved to the surface, lifting Sofia's body with me. It was impossible to keep from gasping as we broke the surface, loud sucking noises as we pulled air into our tortured lungs. I expected to see men standing on the bank, men with guns in their hands, evil men with grins on their faces to see us naked and helpless, men who would pour bullets into our bodies and laugh as the water turned color.

The only thing there was the ever-fainter sound of the jeep on the right side of the hillock as it moved down and away. We could not tell how close it had come to the water hole, and I glanced in panic where our clothes had lain. They were in the open, but on the side where the jeep had come from, a bush intervened, a gift from Mother Nature to us. The sound died.

Neither of us bent to retrieve our clothes, but picked our way carefully through the brush, feeling but ignoring the rough stubble pushing into the bottom of our feet.

However, by the time we reached the center of the grass where the shirts with the vegetables and all our guns had been placed, awkwardness had replaced the fear and relief.

There we were in the middle of an open field, small though it was, stark naked in the daylight, the sun beating down on our wet bodies, and the possibility of armed men suddenly reappearing. I looked down at the guns and thought how stupid it had been to go to the water hole without them, how helpless we had been for those minutes. Then I looked back at Sofia, who was standing with her eyes closed, probably because she was embarrassed to open them. I sank to the grass, pulled her down alongside me, and placed my arms around her thick body as best I could.

"I was awake all last night thinking of your hands on me," she said, her eyes still closed with traces of wetness below them that I knew were not pond water. "Here Doc was dead and I was thinking of you putting your hands on me. I wanted your hands on me. I've never made it with a man, never, and all this year I have kept thinking and hoping that someday Doc would do with me what Tullio . . ."

She opened her eyes in horror and stared at me, then closed them again.

"It's all right," I told her. "It's a long time ago. It's over."

"All the things that Catherine ever told me," she said in a monotone, "all those things I have dreamed about for myself. And now I want you to do it to me. I decided that in the water when I thought it was the end for us. I know there will never be anybody else. In my heart, I know it. But you were Catherine's husband, and that makes you the same as my husband. And I want you to do it."

I didn't quite follow her reasoning, but my erection had returned, and I knew I was going to do it no matter what goddamned reasons were put forth by either her or me. I believed her when she said she had never done it, partly because I felt that Sofia was not a liar, and partly because there were probably few opportuni-

ties for a girl with her kind of looks. I knew that much
of the scum who had spent time at the Villa Marchese
would have fucked a barber chair or anything else with
hair around it if they had the opportunity, but I figured
that most of them would have been afraid to fool around
with the boss's daughter, especially when word went
out on what had happened to Tullio after Sofia had
whispered in her Papa's ear.

But I wasn't afraid of her father and I was very, very
fond of Sofia, so I wanted her first time to be good, to
be beautiful, to be right. It was as if I were two people,
one doing the work and one standing off and advising,
cautioning, coaching. I carefully kissed her lips and her
face and her eyes and tender parts of her body as she
tensely lay there flat on her back, the sun burning into
my own skin as I moved about her on the grass, working here and there and what seemed like everywhere.

Finally, in desperation more than desire, I spread
her massive thighs somewhat further apart and entered
her rather dry and rubbery interior. Trying to be as
tender as possible, I moved slowly at first but then
faster and faster as the dryness excited me in proportion
to the rubbing together of the two skin areas in contact.
It was probably the same as starting a fire by rubbing
two dry sticks together, and basically just as crude.

Even when I finally came, I felt no spurt of fluid.
Dryness was all and I pulled back and rolled over to my
side. Sofia had neither moved nor opened her eyes
during any of this, and after watching her for a few
moments I stood up and retraced my path to the pool to
retrieve our clothes.

When I returned, she was sitting up with the knife in
hand, cutting the cantaloupes in half and cleaning out
the seed cavities. I placed my pants on the ground and
sat down on them because the stubble had started to
irritate my skin. Sofia skillfully cleaned off and cut up
vegetables, and we ate as we were, naked and sun-
drenched. We did not talk, not a word.

As I watched her slicing the blood-red tomatoes in

half, I remembered the sound the knife had made as I had dredged it out of Giuseppe's body, and as I bit into the juicy half that was handed me, I probed with my tongue to see if I could detect any extra saltiness.

We ate more than half of what we had brought and wrapped the rest in my shirt. I picked up one of the guns and went back to the pool to cool myself off again, crouching in the middle of the water with my right hand stuck in the air to keep the weapon dry. If anybody busted in on us now, at least I would be able to get some naked shots off in return.

When I went back to the clearing, I found Sofia dressed again, even her shirt, and when the sun had dried me a bit, I put on my shorts and pants and socks and shoes. We moved to a side of the clearing where we could get some shade, and I fell asleep, my body soaking it up as it had the sunlight before.

When I awoke, the dusk was just beginning to fall, and I suggested we move back to the bunker for the night, where we would be out of the dew. Sofia started off without saying a word, and in half an hour led me to the first clearing again. I had thought we would stay out until it started to get really dark, but the mosquitoes began buzzing around us, and we went inside, closed the door, and lit the lantern.

I checked through the pistols and the tommy gun again while Sofia sat with her back against the wall. She hadn't said a word, and I wanted to explain to her that something had gone wrong, that it really could be much better than it had been, that she was nervous the first time, and probably it had been my fault. But I didn't know how to start it and I wasn't sure what I would do with it if I did get it started. I even thought of telling her that it would have been much better with Doc, whom she loved, but it was just one of those stupid passing thoughts you get when you're desperate. And most stupid of all, I even thought of trying to do it with her again, hoping for second-time-lucky. But even if I had wanted to, I knew that my body wouldn't have cooperated in the venture. Because of what we were going through, because of what lay ahead, because of my state of mind and body, I was literally fucked out.

And when we blew out the lantern and lay there in the dark, I knew that she was just as wide-awake as I was and would remain so during the long, long night ahead. There has been enough of this shit, I told myself. Tomorrow you are going to that house and blow those sons of bitches out of there. And such was my state of frustration that I almost believed it.

21

Walpurgisnacht.

When I was taking courses in criminology at the community college in Boston, the last thing most of the so-called students were there for was an education. There were some who planned to transfer to four-year colleges for a degree in whatever they hoped to make their living at, but my enrollment was typical for all the others. Since he was about as Jewish as you can get in the United States of America without being really religious, my father felt that you were nothing without a college education. He never had one because he was so good with the violin that he started working his way up the symphony ladder right after he graduated from high school. He wasn't a virtuoso who could make it as a soloist, but he was good enough to make any symphony he tried for.

However, to his mind, the thing he lacked, the reason he wasn't a virtuoso, was a college education. The Jew can explain anything away through lack of a college education. Remember the old joke about the hooker with the Vassar diploma on the wall and the john asks her how come she's doing this for a living and she says, "Just lucky, I guess"? Well, the guy who asked her had to be Jewish.

In any event, I didn't want to go to college, but to shut my father up I went to community college and that's how I took all those courses in criminology and the novel and poetry. It hooked me on reading books and using words with more than two syllables, much to the disgust of my captain, who can't say a word as long as

"Mediterranean" without throwing a "fuck" into the middle of it.

In one of my classes—"The Contemporary Novel," it was titled—there was this crazy little guy named Phil Miles. He was one of those nervous people who hovered around you like a hummingbird, and he kept your attention with the strange words he used. His favorite of favorites was *Walpurgisnacht*. If you asked him if he wanted to go get a grinder, he would say "*Walpurgisnacht*, baby, *Walnpurgisnacht*." Or if someone asked him what a certain girl was like, he'd moan, "She's *Walpurgisnacht*, man, *Walpurgisnacht*."

I asked him once what it meant, and all he did was stare at me funny for a moment and move off. So I went and looked it up, and found out it was a situation that was like a crazy nightmare because in medieval times people believed that on the eve of May Day, all the witches gathered together to celebrate their sabbath, a kind of witches' ball, and it wasn't anything like the sophomore hop in predrug days. And when I took the course on the Holocaust in college, the professor used that term to describe Germany at the height of the Nazis. It's a word you don't forget once it gets down your throat and into the intestines.

So as I lay there in the concrete bunker with Sofia a few feet away, my own concrete state of mind began disintegrating as my fears jackhammered away chunks at a time. I was like that little kid in the Bloom County comic strip whose anxieties come out of the closet every night.

There were the two of us, me and Sofia, right? Over at the house there were fifteen to twenty guys, maybe more by now, who had guns and no hesitation about using them. The good news was that they didn't want to kill me because once I was dead, the five million bucks was out the window. But the bad news was that they could sure take it out of my hide while getting me to sign over that five million, and once I did, bye bye Benny.

Sofia could lead me out of the jungle to a place where I could call the cops, but Pascaglia had sworn to kill her family if I did, and if that happened, I would have betrayed my "wives" two times over.

It was probable that Pascaglia couldn't hope to stay much longer in the area without something going wrong for him, and that he would be forced to return to New York without obtaining what he wanted. All we had to do was sit tight and wait him out.

But then again, he could lose patience and send his crew out looking for us with Marchese's soldiers as guides and we would be flushed out like animals and carried out on poles. We had been lucky the day before at the water hole, but that didn't mean that the gods would smile on us the next time. Time had to be running out. From here on we had to make our own luck.

"Before the Israelis," my father used to say, "the Jews would always run when they were chased. Some would make it and some would not. But the Israelis changed the rules. They kick you in the balls and then ask if maybe you were planning to chase them. You know what the Israelis really are?" he would ask me. "Do you know? Do you know?"

Even though he had told me the answer a dozen times before, I would never dare to reply, sitting there with my eyes locked on his, not even breathing for those few moments.

"They are Jewish *goyim*," he would yell. "Jewish *goyim!* They are the only people in the world who ever really learned anything from history."

And what about my mother's brother who tried to take out a Protestant police station all by himself? Did I have any of his craziness in me too? The church people who had held me prisoner had scared me to the point where I wasn't sure who I was anymore. And now these Mafia scum were trying to finish the job. It was time for me to find out who I had been and how much was left of me. So I started to make my plans as I lay there in the dark. How we were going to flush out or kill off or chase away those sons of bitches, and without any of Sofia's family being hurt in the process. I had to bring that factor in because I knew I would never be able to live comfortably if something happened to even one of her people, including Uncle Vinnie, the little prick.

So I started to make my plans. And every time I started to make my plans, I would realize that I couldn't think of one goddamned plan to make. It was like that Shel Silverstein cartoon with the two guys chained upside down to the wall of the dungeon, and one looks at the other one with a little hopeful grin on his face and says: "Now, this is my plan."

Sofia and I were the equivalent of the two guys upside down. We had an antique tommy gun and a shotgun that might or might not work. We had two pistols and a knife. Only God knew what those people had for armament. They probably had enough stuff to cut down all the trees in the forest if they blazed away for a few minutes.

So I started all over again to make my plans. And I realized that if I kept to that hopeless approach much longer, I would probably burst into tears. I sat up and scrabbled around with my hand until I found the box of matches and struck one. It was twenty-five minutes past ten. Sophia sat up and watched me until the match burned out.

"Sofia," I said into the darkness, "can you lead us back to the house?"

"Now?" she asked.

"Now," I told her. "In the dark."

"Why?"

"Because I've got a plan," I told her.

"What is it?" she asked.

"I won't know until we get there," I answered.

I could hear her moving up onto her knees. If I wanted to go to the house, she was going to take me.

We lit the lantern again and I checked out all the weapons.

"You'll have to carry the shotgun," I told her, "because this other one weighs a ton."

I blew out the lantern and we waited in the dark until our eyes adjusted. Then I slowly opened the door and we moved out into the open again. There was only a quarter-moon in the sky but it afforded enough light to make out trees and bushes. The air had a little bit of nip in it, notice that September wasn't that far off.

"We'll go slowly and carefully," I whispered, "because we can't do anything until they're asleep anyway. Take me to the tree with the hideaway hole at the bottom."

She moved off through the bushes and I followed closely behind her, the tommy gun held at port arms. I didn't feel scared at all, maybe because I didn't know what we were going to do when we got there, or maybe because my Irish and Jewish blood had finally fused into the right combination. Or maybe it was because I really did have a plan.

What we were going to do one way or another was kick them in the balls and find out if they were planning to chase us.

22

*W*alking through a forest in the dark is a special experience by itself. The only thing you're sure of is how unsure you are of everything. I don't know how many times we went on our faces or our asses, always painfully. Usually we went down separately, but sometimes Sophia would trip and I, trying to keep close, would stumble over a leg and go down on top of her or to the side. Sometimes I fell down by myself, my foot caught by something that she had missed ahead of me. We were gashed and scratched and stabbed and gored, but we would always get up without a word and start going again.

Time loses all bearings in the darkness, and I don't know how long we had been out there when I started to have some qualms about the time it was taking to get back to the house. Twice I opened my mouth to say something, but I was trying to make as little noise as possible under the impossible conditions, and the human voice can seem louder than a bugle in the dark woods. So I just slogged along with the tommy gun and extra magazines getting heavier with each step, and the mosquitoes moving in whenever we stopped for even a split second. Everything they say about New Jersey mosquitoes is true, and there were times when I was this close to pointing the gun up in the air and blasting away in hopes of winging just one of those vicious mothers.

Sophia stopped suddenly and I whacked her shoulders a hard one with the side of the gun before I was able to stop moving and pull back. She ignored what had to have been extremely painful.

"I don't know where we are," she said.

"What do you mean you don't know where we are?"

"I must have taken a wrong turn somewhere because I can't find anything I recognize."

We were talking in normal conversational tones that could be heard quite a distance away, I am sure, but at the moment I couldn't have cared less. I wanted to scream, swear, shout, beat my head against a tree. If Pascaglia's men had suddenly charged us, I would have regarded it as a boon from heaven to take them on, the whole freaking crew. I took two deep breaths, sucking a mosquito into my nose on the second one, who died when I banged my fist as hard as I could against the nostril. I wanted to hurt me as much as I wanted to hurt him. Or rather, her, because it's only the females who bite. I hated all women at that moment, especially the dumb bitch standing before me who had got us lost.

"What can we do?" I asked.

"We can wait here until it gets lighter and then I'm sure I'll recognize something."

"There will be nothing left but bones if we spend the night out here," I said. "And it will be an agonizing death. It can't be more than half-past eleven. We can't stay out here. You've got to figure out something."

She thought for a moment. Meanwhile, the Stukas were settling all around my head, the buzzing increasing in intensity as they went into their bombing runs. I was past the stage of even slapping.

"Come on," she said, turned to the right, and started off again. I followed. We had walked maybe ten minutes when she gave a grunt and stopped. Something big and black loomed ahead. She walked toward it slowly and I followed with the tommy gun at the ready. As we drew close, I could see it was a small house and that some of the windowpanes were broken out, darker shades among the slight reflection of the moon from the glass that remained.

"This was where Catherine and Hermie lived for a while," said Sophia. "There's nothing in there now."

But there was. Cathy was in there. I could feel her presence. Nothing ghostly or any of that crap. Just the fact that she had once been in there, lived there, left her mark forever. I'd like to have thought that she had sent out some signal to Sofia, a beacon for her to follow so we could get our bearings. But I knew better than that. Just as I knew that now we would be able to find our way to where we wanted to go. A good omen. The kind you need before you go into battle. A little touch of Cathy in the night.

I think Sofia felt something too, because she paused for only a few seconds and then said rather gruffly, "Let's go!"

I followed her carefully and about twenty minutes later she stopped again, turned and squeezed my arm, then pointed to the right through the trees. Dim light was filtering through, man-made light.

We both crouched down a little as we walked forward, an instinctive rather than a meaningful move, and two minutes later we were at the big tree and then in our safe hole.

We sank down and let the guns drop to the ground, both of us drenched with sweat and exhausted. I knew if I let myself, if I closed my eyes and leaned back against the wall, I would fall asleep instantly, and I was sure the same thing would happen to Sofia.

"They seem to have all the lights in the house on," I whispered, and she leaned forward to take a look, her knee grinding the back of my hand into agonized mush.

"Jesus," I yipped, and out of the dark somebody yelled "Who's there?"

We froze. Then I slipped my gun out of the holster and moved it up to rest beside my chin on the bank. I could hear Sofia breathing beside me and wondered if it could also be heard by whoever had asked the unexpected and, as far as we were concerned, unanswerable question. Nobody but us poor kosher chickens, I wanted to tell him, but he wouldn't have believed me so I tried to make my own breathing as soft as possible.

After what seemed an eternity, there was the sound of footsteps through brush, and then silence again.

"Anybody out there?" a voice asked uncertainly, a rough man's voice, a voice that wasn't comfortable being alone in the woods on a darkish night even when he was only that many yards away from the security of his many friends.

The front door of the house opened and a man came out on the porch. I couldn't make out his face, but I could see that he was wearing a shoulder harness with a gun in it.

"Hey, Tony," he called out, "where the hell are ya?"

"I'm over here," said Tony, and he couldn't have been ten steps away from the tree.

"You wanna beer?" asked the guy on the porch.

"I wanna get the hell out of here," said Tony. "I keep hearing weird noises. I don't like it out here."

The guy on the porch laughed.

"You got another half-hour before Joey takes over," he said. "You sure you don't want a beer or maybe a shot?"

"Why don't you stay out here with me?" said Tony. "I shouldn't be out here all alone."

"There ain't nothing going to happen out here," said his friend. "There ain't no bears out there. And besides, we're watching *The Godfather* on the television. I ain't never seen it before."

He stretched, turned, and went back into the house, closing the door after him. There was silence for a moment before the steps began again and Tony finally moved out to where I could see him. He was a medium-frame stocky guy, but I couldn't make out his features because of the lighting. He walked toward the house and went up the stairs for a few minutes, peering into one of the side windows on the door.

Then he came back down and walked around to the back of the house before coming around the other side.

He had obviously been assigned the perimeter. A half-hour. He had another half-hour before anybody came to relieve him.

I slipped my gun back in the holster, pulled the other pistol and the knife from my belt and laid them down beside the tommy gun. I picked up the shotgun and stuck it out of the hole, laying it carefully down on the ground. Then I took the extra pistol and placed it in Sofia's hand. I put my finger on her lips to indicate that she was to keep silent, and then I crawled slowly out of the hole.

Cradling the gun, I elbow-and-knee-walked from tree to tree, moving closer and closer to the house until I reached the spot where Tony came closest on his circle. I wasn't sure about what I was going to do; I was only sure that I was going to do something.

When he finally showed up on his slow ramble, I let instinct take over. Despite his unease at being out all alone in unknown territory, he wasn't on the tip of his toes but was just drifting along with whatever thoughts were running through his head. As he walked by, I reversed the gun in my hands so that I was holding it by the barrel rather than the stock, stepped out from behind the tree, and swung with all my might. I think I was aiming for his back in the middle of his shoulders, but the barrel slanted and my swing went up instead of straight and even, and the stock cracked him square in the back of the head with the peculiar sound of polished wood meeting bone covered only by a little bit of hair and skin. I say it was a peculiar sound because I had never heard anything like it before, and I'm sure I don't want to hear it again. He went down like anybody else who's ever been poleaxed. I thought he might be dead, but I didn't bother to check because the only important thing at the moment was that whether he was dead or alive, he was not going to be able to interfere with anything I might do.

And what was I to do? What could I do? I was armed with a shotgun and a pistol. Whatever I was going to do, they were the things I was going to have to do it with.

I looked up toward the house and I happened to be standing opposite one of the windows to the living room, and through the curtains I could see figures moving about, talking and throwing their arms around and moving their heads back to guzzle from cans of beer. I couldn't make out who they were, but there were a lot of them, and I figured that this was where *The Godfather* was being shown.

I instinctively pulled back because it seemed obvious that if I could see them, they could also see me, but I was in the shadow and nobody was looking out. So I moved forward again real close to the window, reversed the gun to its normal position, held it up so that it was pointing straight in to the middle of the glass, and pulled the right-hand trigger. It clicked. The shell was a dud. I could feel my hands shaking and it suddenly occurred to me that Sofia's family might be in the room, but I couldn't stop myself and I pulled the left-hand trigger. It clicked. The other aged shell was also a dud.

I broke the gun open, uncaring about the noise it made, pulled out the shells, and replaced them with two from my pocket. Sofia's family couldn't be in there with this mob. They were probably still prisoners in their bedrooms. To tell the truth, I didn't care. I was so worked up that I had to shoot that gun off or explode myself.

I pulled the right-hand trigger and the noise of the explosion and the backlash almost ripped me over backward. But like a jack-in-the-box, I sprang back into position and pulled the left-hand trigger. This one didn't seem as loud because I guess I was partially deafened by the first shot, but the backward pull was just as strong and this time I went down.

As I scrambled to my feet again, the screams and yells coming through the smashed window spurred me into backpedaling so fast that when I smashed into one of the big trees at the side of the house, the shock took all the strength out of me and I slid right down on my rear end. The shotgun was still in my hands, held in an iron grip that nobody could have broken loose.

The yelling inside seemed to get louder and louder, and all of a sudden a face poked through the broken window and a hand appeared holding a gun. Instinctively I pulled my own weapon and fired every bullet in the magazine. The gun, the hand, and the face disappeared. Turning over, I crawled behind the tree and then went into a low crouch as I ran around the house to where our fortress tree was situated and threw myself into the hole right on top of Sofia, who didn't have time to scramble out of the way.

I was as soaking wet as I had been in that little pond we had cooled off in that day, and my throat was so dry that I was unable to speak.

"Are you all right?" she whispered, her hands feeling over every inch of my body from the top of my head down to my shoes.

I nodded in the dark.

"Are you all right?" she whispered more urgently, and I reached up and put my hand on her face to show that I was all right. She kissed the palm and then held the fingers in her two hands, stroking them gently. She pulled me up and held me close and it almost felt as though she were rocking me just as you would a little baby who has had a fright and needs reassurance.

"I'm all right," I said in a hoarse croak that sounded like that ventriloquist who uses his own hand for a dummy. The dummy was all right.

Lights were being turned off all over the house except for places on the second floor. Whoever was up there, and it might have been the rooms of Sofia's family, obviously didn't know what was going on and what the procedure should be. Then even those lights went out, and silence matched the darkness.

"What did you do?" she whispered. "I couldn't see anything from here."

"I fired into the window of the living room," I told her.

"Was my Papa there?"

"No," I said. "It was only the other ones."

I am not a liar and I can't stand liars. When somebody lies to me even once, and I know it to be a fact, that's it from then on. The relationship is never the same again. This can be a drawback when you're in police work because everybody lies to you all the time. But I was able to differentiate between business and personal. I expected the people I had to deal with professionally to lie to me and acted accordingly. I'll never forget the first time I had to testify in a criminal trial and I sat there listening to the judge instruct the jurors.

"Don't try to decide who is telling the truth," he said to them. "Just try to decide who is telling more truth."

And I was dumbfounded because I felt that this was no way for a judge to talk. In a trial, you must deal with absolute truth, pure and simple. But as the trial went on, I realized that many of the witnesses thought they were telling the truth when they were not. Some of them were out-and-out liars, to be sure, but the rest were just trying to tell the truth as they saw and understood it. What one witness saw or understood was just the opposite of what another witness thought he had seen or understood. That judge was a wise man, a student of human nature.

Had I just lied to Sofia? I was pretty sure her father wasn't in the room, or any other member of her family, when I pulled those triggers, but I wasn't positive. I had told the truth as I wanted to believe it. But it bothered me; it left a cold feeling in the pit of my stomach. Suppose I had killed or wounded her father or a member of her family? I would never be able to look my Sofia in the eyes again. No, I told myself, Papa was not in that room.

"Hey, cop," someone yelled from a window in the house. "You out there, cop?"

I almost smiled. Who the hell did they think was out there? I almost smiled again at the thought that I had almost smiled. I didn't feel scared, not at all. Either I was numb from the double jolt of the shotgun or something had happened to Benny's psyche. I had often thought about the commandos and the Green Berets and the paratroopers and the Israelis who had pulled those people out of Africa, and wondered what they were like. We had guys on the police force, especially the SWAT-ers I had met, who almost drooled at the thought of going up against someone in a life-or-death situation. There weren't a hell of a lot of them; most cops were like me, just this side of shitting their pants whenever the fat seemed about to or actually did fall in the fire.

But here I was for the first time in my life reasonably calm when there were all those guys in the house who wanted nothing more than to blow my brains out. There hadn't been anything like this when the church people had me and I broke loose. My so-called heroism during that whole piece of absurdity all took place with my hands trembling, my knees knocking, and my scrotum trying to turn itself inside out. But right then at that moment, I felt like smiling. I replaced my pistol in the holster, shoved the knife back in my belt, and picked up the tommy gun from the bottom of the hole. I wondered if all or any of the bullets, which had to be as old as the shotgun shells, were capable of firing. It looked like we were going to find out.

I laid down the tommy gun, broke open the shotgun, replaced the shells, and handed the weapon to Sofia.

"You stay in here no matter what happens," I whispered to her. "You've got the two guns in case somebody sticks his head in. But don't go looking for trouble. I have no idea what these guys are going to try, or what I'm going to do when and if they do, but I've got to know that I don't have to worry about you."

Her head went up and down in assent. One thing about these Mafia people: they train their women to take orders. I'm not a male chauvinist pig, and my wife, Cathy, took no bullshit from any man, especially me, but right then I liked the system. Sofia would follow instructions to the letter, and I would only have to worry about myself. Which, despite my new assurance, I certainly did.

"Cop!" It was Pascaglia himself doing the yelling. "We've had enough of this bullshit. I'm raising the ante to twenty-five percent. We're going to come out and all we want to do is talk. No guns, no bullshit, no nothing. Just talk. We're coming out, cop. Don't do nothing crazy. All we want to do is talk."

The moonlight was gone now and all you could really make out was the huge black mass of the house. I heard the creak of the front door opening, and then footsteps on the wood and on the stone, even though they were obviously trying to muffle the sound. How many were coming out? Were they coming from the back too? Were they fanning out in a semicircle, their guns ready, set to blast us to kingdom gone if we were sucker enough to believe the offer and come forth? What do we do now, coach?

I decided to wait them out awhile. They knew I had a shotgun, which was a close-range weapon, and a pistol, which was even less deadly from a distance. Would Pascaglia dare yell again even in the dark? They were probably hoping to suck me into saying something or maybe even getting a shot off so they could concentrate their fire and pulverize the whole suspected area.

I reached to the back of the hole and found the empty water bottle that Brachi had pissed in, pushed myself as far out of the hole as I could without taking my feet off the floor, and heaved the bottle as hard as I could to the left.

I don't know what it hit but it made a most satisfactory smash, and immediately from the front of the house maybe eighteen guns started blazing away, the collective muzzle blasts lighting up the area enough for me to see the dark figures of the men, all bunched together at the front. These were street fighters, a gang, rather than Minute Men from Concord and Lexington, and the only way they knew how to battle was in a group formation.

I slid out of the hole and ran to the left so that my line of fire would be directed toward the gang but would not have the house behind them. Stepping from behind the tree, I pointed the tommy gun toward where I figured the middle of the group had to be and pulled the trigger.

I don't know about them, but it sure surprised and scared the hell out of me. The backlash and pull were such that the muzzle of the gun climbed up and away beyond my control, and what started as ground-level shots ended up with me practically shooting straight into the sky.

But the noise and the muzzle blasts were fantastic, and by the time I had emptied the magazine and the echoes had died, there was the sound of men running, men running and yelling and swearing marvelous obscenities, running for the safety of the trees on the other side of the house, running and running to get away from my totally unexpected machine of devastation. The field was ours.

I swung behind the tree, unhooked the magazine, and slid another one into place, just as I had practiced in our concrete bunker for two nights. I had forgotten what the FBI guy had said when he demonstrated the weapon in my one tour of the Washington headquarters. "The muzzle velocity is such that the weapon climbs like it was a jet plane," he had said. I had laughed along with all the other tourists at the time, never dreaming that one day I would be using it as an attack weapon in a firefight with a battalion of Mafia men. There I was standing behind the tree in the dark, and it almost made me smile.

"I think they all ran away into the woods," said Sofia in my ear, which were almost the last words she ever said, because at the first sound I started to turn, bringing the butt of the tommy gun up in the air to smash into the jaw of whoever had sneaked up on me. I couldn't stop the follow-through until it was too late, but I missed her in the dark.

She heard the sound and felt the air going past her, however, and must have jumped back and tripped, because there was the noise of something going down heavy, and then a shotgun blast ripped past my ear into the trunk of the tree and the air. Her finger must have been on one of the triggers, and the shell definitely was not a dud.

"Benny," she gasped from the ground, "what the hell are you trying to do?"

"You all right?" I asked.

I heard her scrambling up again, but I really couldn't see her.

"Do you have your finger on the trigger of the gun?" I asked. "If you do, take your finger out and be careful not to pull the trigger."

"We've got to go into the house," she said.

"There may still be some of them in there," I whispered back.

"I've got to know whether my father and Mama Maria and the rest are all right."

"Give me the shotgun," I told her, "and go put this back in the hole. I'll wait here."

I handed her the tommy gun and she disappeared. She had not followed instructions. Goddamned Mafia women were like any other women. I could have taken her whole head off with the butt. And now we had to go into the house. I extracted the used shell from the shotgun and reloaded.

"You still got your handgun?" I asked when she returned. She must have eyes like a cat, I figured, because she was back in no time. All I could see was darker-than-light and lighter-than-dark. Maybe she should lead the way into the house.

"Follow me," I told her, "and go as quietly as you can. The problem will be not to shoot any of your

family and not to be shot by anybody else. Don't keep
your finger on the trigger of the gun; keep it just on the
outside. But if you have to shoot, shoot. Don't hesitate."

So there we were, sneaking up on the big house just
like two cat burglars, with Pascaglia men scattered in
the woods and maybe scattered in the house. Death
outside and maybe death inside. And once they got
their balls back, they might decide to retake the fort.
Except that they had been running pretty hard according to the noise they made, and they must have gone a
ways in, and without Sofia for a guide, it would take
them a while to get back. By that time we might be
able to arrange a little reception party with the help of
the Don. Provided he was on our side. If we get through
this, I told myself, maybe you ought to start keeping a
diary. I almost smiled.

23

I fell down twice going up the front stairs, and Sofia impatiently moved ahead of me.

"Don't go so fast," I hissed. "We've got to stay together."

She slowed down, but not by much, and as soon as we were inside the house, she started calling out "Papa. Mama Maria. Elena. Vinnie. Marina." Over and over again, repeating the list exactly the same each time.

I kept waiting for the muzzle blast from the dark, the one that would take her or me or both of us out. Could every one of those guys have come out of the house in the attempt to cut us down? And were they all still outside or were they starting to creep back in? It was so frustrating that I almost looked for a light switch so that I could see where the hell we were and what was around us. Instead, I put my hand on Sofia's left shoulder and followed wherever she went, listening to her call for her Papa and her Mama Maria and the rest of the family. Nobody answered. This was definitely not *The Waltons*.

I felt Sofia's body lift and searched desperately with my toe for the stairs that I knew we were about to ascend. She went up quickly and then we were on the landing.

"Papa!" she yelled. "Where are you, Papa?"

"Sofia," echoed a voice out of the darkness, "we're here, Sofia."

She quickly brought me down the hall and we turned right into a room where I heard her body smack into another.

"Papa," she said. "Are you all right, Papa? Is everybody all right?"

"We're all right," said the Don. "What has happened? We were all in Elena's closet and we couldn't hear anything through the dresses."

I visualized Elena's closet, as big as an ordinary bedroom, with scores of expensive designer gowns hanging on the racks, boxes of shoes piled neatly, a veritable fortress of fashion. About as safe a bomb shelter as any during an emergency.

"Benny made them all run," said Sofia. "We think they went into the woods, but they could be coming back at any moment."

"They are pigs, not men," said the Don bitterly. "They have broken the code in the way they have treated us, and I will report them to those in authority."

What the hell was this Mafia, an adjunct of the bar association? The Don was going to report Pascaglia *to those in authority!* Pascaglia would then probably be fined or dis-Mafiaed, or if they thought he had been real naughty, wasted. Hey, Pascaglia, nothing personal, but rules are rules.

And thinking of nothing personal reminded me that the Don had put the finger on me at his dinner table. Who was I supposed to report that to? But it was no time to bring that up. What we had to figure out was how we were going to protect ourselves when those guys tried to blast their way back into the house.

"We've got to act fast," I said, breaking up the reunion and the complaints. "I've got to call the police or the sheriff's office."

"The phones are gone," said the Don. "They cut the wire outside the house. Pascaglia said he was going to burn the whole place down when they leave."

"What's the best way to defend the house against them coming back in?" I said. "Is there a place to hole up where they can't get at us? They can't stay here forever doing this. Something's got to give."

"I have a few *pistole*," said the Don, "but we haven't been keeping up lately and there's no heavy stuff."

"Well, we've got to get moving," I said. "We can't just stand here and—"

The door burst open and men poured into the room, black shapes in the gloom, shouting words I couldn't understand, and I lifted my gun to shoot when Sofia, sensing my move in the dark, swung the shotgun square at me, whacking me in the side of the shoulder and knocking me right to the floor. Despite my amazement at her going crazy, I still tried to get the gun up in the air, and she dropped the shotgun and fell on top of me, pinning me and my arms to the floor. I have commented before that Sofia was huskily built, which I noticed even more when I was on top of her. But I had no idea how heavy she was until she was on top of me. The air left my chest in a whoof and I lay there completely helpless while she swung her arms around me and hung on with all her strength.

The Don and the four men—I could make out four separate shapes in the dark despite my dizziness—were yelling at each other in Italian, back and forth, back and forth, arms waving, some with guns in them, spit flying and excitement rising.

Holy shit! One of them had to be Angelo. Which meant that the other three had to be the Don's soldiers too, reporting for duty. I didn't know where they had been while everything had been going on, or from whom they had taken orders, but it now seemed that the regular chain of command had been reestablished and we had a force of our own.

When Sofia realized from the untensing of my muscles that I now comprehended the situation, she released my arms, rolled to the side, and left me free to breathe again. I sat up, flexing my arms, checking my bones, regaining my poise. There is something about being decked by a woman that doesn't rest easy in the ego, no matter how sympathetic you are to feminism. Nobody there thought any the less of me because of

what happened, and Sofia was now crooning over me
and checking me for booboos, but the whole episode
took my mind off the major problem for a moment. It
wasn't until I regained my feet that I was able to forge
into action again.

"What are we going to do?" I almost whined to the
Don.

"I've got a master switch in my bedroom," he said,
"that will throw lights all around the house. We've got
enough people to cover each side, and if they try to
rush us, we'll cut them down. Once Pascaglia realizes
that he has crossed the wrong man, he will ask forgive-
ness and leave. But he has also insulted the wrong man,
done things to my beloved daughter that are unforgiv-
able, and I will see that he pays. Marchese does not
forget."

This was no seventy-year-old hypochondriac anymore.
He seemed twenty years younger, his voice was stronger,
and he moved around like he could hold his own with
Marvelous Marvin Hagler. I glanced at Elena's svelte
shadow and was positive that I was looking at a woman
who was satisfied sexually. This was no Don to Fugaroun
with.

Marchese went to the wall, pulled back the picture
that was hanging there, and flicked the switch that was
underneath it. I could see lights flash around the windows outside the room, coming from somewhere on the
edge of the roof. The Don barked orders in Italian and
his four men scampered out, presumably each to his
designated area.

"You, me, and Vinnie," said the Don, "will stay
upstairs and go from side to side, and if they hit from
any one place, we will rush there to help."

"We've got a machine gun hidden outside," I said,
"but it would probably be too dangerous to try to get
it."

"Nobody goes out of the house," said the Don decisively. "We hold out until morning and then that piece
of cat meat will come begging to talk."

A shot rang out from the other side of the house, and the Don ran out of the room with the rest of us following. We could see fairly well inside from the lights that were shining on the outside, and the Don stopped at the head of the stairs to call down something in Italian. One of the men answered.

"What did they say?" I asked Sofia, who had yielded up the shotgun to Vinnie. From the way she had been talking before, I was sure she was going to shoot Vinnie with the shotgun the next time she saw him, but she had just handed it over when he made a motion with his hands. Blood is thick with these people, and family comes first.

"Angelo said he saw somebody coming out of the trees, but when he fired at him, he ran back in. They must be out there now. I don't know if we can hold them off if they rush us."

"I don't think they will," I said. "They have no idea how many of us there are or what weapons we have in here. They probably think we still have the machine gun."

I could have kicked my ass ten times over for leaving that outside, but it was too late to do anything about it now. The goddamned thing was so inaccurate and so tough to handle that I hadn't wanted to bother with it once it had scared them off. If I had it now, I could probably scare them off forever. But we'd have to make do with whatever we had. I wasn't sure what the situation really was. Did they have us trapped in the house or did we have them trapped in the woods? I went to the side of the house where I had slugged the guy with the shotgun. His body wasn't lying there. Either he had come to and scampered off with the rest of them or they had dragged him away.

A shot rang out from the other side of the house, and we all rushed there immediately. If we'd been in a boat, it would have capsized. It was also stupid in that anybody could be hit by a stray shot. We were a ragtag army at best, and our only hope was that the group outside was even ragtaggier.

Two more shots rang out from the woods and one of the lights on the roof shattered and went dark.

"Hey," yelled a voice from somewhere out there, "don't shoot out the lights. How the hell do you expect us to see?"

Ah! They didn't want to be in the dark in the wild woods. They were feeling just as insecure as I was. I thought of the American troops in Vietnam, thousands of miles from home, fighting in jungles where you couldn't see a foot in front of you, strange noises, poisonous snakes, booby traps, an enemy you could never find but who you felt was everywhere around you. And those little brown men in their black pajamas, accustomed to little food and no comfort, able to sit still for hours at a time if need be, in holes, in caves, in underground tunnels. Fighting for their own country and their families and their land. Guess why they won and we lost.

Pascaglia and his people were working under somewhat similar circumstances. They needed sleazy bars and small restaurants, vacant lots near municipal dumps, the capacious trunks of Cadillacs and Lincoln Continentals and people who could be bribed or scared into looking the other way. They were out of their depth here; still dangerous, deadly dangerous, but out of their depth.

Sofia came and stood beside me in the hall. The lights from the outside reflected enough through the windows so that you could even make out people's faces close by. I pulled on her arm and she squatted down beside me.

"Don't walk in front of windows," I told her, "and stay as low as you can because a bullet can come through and hit you or ricochet around and do real damage."

"Tomaselli's unconscious," she said. "Mama Maria thinks he's going to die."

It took me a second to remember who Tomaselli was, but then I nodded.

"Papa told Uncle Vinnie and the boys to play along with whatever Pascaglia said until the right time came," she said. "Their honor is intact. And it was the same when he told Pascaglia who you were. His honor is intact. He also told Marina to help you in the cellar. He also said there was nothing he could do about . . . do about . . ."

She couldn't make it any further. I put my face against hers and felt the hot tears coming out of her eyes. She had convinced herself that her father would have saved Doc if he could have. But Doc didn't have a five-million-dollar trust fund as a life-insurance policy against his being mashed, and there had been something in Pascaglia's eyes that first night when he looked at Doc that seemed in retrospect to have been a foreshadowing of death.

"Does your father have any plans?" I asked her, as much trying to shift her mind as find out if some miracle had been concocted.

"He keeps saying that once Pascaglia realizes how much he has dishonored himself he will apologize and leave immediately," she said, "but I'm afraid Papa is out of touch with how things have been the last five years and how much things have changed since he was active in the business."

A delicate way of describing garbage, but there were two Sofias and she did the best she could in allowing them to live in one brain and heart.

I was too exhausted to come up with any brilliant solutions of my own, but before either of us could say anything more, this tiny shape glided up to us bearing something big and round in its arms. It was Marina with a tray of sandwiches and drinks, and as she bent to offer me whatever I wanted to take, without thinking about it I suddenly rolled over backward and came up two feet away with my gun pointing straight at the little woman. She and Sofia froze where they were, and I realized that I was as mystified as they were. What the hell had come over me?

It wasn't until I realized that I was staring at her right arm that I understood my action. Was the hand under the tray holding a butcher knife to slide into my belly? Of course it wasn't. Or was it? If the Don had given the order, it would have, and that would have been the end of that.

"It's Marina," said Sofia crisply. "Who did you think it was?"

"I guess I'm a little jumpy," I said, crawling forward on my knees to take a sandwich with my left hand, place it on the floor, and then a drink with my left hand, never loosening my grip on the gun. "The dark got to me."

Sofia took a sandwich and a drink and Marina left to finish her rounds. We sat there munching and drinking without saying a word. The meat tasted good after our vegetable-and-fruit diet.

The Don came out of the bedroom and I asked him if we should take turns guarding the four sides so some of the people could get some sleep.

"No," he said, "it won't be that long before morning and my boys know every blade of grass out there. You just stay ready in case they go crazy and try something."

He started to walk away and then came back.

"Sofia told me what you did when that pig was going to cut her," he said. "They had us locked in the bedroom and I didn't know. If God had given me a son, I would have asked for no more than you."

He turned and walked down the stairs to check his soldiers. I sat and thought how I would have felt if my own Papa had ever said that to me.

24

*T*he first false light of dawn tickled through my eyelids, and I woke to find myself leaning against the
spindles of the stairway, Sofia curled on the floor by my
side. My back felt as though the skin would carry a
permanent impression of every knurl in the elaborately
carved spokes, and both my knees cracked when I
straightened and stretched my legs before me.

There had been no more shots in the night, and I
wondered what kind of shape Pascaglia and his men
might be in after their several hours of survival training
in the woods. Had their anger and frustration built to
the point of rushing in at us and the hell with who
might be gunned down? Or had it sapped their strength
and resolution to the point where they would be ready
to pick up their dolls and go home? My answer came
almost immediately.

"Marchese," shouted a voice from the right side of
the house. "Marchese!"

The Don appeared almost immediately from his bedroom, the long-barreled *pistole* dangling from his right
arm. I could tell in the ever-increasing light that he was
newly shaved, and the crisply pressed gabardine was
not the suit he had been wearing the night before. My
admiration for the dude increased even more. I personally felt like something the coyote had shit over the
edge of the cliff, and as I experimentally moved my
tongue around my mouth and waggled my jaw, I became aware that the pepper ham sandwich I had eaten
the night before was still going through the digestive
process in the cracks between my teeth. I remembered

a line from an old Marx Brothers movie that had tickled
my fancy. Groucho would look pensively up at the
ceiling and say, "Shelley, ah, Shelley. They don't write
stuff like that no more." The Don, ah, the Don. They
don't make Mafia men like him no more.

Marchese moved to the side of the window at an
angle from which no bullet could get to him and shouted
back through the broken panes. What he yelled sounded
something like *"Che fa?"* but I have no idea whether it
was English or Italian or whether I heard it correctly.
Whatever it was, Pascaglia understood it.

"It's time to talk," he yelled back from behind a tree
somewhere. "It's time for a meeting."

A shot rang out from the other side of the house and
a slug thudded into the brickwork and scattered lead
and pieces of stone into the air. There was no answering shot from our man.

"Who the hell did that?" yelled Pascaglia. "Goddamn
it! Who the hell did that?"

Nobody answered him. If I had fired the shot, I
wouldn't have owned up to it either. They were all
sitting out there with their fingers on the triggers, cold
and wet and pissed off. But the boss had just yelled out
that he wanted to parley, so it was no time to be
throwing a bullet into the works.

The Don decided to take advantage of the mishap.

"Is this how you want to talk?" he yelled out. "Is this
your idea of a meeting? You are a disgrace to the family
you represent."

"That was a mistake and I apologize," Pascaglia yelled
back, and you could tell from the gargled sound of the
words how much it cost him to utter them. "I agree
that there have been mistakes on both sides, but I think
we can work out something to mutual satisfaction."

"Mistakes on both sides?" thundered the Don. "You
have invaded my house, you have laid hands on my
daughter, you have treated me like I was dirt, you have
killed one who was like a son to me, you have injured
my servant, you have dishonored the code, and now

you have the nerve to say that there have been mistakes on both sides. You cannot be the real Pascaglia. You must be a G-man impersonating Pascaglia."

A G-man, he said. The Don was fifteen years behind the times with his codes and his honor and his association of the depths of dishonor with G-men. Where had he been during World War II? He was dealing with the Nazis of crime, not General Braddock.

"We are ready to leave," Pascaglia yelled, "but first I must talk to the cop. I am ready to make a deal that will be satisfactory to all parties. I am ready to make a deal that will also satisfy your honor and your needs, Don. There can be money in this for all of us. But we must talk, we must work it out."

I could tell by the tilt of the Don's head that Pascaglia had reached him a little. *A deal that will also satisfy your honor and your needs.* Times were tough for the Marcheses with only the pizza parlors and the bakery to keep them going. Elena Marchese was an expensive proposition. The Don's ego had been simmering on the back burner for how many years, and here was an opportunity not only to be respected again but also to get a share of the big money. I wondered right then if my life was worth two cents, if I was part of the deal that was to be put on the trading block. Sofia had said the Don's honor was intact, but how honorable was that honor to begin with? I began to get a squeamish feeling in the pit of my stomach.

"Talk," yelled the Don.

"We can't talk like this," Pascaglia said. "We must meet face to face, eyeball to eyeball."

"Where?"

"In the front of the house, on the driveway," said Pascaglia. "A few of us, a few of you. Covered by both sides so that a wrong move means instant death."

Showdown at the O.K. Marchese. We were outnumbered at least three to one, but there would be people in the house covering the proceedings on the driveway with rifles, and if Pascaglia was going to put

his own ass on the line out there in the open, the
danger should be minimized. Unless he had something
special up his sleeve, which I was sure he did. What it
was we wouldn't know until we got out there with him,
but we had to take whatever chances were offered
before something exploded and a bloodbath occurred.
There wasn't much we could do on our end except go
along and hope for the best. If it occurred to those
Indians out there to shoot a burning arrow into the
house and then cut us down as we tried to escape, they
could be the hell and gone before anybody outside the
estate noticed the fire and put in an alarm. We might as
well have been in the wilds of the Amazon as in those of
New Jersey.

I sank to the floor and started doing push-ups while
the Don considered Pascaglia's offer. Even though Sofia
had become somewhat accustomed to my sometimes
bizarre behavior, she still looked at me rather peculiarly.

"We meet," yelled the Don. "But remember that
you are on your honor."

What was it the Red Queen said to Alice? Something
about words meaning what you want them to mean. I
would have loved to make Pascaglia write his definition
of honor fifty times on the blackboard.

The Don called a council of war in his bedroom, and
the women automatically moved outside the inner circle of men. I didn't know whether or not I was supposed to be included, but since there were only the
Don and Vinnie, what with Angelo and his boys still
guarding the perimeter, I moved in to make it an
official holy trinity. Since I was the only one with any
authentic Jewish blood, plus it was my five million that
was going to be dickered for, I wasn't going to give up
any of my dick without putting my two cents in.

"I think he's going to try something dirty out there," I
said, venturing the first penny.

"Of course he is," snapped the Don, just a bit annoyed by my naïveté. "Right now he is just trying to
save his face in front of his men, wanting to leave here

with some dignity. But he may have some plan to have
his people rush the house while we concentrate all our
guns on the front. Which means we have to leave
everybody where he is, and just the three of us go out
to meet them. They won't really know where everybody is, and if we hear one shot while we are out there,
the man with the rifle has to waste Pascaglia first and
then whoever else he can get while we do our own
thing."

This all would have sounded pretty stupid to me
except that I once read a book about the high command
in World War II and most of those guys didn't know
what their asses and elbows were doing either despite
their huge staffs and technical equipment. And despite
what my father said, the Israeli leaders quite often
pulled blunders in their wars with the Arabs. If the
Arab sheiks didn't have a gift for fucking up, the results
could have been much different. It was like the judge
had said about truth. The wars were won by the people
who made less blunders and had whatever the hell else
Napoleon said they needed. Pascaglia's plan, whatever
it was, probably was the equal of what the Don was
laying out for us. No better and no worse.

"He's going to want a piece of my five million," I
said.

The Don considered this for a moment.

"Whatever is agreed to out there," he said, "is fly
shit in the wind. He isn't going to keep his word on
what he promises us, and we should not expect to keep
our word on what we promise him. We must act as if
we are dealing from the heart, we must not give in too
easily on anything, but all we are trying to do is get
them out of here without any of my family getting hurt.
Once he is out of here, I can make some calls. I still
have friends in high places, and Don Marchese is not
without influence among those who are important."

I had a feeling that he was overestimating both his
friends and his influence, but it was no time to ask for
references. Vinnie didn't say anything during all this

time, and I realized it was because he had nothing to say. Vinnie's forte was bitching about how life had treated him, but life had treated him that way because the only thing he was good at was bitching.

"All right," said the Don, "the four of us will go out to meet them."

"Four?" I questioned.

"Four," said the Don. "You, me, Vinnie, and Marina."

"Marina?"

"In case we have to send back to the house for anything," said the Don. "We will not want to send a gun back in the house."

That made sense. Vinnie had the shotgun, which could cause quite a bit of havoc at close range. But first we had to get some fresh shotgun shells from Angelo. We didn't want any click-clicks out there the way I had at the window the night before. We wanted boom-booms. The Don had his *pistole*, which was impressive looking but of doubtful firepower, and I had my own gun and the one I had picked up from Giuseppe. I had laid the knife down somewhere in the house, but couldn't remember where.

The Don went back to the side of the window and shouted out.

"Three people," he yelled. "You, Brachi, and one other. There will be three of us also."

"Four," I said in a piercing whisper. "There will be four of us."

The Don shook his head impatiently. Obviously women didn't count.

"Three it is," Pascaglia yelled back. "Will you be carrying guns?"

"We will be carrying guns."

"Then we will be carrying guns also. But no tricks. The rest of the guns will be dead on you."

"And on you, too," shouted the Don.

It began to remind me of the rock fights we had in the fields of Boston when I was growing up. We would be behind our fort and they would be behind their fort, and we would be shouting rules back and forth before the first missile flew. Almost nobody ever got hit, but a couple of times kids went home with bloody heads, and once Bobby Mills almost had his eye put out. Missed it by that much. At least grown-ups had guns in our civilized world. After the nuclear holocaust, whoever was left would have to be content with rocks again, but at least we still had guns. I was so hyped up that I would have loved to do a hundred push-ups, but realized that this might make my colleagues nervous.

"Okay," said the Don. "Let me do the talking."

He went to the head of the stairs and shouted for Angelo, then spouted Italian for five minutes. Angelo answered with a simple "*Si*."

"Let's go," said the Don, and started down the stairs, followed by me and Vinnie and Marina. I hadn't seen the Don give her any instructions, but perhaps that had been part of what he had called down to Angelo. In any case, there was this midget following behind us.

"As soon as we get outside the door," said the Don, "spread out. And if you just hear somebody fart, get back in the house as quick as you can. I want the shotgun ready for Pascaglia, I will cover Brachi, and Benny will cover whoever else is out there."

I hadn't been thinking about Brachi at all. The Don assumed that Pascaglia would want his lawyer out there, and it made sense. I would have laughed at the idea that we needed a lawyer for this kind of thing, but there was no laughter in me. But I didn't feel that scared, either. Something had happened inside me in the last couple of days; something had burned out or been replaced. I would have to spend some time finding out about the new Benny. Right then I hoped I would have the time.

The Don opened the door and stepped outside, then Vinnie and then me and then Marina. We spread out a little and then stood there waiting, not wanting to get too far from the doorway so that we could jump back inside if even a bird flew by.

A few seconds later, Pascaglia appeared from behind a tree, then Brachi came into view, moving slowly, obviously nervous about being a part of field action, and finally the young guy, the one they called the Crusher, stepping quickly, flexing his muscles, moving the gun back and forth in his hand, wanting to kill, his eyes fixed on me.

"All right," said the Don, starting to move forward, "keep apart and watch everywhere."

We went down the porch stairs and they came out toward the driveway. Your mind plays you tricks in tight situations. You're concentrating on what is important, but errant thoughts go through your head at the same time. I remembered once when I was touring Gettysburg with two buddies from college. One of them was from Pennsylvania, and we were visiting his folks for a few days, and somehow we ended up at Gettysburg. And we stood on that little hill where the Northern troops first saw that incredible wave of Southerners coming out of the woods into the open fields.

And I wondered then what it must have been like to have seen all that death advancing on you. Ours was a small-scale, shitty little thing compared to Gettysburg, but I finally knew something I hadn't ever thought I would find out. I knew what it was like to have death advancing toward you over an open field.

=== 25 ===

Even when I'm in a tight situation, say maybe walking down a dark alley where a suspect might have run, or even going through a warehouse where the burglar alarm has sent in a silent alert, I always keep my finger on the side of the trigger guard rather than on the trigger itself. I don't know how many times I would have wounded or killed or maybe scared half to death some innocent party or pussycat who happened to be in the wrong place at the wrong time and popped up near me. It could be that the split second it takes to slip your finger inside the guard and pull the trigger will cost me my life sometime, but I've always felt that I'd rather have that happen than live with the burden of having destroyed innocence. The Germans destroyed innocence, my father used to tell me all the time. There can never be innocence again, he would say. But I didn't want to take any chances in case there was still a litte hanging around.

However, as I walked out on the driveway that day, my finger was right on the trigger. There was the chance that I might trip over something and shoot one of my own people, but I was willing to take that chance. In the back of my mind was the question of what Pascaglia and his lawyer and his thugs might have done to me in that cellar to get me to sign those papers if Marina hadn't ridden to my rescue. I could feel the rage building in me with each step, but it was being channeled into the right place and filling my body with the right feeling. I wasn't relaxed like I was going out to bring in the mail; I was relaxed like I might have to shoot and kill somebody.

Close up, Pascaglia and Brachi looked a mess from their night in the woods. Their unshaven faces, baggy eyes, sleepless wrinkles, and dirty clothes would have been appropriate for a mission soup kitchen, and they looked more desperate than dangerous. The Crusher, on the other hand, was all bouncy, flexing the gun in his hand, a little smile on his lips, and his eyes—ah, his eyes; what was it with his eyes? They were the eyes . . . they were the eyes . . . they were the eyes of all the druggies I had encountered in arrests and police stations, eyes that showed the person was bombed out of his skull from some chemical substance that made him think he was king of the world.

There's this old joke about a guy going by a stable just before a big track race, and he looks in the window and sees a trainer forcing a pill the size of a golf ball down a horse's throat.

"Tell me, friend," says the casual passerby, "has this steed got a good chance of winning?"

"Win or lose, mister," says the trainer, "he's going to be the happiest horse in the race."

Win or lose, shoot or be shot, the Crusher couldn't have cared less. His eyes were pinpoints and his feet were barely touching the ground. He had not spent a miserable night in the woods; he had transported himself to a suite in Valhalla. I decided to watch the gun. If it swung up even two inches, I was going to shoot.

We stopped maybe three feet from each other. From the corner of my eye I saw that Brachi didn't have a gun. That gave us three to two right there, but we only had one rifle trained on the bunch from the house while they had maybe a dozen handguns on us from the trees. Except that Pascaglia didn't know we had only one rifle on him. And we didn't know where his dozen men were, either. They could by now be all the way around the house and ready to go in the back door. I kept my eyes on the Crusher's hand.

"Talk," said the Don.

"We go out of here," said Pascaglia, "all of us. And

we cut you in on some of the big action from now on. It has been so long that I had forgotten how useful this place could be. It's far away from everything with nothing and nobody to bother you, and yet it's close enough to the city to make things easy. You'll be big again, Don, with money as well as respect."

"And what do you want?" asked the Don, knowing that you do not get something for nothing.

"Him," said Pascaglia, turning his face toward me. "We take him with us. He has five million dollars of my money, and he belongs to me."

"No," said the Don, "he belongs to us. He is family. Five million. Fifty million. Five cents. It makes no difference. He is part of my family and he stays."

"For Christ's sake," said Pascaglia, "he's not family. He's a Jew, for Christ's sake."

"He was married to Catherine," said the Don, "who was the daughter of my wife's second cousin. He is family and he stays."

Jesus. Winston Churchill never gave a speech that could match the Don's at that moment. To me, it was his finest hour.

"I am not a man to cross," said Pascaglia. "If I leave here without him, I will be back. I will be back to your sorrow."

"I still have friends in high places," said the Don. "The sorrow will be on your head if you pursue this further. We will let you get in your cars and go, and that could be the end of it. Don't make it worse on yourself than it already is. You are in big trouble."

"Fucking Jesus," screamed the Crusher, and in surprise my eyes lifted to his face despite my determination never to take them off the gun. His features were distorted into a hundred different lines, and he threw his gun down on the ground and started coming toward me.

"You fucker!" he was screaming. "You fucking fucker!" Over and over again.

I was as surprised as anybody, frozen into place as he

came closer and closer until his right arm, the one that had held the gun, snaked out and banged me on my right wrist, paralyzing it instantly so that my fingers froze and the gun dropped to the ground.

His arms went around me, lifting me straight up in the air, and he twisted to the side and brought me down hard, so hard that the wind was partially knocked out of me, but by the time I had recovered from my shock, he had dropped down on top of me and was strangling me with his incredibly powerful hands.

I kicked up with my feet and managed to get them around his head and gave a convulsive heave that tore him loose. It was only for an instant because he was immediately back and punching away at me, his fists smashing into my chest and side and shoulders. If even one of them had caught me on the head it would have been all over.

No one was moving around us, their eyes on each other's guns, and nobody could shoot either one of us for fear of hitting the other. I don't think anybody could have moved anyway, because when two men are going at it, the mob psychology is to let them finish what has been started without anybody thinking of the consequences.

So there we were, him and me, me and him, and I knew it was just a matter of seconds before one of those fists finished it off, just as I knew that his body was impregnable to anything my own hands might do.

I twisted to the side and one of those iron fists smashed by me into the hard ground, causing him to pause in pain for just one instant, and in that moment I shoved forward, grabbing the back of his head with my hands and sinking my teeth into the side of his throat. It is one thing to bite somebody; it is another to sink your teeth into him, just as a dog or a lion or a tiger or any small animal that has been cornered will use the teeth as a last resort.

This was my last resort, and the sharp edges of my uppers caught on to something and ripped, and I bit in deeper and deeper, using my bottom teeth as a wedge or a fulcrum or whatever it was that made the uppers as deadly as a knife. I felt something give and the blood that spurted out covered my whole face so that I was blinded for a moment, but I did not relent and held on for my dear life as I heard him scream once, and then his grip on me slackened and I let go as he fell backward on the ground, blood still pouring out from his throat.

I tasted the salt and through my mind went the memory of that tomato Sofia and I had eaten from the Doc's vegetable garden, that blood-red tomato that she had sliced with the knife that had finished off Giuseppe. I used the fingers of both hands to clear my eyes and looked around at the horror on the faces of the four men standing near me; only Marina's expression remained unchanged.

"You," I grated at Pascaglia, the vomit trying to crawl up my throat, "look what you made me do."

His right hand started to move up and I could tell that he was going to shoot as soon as the arc was completed, but he was five feet from me and I braced myself for the impact even as the Crusher's body gave its last shudder and stopped still.

"Marina," said the Don, and she moved one step forward and sank her knife, which always seemed to come from nowhere, square into the middle of Pascaglia's belly. Jesus, I thought to myself, she has to be one of the top hit men in the East. We'll take her with us in case we need someone to run back to the house for something, the Don had said, and in the excitement I hadn't questioned that. Why the hell would anybody take a little old lady out to the middle of almost certain mayhem? That's why, I thought, as Pascaglia sank to the ground, his eyes trying to force their way out of his head.

If what I had done to the Crusher had caused shock, this final blow had finished it off. Not one shot had come from wherever Pascaglia's men were hiding in the woods. They had obviously shit or gone blind, but whatever it was, it had paralyzed them.

I reached to the ground, picked up my gun, walked the four steps and grabbed Brachi around the throat with my left arm, turning him so that he was facing the woods.

"All right," I yelled, "I'm a police officer and you're all under arrest. Throw down your weapons and come out with your hands up, or this little creep dies first and then the rest of you afterwards."

"Do what he says!" Brachi started shrieking. "Do what he says!"

Maybe it was because Pascaglia and the Crusher, one the leader, the other the enforcer, were dead, or maybe it was the night in the woods, or maybe it was because with Pascaglia gone Brachi was now the chief, or maybe it was because they had undergone enough, or maybe it was because they had seen me rip a guy's life from his throat with my teeth and who knew what this blood-covered nut would do next, but they started to come out, first one, then another, then the rest, all thirteen of them.

I waved them toward me and as the first one got close enough, maybe from habit or because I wanted to assure myself that I was a policeman and not a crazy killer, I started the chant.

"Before asking you any questions," I said loudly, "it is my duty to inform you of your rights. You have the right to remain silent. If you choose to speak, anything you say may be used against you in a court of law or other proceeding . . ."

I don't know how it started. Maybe one of the hoods had a sense of humor, or maybe they were trying to placate a maniac whose face was covered with blood and who was waving a gun in the air in their direction, or maybe they didn't even know they were repeating aloud something they all knew so well, but by the time I reached the word "proceeding," two of them had joined in, and by the end they were all saying it like they were reciting the Boy Scout oath.

"You have the right to consult with a lawyer before

answering any questions," they chorused, "and you may have him present with you during questioning. If you cannot afford a lawyer and you want one, a lawyer will be provided for you by the state without cost to you."

They stopped, waiting for the high priest.

"Do you understand what I have told you?" I yelled.

"Yes!" they shouted.

"You may also waive the right to counsel and your right to remain silent," I informed them, "and you may answer any question or make any statement you wish. If you decide to answer questions, you may stop at any time to consult with a lawyer."

I unfolded my arm and pushed their little lawyer toward them. They all still had their arms in the air, and Brachi put his up too. He didn't want to stand out from the crowd at that moment.

"What are you going to do now?" asked the Don, his *pistole* held loosely in his hand. He didn't seem at all concerned about any of these men still being dangerous.

"I'm going to take them into West Orange to Lieutenant Cibelli," I said, "and have him book them on every charge in the New Jersey statutes."

"I thought that's what you had in mind," sighed the Don. And then almost as an afterthought, he said softly, "Vinnie."

And the little guy smacked me on the back of the head with the barrel of the shotgun, coldcocked me as smoothly as Marina worked with a knife, and as I felt blackness descending and my body sinking to the ground, the word that was echoing through my head like I was in a giant cave, the kind that has thousands of bats sleeping at the top, the word that drowned out everything else, was *family*. It was one hell of a way to run a *family*.

***D**éjà vu!*
I pulled my arm out from under the sheet and
heard a rustle like a hundred snakes moving in the grass.
Silk on silk. I was wearing silk pajamas and tucked in
between silk sheets. Lifting the hand slowly, I reached
to the back of my head and pushed gently. Even so the
pain was enough to light a fire behind my closed eyelids. The last thing had been Vinnie whacking me on
the back of the head with the barrel of the shotgun. At
the Don's order. Let us reconstruct the crime, Dr.
Watson.

I had told the Don I was going to take all of Pascaglia's
thugs into West Orange and have Cibelli book them.
He obviously didn't want that done so he had given the
nod to Vinnie who had put the quietus on me with his
bare shotgun. Then they had lugged me off to my old
room in the dorm, Sophia, maybe with Marina's help,
had stripped me naked and slipped me into these cool
pajamas. I opened my eyes, closed them again when
the light hit, and then opened them again slowly. What
color were my pajamas? The same purple ones like the
first time? No, these were pink. Who the hell bought
these pajamas in the first place? They were the equivalent of classic Christmas neckties.

I could see sunlight outside the window, bright sunlight, and wondered what would happen if I tried to get
out of bed. I'd probably be a little dizzy, but it shouldn't
be as bad as the food poisoning had been unless I had a
major concussion or a fractured skull. But it didn't feel

that bad. And besides, the Don owed me an accounting. I had to get up. There was a lot to do.

I turned my head and there was Marina's face suspended in the doorjamb and as quickly gone. I could probably expect a luncheon tray in five minutes. It would have been funny if I hadn't been so pissed off. Okay, the guy fingered me to Pascaglia, but he explained that, at least to Sofia's satisfaction. Okay, he had Marina save my life twice. That put him one ahead even if he was really one behind. But then he had me whacked. Whose side was he really on? I started to lift my head from the pillow to get leverage for sliding off the bed, but there seemed to be no strength in any part of my body. Why was I so weak? Maybe there was a concussion or a fracture. The little son of a bitch.

Sofia came hurrying into the room, her face showing her concern.

"How are you feeling?" she asked. "How is your head?"

"It hurts like hell when I touch it," I told her, "but it always takes a couple of days for a bump to feel better."

"But it was three days ago," said Sofia excitedly. "It should be much better by now."

I sat up and to hell with the pain and the weakness.

"What do you mean three days?" I said. "I've been knocked out for three days?"

"Well," she said, "they've been giving you shots. I wanted to call a doctor but they said that if they kept you quiet for a few days it would be much better all around."

I could hear the voice of the first aid instructor telling us how you have to keep the victim of a bump on the head awake until you know whether it's a concussion. Three days! They could have killed me. What the hell was going on?

"Get me some clothes," I told her.

"Are you sure it's all right to get up?" she said. "Let me go ask Papa."

"Don't you leave this room," I ordered. "Get me my clothes."

She went to the closet and brought out my pants and sports jacket, which had been cleaned and pressed again, and found me a shirt and socks and pulled my loafers out from under the bed.

A lot of water had gone over the dam between us so I stripped off the pajamas in front of her and then quickly dressed. She didn't even look at me but carefully folded the pajamas and slipped them over a hanger in the closet. We could have been married for twenty years.

"Where is your father?" I asked.

"He's in his study working on his book."

Well, I thought, he's had some hot chapters to add from the last couple of days. And I was about to give him a couple more.

I headed out of the room toward the study, not even looking to see if Sofia was following. I thought of telling her that this was between her father and myself, and since I was a man, she might have obeyed, but she and I had been through too much crap together to shut her out now. Whatever went down between the Don and me was her business too.

The Don was sitting at his desk scrawling away, dressed in his Colonel Sanders suit, his face pink under the close shave, impeccable. It took me a few seconds to realize what was wrong. There weren't any broken windows. There weren't any bullet holes. There was fresh paint on one wall; it contrasted nicely with the faded look on the others. Three days. They'd neatened up while I was in la la land. I had the feeling there wasn't a broken window in the house. Nor bullet holes. That quite a few gallons of fresh paint had been spread around.

And last but not least, that a few bodies had been added to the area around the swamp. Three days. They had kept me under wraps for three days while all the filth was swept under the rug. It could be described as keeping it in the family.

The Don looked up and smiled, but before he could utter any pleasantries, I broke in.

"Where are Pascaglia's men?" I asked, knowing the answer as I asked it.

"They have gone home," he said quietly. "Brachi is now the leader of their branch, and he has assured me that nothing more will be heard from that quarter. He said the money was yours as far as he was concerned, that there was plenty to go around."

"Do you believe him?"

"Yes. But I also made some calls to old friends, and they have assured me that they will see to it that he keeps his word."

"Will they keep their word?"

He nodded. "They are men who keep their word."

"So this is the end of it?"

He nodded again. "This should be the end of it. No one will be reported missing. No one will go to the police. No one will go to the families. The seal of silence has been put on the whole affair. Anybody who talks will end up with a dead canary in his mouth."

"Just like that?"

He nodded again. "Just like that."

"But I am police," I told him. "Suppose I go to the police."

"It would be difficult for you to prove anything," he said. "No one here, nor any of the others, would testify. And you would also cause trouble for your family."

I half turned and Sofia was standing in the doorway of the room, standing respectfully as she listened to the discussion between the men in her family. I had always wanted a family, a real family. Wasn't there an old saying about not wishing for anything because you just might get it? If there is a God, I thought to myself, he must be pissing his pants right now.

"I am leaving," I told him.

"God go with you," he said, not knowing how ironic that sounded. "But first I would like to speak to you privately for a moment." He looked over to where Sofia was standing, and she immediately left the room.

I walked closer to the desk and stood before him, wondering how I really felt about this old enforcer, this murderer, this gangster, this guy who had spent most of his life on the other side of the law, whose ideas and ideals were the opposite of everything I had every believed or stood for. I guess I kind of liked him.

"I need a favor," he said.

I waited.

"We can make a living out of the pizza parlors and the bakeries," he said, "because Sofia is a good businesswoman and she and Vinnie work hard, but we need new equipment and some capital. I would like to borrow some money from you."

"How much?"

He hesitated. It was the first time I had ever seen him hesitate. He was wondering how soft a touch I might be with my five million dollars.

"A hundred thousand?" he ventured.

"My checkbook is in my suitcase," I said. "I'll go get it."

"We'll pay you back," he called out as I was about to leave the room. "We'll pay you back with interest."

Sure, I thought, with the money you'll make from your book.

When I got back to the bedroom, Sofia had my suitcase on the bed and was carefully folding my clothes preparatory to putting them in.

I looked inside the bag and saw both my checkbook on the bottom and my gun neatly wrapped in its straps. I was going out the way I had come in.

I removed the checkbook and walked over to the bureau. I almost wrote Don Marchese on the check, and then it took me a few moments to remember that his name was Alessandro. A hundred thousand dollars. I was writing a check for a hundred thousand dollars that I would never get back, and it wasn't bothering me one bit. It's good to be a king.

I started to turn to put the checkbook back in the suitcase but stopped and thought for a moment. Then I made out a check for another hundred thousand, only this time the recipient was Sofia Marchese.

She had finished tucking everything in neatly, and I handed her the check.

"Why are you giving me this?" she asked.

"I don't want you to tell anybody about it," I said. "Deposit it in your name and use it for yourself or for the family if they need it. Save it for emergencies if you want, but I will feel better knowing you have it."

"But why do you want to give it to me?"

"Because you are my wife," I told her.

She folded it and, true to her blood, she tucked it into the cleavage of her bosom.

I dropped the checkbook into the bag and strapped it shut. She did not follow me as I walked back to her father who was sitting at the desk staring at nothing. I placed the check down beside him.

"The telephone is for you," he said.

Surprised, I looked down at the desk and sure enough the receiver was lying off the cradle. I picked it up.

"Hello," I said.

"Mr. Freedman?" a man's voice asked.

"Yes."

"This is Del Bramini."

Del Bramini. It took a moment. Bramini. From Boston! "Yes."

"I have been in contact with attorney Brachi in New York, and he has filled me in on recent occurrences."

The voice was actually cultured. He could have been a cousin of the Kennedys, for Christ's sake.

"Yes?"

"He says that he has virtually canceled the debt you owe his organization."

"I understand that to be the case."

"Well, we are about to have a final reckoning with Bandini, and I just wanted you to know that my brother and I still feel most strongly that you also owe us a large sum of money, and we hope that you will be sending it to us as soon as possible."

"When you send me your mother," I told him.

The line clicked dead.

"Brachi put them on you," said the Don. "He hopes they will do what he has been forbidden to do because of me."

"I'll worry about them when the time comes," I said, starting to worry right then.

"I know little about them," said the Don. "They are of the new generation."

"And how is that different from the old generation?" I asked him, curiosity mixed in with annoyance and unease.

"We were what we were," the old man said. "Today it is all so mixed in together that it is hard to tell where crime ends and government begins."

I nodded wisely, not sure of what he meant and not completely unsure. I was unsure of what I was, a cop with six million bucks of dirty money. That was going to have to be worked out sometime.

I reached out my hand across the desk, and we solemnly shook, looking straight in each other's eyes. A lot had happened and nothing had happened. If I kept up with this kind of thinking, maybe I should go back to my old junior college and teach philosophy. At least I could do better than that fucking rabbi. Deuteronomy indeed.

Which brought me out front to my car where Sofia was standing with all the other members of the family, including Tomaselli, who had hobbled out in his dirty white jacket. I looked past the driveway from the top of the stairs to the place that had been the field of combat three days before. There would never be markers there like at Gettysburg, but the battle had been as important to me as it had been to anybody in blue or gray. Pascaglia and the Crusher. Out somewhere in the swamp. With the Doc. I hoped they were buried at his feet.

Angelo was giving the front fender of the convertible a final polishing with a big rag, and for a moment I had the crazy idea of buying the car from the rental agency and giving it to him. After all, I could afford it, and he seemed to love it. But the thought of him driving that beautiful convertible, smashing it into whatever was available, was too horrible to contemplate.

Elena had obviously come from a sunbathing session, and her whole body, except for the tiny little spots covered by the bikini, was slathered with suntan oil. As I shook her hand, I remembered that she was going to get a new car just for uncovering those three little spots to Vinnie's eyes, and I gave him a farewell hug, to his surprise, in honor of his impending treat. He had been wary as I approached him because he wasn't sure of how I felt about his clubbing me on the head. The thought of decking him passed through my mind for a moment, but he was so small and so basically insignificant that I grinned wryly and let it go at that.

Mama Maria gave me a big hug, sobbed about her Catherine for a moment, called down all of God's blessings, told me I must come visit often, and then handed me a bag with sandwiches for the trip.

Marina just stood there looking at me, and I approached her warily, not knowing where the knife might be concealed and what her current attitude was toward me. She mumbled something in Italian, and I turned questioningly to Mama Maria.

"She says you're a good boy," said Mama Maria.

"And you tell her she's one hell of a girl," I said.

"I'm going to ride down to the gate with you," said Sofia, as she opened the door of the car and got in on the passenger side. I threw the bag on the back seat, and we started off.

We didn't say a word all the way down the driveway, and when I stopped before the gate, she jumped out, pulled whatever switch was necessary, and then started to haul the gates over the rough spots. By the time I got out, there was only need to help her with the second one, and we ended up holding on to the same end bar with our hands extended up it.

When they came down, they encircled us in an embrace, and Sofia was crying big tears into my shoulder, holding on so tight that I thought we might fall over.

"Now that I've known you," she sobbed, "how am I going to live without you?"

I was a widower less than two months, and here I was looking down at one of God's homeliest women and wondering what it would be like to spend the rest of my life with her. I wasn't going to live at Villa Marchese, that was for sure, so she would have to come to San Diego.

She gave me a final squeeze and pushed back.

"You must go," she said, and I realized then that she knew that as much as I cared for her, I didn't love her as she wanted and needed, and she was too much woman, too much person, to go for that. Her push had also pushed the realization into me.

"If ever you need me for anything," I said, "you have only to call. And if you want more money, you have only to ask."

"We will be fine," she said. "Everything will be fine. And you must always remember that you have a family here. Now go."

I thought of kissing her good-bye, but it would have been awkward so I just got in the car and drove away. When I reached West Orange, I drove down the main street and almost stopped at the police station to see Cibelli. But then it occurred to me that he might extend an invitation to dinner and I drove on.

It wasn't until I was almost at the George Washington Bridge that the realization hit me, and I slammed on the power brakes, which almost instigated an umpteen-hundred-car pileup. Red-faced and with the top of the convertible down so the whole world could see who the idiot was, I started forward again to the blaring chorus of innumerable horns.

Remember that you have a family here, she said. Sofia was definitely not on birth-control pills, and no precautions had been taken during our bucolic idyll. Suppose I did have a family started there at the Villa Marchese?

It did one thing for me. It took my mind off those mother-loving Bramini brothers.

About the Author

Milton Bass lives in the hills of western Massachusetts
with his wife and youngest offspring. He is a columnist
for the *Berkshire Eagle* and an avid vegetable gardener.
His first Benny Freedman novel, *The Moving Finger*,
is available in a Signet edition.